THE
COLLECTED
NIGHTMARES

Fred Wiehe

The Collected Nightmares
A Black Bed Sheet/Diverse Media Book
April 2019

Copyright © 2019 by Fred Wiehe
All rights reserved.

Cover art/design by Ian Brenner-Wiehe
Copyright © 2019 by Fred Wiehe and Ian-Brenner-Wiehe

The selections in this book are works of fiction. Names, characters, places and incidents either are the product of the author's imagination or are used fictitiously, and any resemblance to actual persons, living or dead, events, or locales is entirely coincidental.

No part of this book may be reproduced, stored in a retrieval system, or transmitted by any means, electronic, mechanical, photocopying, recording, or otherwise, without written permission from the author.

Library of Congress Control Number: 2018967050

ISBN-10: 1-946874-11-6
ISBN-13: 978-1-946874-11-5

The Collected Nightmares

A Black Bed Sheet/Diverse Media Book
Antelope, CA

COLLECTED PRAISE FOR FRED WIEHE

On ALERIC: MONSTER HUNTER:

"With *Aleric: Monster Hunter*, Fred Wiehe breathes dangerous new life into urban fantasy. With a lightning-fast pace, dangerous twists and action that will leave you breathless! Disturbingly entertaining!" **–Jonathan Maberry, New York Times best selling author of DUST & DECAY and DEAD OF NIGHT**

"Fred Wiehe's latest novel *Aleric: Monster Hunter* is an ambitious book that ties fast paced action into well-researched gypsy custom." **–Read Horror**

Aleric: Monster Hunter is one thrill-ride of a monster mash." —**Jeani Rector, The Horror Zine**

On HOLIDAY MADNESS:

"Ghouls and Santa, Ghosts and Aliens—a stocking full of bloody holiday stories hung with care. Scrooges of all ages will shriek with delight!"—**Del Howison, author, editor, part-time actor, and owner of Dark Delicacies Bookstore in Burbank, CA**

•

This book is dedicated to
the accident that almost killed me,
to the agonizing pains during a long
recovery,
and to the chronic pain that follows me
even today.
It's dedicated to
the mean-spirited people
and to all the bullies
that haunt the waking world.
It's dedicated to
the dead,
to the ghosts,
and to all the nightmares
that haunt restless nights.
Without all of you,
this volume would not
have been possible.

Table of Contents

Pretender......................1
Penny's Song...................27
A Whistle and a Tap, Tap, Tap...28
Nightmares.....................33
It Knocked at My Door.........34
Not Dead......................41
The Collection................43
Shadow Pain...................56
Under the Protection of Witches:
A Novella.....................57
   (Based on the feature-length script
      The Uglies by Fred Wiehe)
Lupine Dream..................191
The Reckoning.................192
Transformed...................212
My Only Daddy.................213
The In Between................226
The In Between, Part 2........227
Holiday Madness...............258
Shoot Me......................259
Evil..........................262
The Alchemists................263
Songs of the Night............274
Creeper.......................276
Burning Soul..................299
Rebirth.......................300
Predator & Prey...............301

Succubus......................307
Bimbai........................308
Resurrected: An Aleric: Monster Hunter Novella...............309
The Devil's Prayer............448
Strange Days..................449
Dead Girl.....................450
The End.......................467

The Collected Nightmares

Fred Wiehe

Pretender

Late for his own book signing, Frank Lester ran across the parking lot. He carried a framed poster in one hand. An easel collapsed and secured in a black case was slung over his shoulder. The case made it appear as if he were carrying some sort of rifle, which always got him worried looks from people around him. This time was no different. He paid them no mind, though, as he rushed up to the front entrance of Barnes & Noble, swung open the door, and hurried inside.

Just inside the entrance, he couldn't help but stop and admire the large sign the store had made to advertise his event. In big bold caps, the sign screamed, HALLOWEEN BOOK SIGNING. It included the time and some review quotes, as well as his picture and the cover of his new horror novel *Bloodshot*. It certainly made quite an impression. The bookstore had gone all out.

Turning away from the sign, he found the table they'd set up for the signing not far away. Stacks of his novel covered the tabletop.

Still, the sight of it dampened his mood. There was no line of people awaiting his arrival, despite the great sign, the advanced marketing, and the fact that he was a good fifteen minutes late. In fact, no one was anywhere near the table, not even one casual shopper lurked nearby.

What did he expect, a line out the door? No. He wasn't Stephen King or Peter Straub or even Jonathan Maberry. Yeah, he had a bunch of short stories and eight novels to his credit, but he was still just a mid-list author. He had just a little over four thousand Facebook followers and really only several hundred of what anyone could consider rabid fans, and they were spread out across the country. No, he didn't expect a line, but still a writer could hope.

Setting the poster down, he unzipped the black case and took out the easel, extending the legs and setting it up next to the table. As he was placing the poster he'd brought with him on the easel, a young woman approached.

"Mr. Lester, I'm Camille, the event coordinator." She extended her hand. "We spoke on the phone."

He shook Camille's hand. "It's a pleasure."

"We're so happy to have you here, Mr. Lester," Camille gushed, "and for Halloween too."

He forced a smile and looked about the store. There were a fair amount of people roaming around, but even with him putting up the easel and poster, no one showed any interest in coming over to see what was going on or to pick up a book. "I'm glad to be here, Camille. The table looks great, and the bookstore did an awesome job on the sign."

Camille blushed. "I designed it myself."

He studied the girl, really for the first time. A very young, naive face stared back at him. Her green eyes shone with zeal and maybe even admiration. Her warm smile appeared genuine. Now he smiled back in earnest. "Well, Camille, it truly is awesome."

Camille blushed again. "Your father thought so too."

"Huh? What did you say?" Frank asked. He lost his smile.

"Yeah, your father stopped by yesterday. He bought a copy of your novel."

He knew someone had to be playing a joke on him, albeit a very sick and humorless joke. His father was dead. "What makes you think he was my father?"

Camille thought for a moment. "He pointed to the sign and said, 'Tell my son I was here.'"

"Are you *sure* that's what he said?" He couldn't stop himself from quickly scanning the bookstore even though he knew his father wasn't there, couldn't be there.

Camille cocked her head and then nodded. "Yeah…is there something wrong, Mr. Lester?"

He continued to scan the store. Someone had to have pretended to be his father. But who could be that sick? Who hated him that much? Those were the questions that plagued his mind. But to Camille, he simply asked, "What did this guy look like? Can you describe him?"

Camille took two steps back. "What did your own father look like?"

He looked hard at the girl. The wide-eyed look on her face and the hesitant apprehension that had been apparent in her voice made him realize just how crazy his questions must've sounded. He forced a half-hearted smile and even managed a chuckle. "I'm sorry." He waved Camille's concern off. "I didn't mean to make a big deal out of it. It's just that my father lives back East, and he didn't tell me he was coming to the Bay Area for a visit."

At that, Camille seemed to relax. "Oh…well, that's a nice surprise then."

He nodded. "Yes…a nice surprise."

The girl smiled back. "Maybe your father will stop by again today."

He glanced about the store. "Maybe…"

"Well, I better go make an announcement. Let our shoppers know you're here." She hurried off.

Frank sat down at the table, Sharpie at the ready. But his attention was focused on the faces around him. When he couldn't see faces, he concentrated on body types and movement. He searched for anyone who might pass for his father as he half-listened to the announcement over the PA system.

"Are you the author?"

That snapped his attention back to the business at hand.

The guy standing in front of the table fidgeted from foot to foot and wrung his hands. He looked possibly homeless—old cowboy boots caked with dried dirt, clothes slightly tattered and ill-fitting, face unshaven and dirt-smudged. He smelled too, like sweat and mold.

Frank again forced a smile. "Guilty as charged, sir."

That didn't elicit even the slightest reaction from the guy.

Continuing the duet with his hands and feet, the guy asked, "What's your book about?"

"It's a cross between science fiction and horror. Do you like scary novels?"

The guy's face contorted. "No," he said flatly.

Two girls in their late teens approached the table. One picked up a book. Heads together, they both silently read the inside flap.

The fidgeting, hand-wringing guy again asked, "What's your book about?"

"Feel free to pick one up, sir." Frank motioned toward the two girls as examples of what to do. "You know…to read the summary."

The guy looked at the books as if they were a nest of slithering vipers ready to attack. "No."

The two young ladies set the book they were looking at down, giving the guy a look of disdain as they walked away.

Frank sighed. There was always at least one crazy at every signing. He needed to get rid of this guy before he ruined another sale—as politely as possible, but gotten rid of just the same. "Look, sir, it's a science fiction-horror story. You said you don't like scary novels." He hoped that would be enough to discourage the guy.

"Do you believe in ghosts?"

Frank stood. That was all he could take. "Excuse me, sir. I need a bathroom break." He turned and walked away.

"Do you believe in monsters?"

Frank kept going. Luckily only the guy's voice followed and not the guy himself.

"I have a friend who's a janitor at a secret government facility. He says he killed a monster there once with his mop. Have you ever killed a monster?"

Frank didn't need to visit the bathroom, so he took a spin around the store to give the crazy guy ample time to move on. As he walked around, he couldn't help but notice that Barnes and Noble was now more than just books, having expanded into carrying music, movies, gifts, and toys. There was even a *Star Wars* display, with *Darth Vader* and *Stormtrooper* masks. But as he continued his short trek, he mostly obsessed over the guy's questions.

Did he believe in ghosts? No. He was a horror writer, but he didn't believe in the supernatural. He had done extensive research into the paranormal for his writing, but he never saw or experienced anything that corroborated its existence. He wasn't even sure if he believed in life after death or a hereafter.

Did he believe in monsters? Yes, but only the human kind.

He finished a full circle, passing Customer Service. Camille, who was manning the station, smiled rather tentatively at him. Probably she was wondering why he was walking around rather than signing books. When he got back to the table, he sat down. Thankfully, the crazy guy was gone.

Within a few seconds, a woman approached the table. "Hello, Mr. Lester, I'd like to get a book. Can you please make it out to my sister, Alyssa?"

He smiled. "Sure." As he personalized and signed the woman's copy of *Bloodshot*, a few more people crowded around the table. The book signing was definitely looking up. Still, even as the day wore on and the books on the table steadily dwindled, he couldn't stop himself from keeping an eye out for both his father—at least whoever had pretended to be his father—and for the crazy guy's return. But what haunted him most throughout the day was his answer to that last question the guy had asked him.

Had he ever killed a monster?

Despite that nagging question, despite the pall cast over the event at the beginning, the day had turned into a successful signing. He signed the few remaining copies before taking down his poster, collapsing the easel, and storing it back inside its case. He picked up everything to leave and then thought better of it when he saw dusk pressing against the store windows. Putting everything back on the table, he revisited the *Star Wars* display. His gaze immediately fixed on the *Darth Vader* and *Stormtrooper* masks as he fidgeted from foot to foot much like the crazy guy had earlier in the day. It was believed by some that on Halloween ghosts of relatives and friends came back to the earthly world, and that they could be encountered while out and about at night. To avoid being recognized by these ghosts, people would wear masks when they left their homes after dark so that the ghosts would mistake them for fellow spirits. Even so, he couldn't quite believe that he would even *contemplate* buying a mask let alone entertain the idea of wearing one.

But what would it hurt?

He stood perfectly still now, gaze riveted to the masks.

What would it hurt? *His dignity and possibly his sanity*, that's what. What the hell was he thinking? Was he losing his mind? There was no such thing as ghosts. Someone very human was messing with him, pretending to be his father. He wasn't sure why, and he wasn't sure whether the pretender meant him harm, but he was sure that a mask wouldn't protect him.

Turning away, he made his way back to the table, picked up his poster, slung the black case containing the easel over his shoulder, and left without further word to anyone. Outside, dusk was quickly turning into night. The soft breeze from earlier in the day was now a strong, chilly wind. He braced himself against it, striding to his car with renewed determination. He wasn't about to let this pretender rattle him. Somehow, he'd find out who this guy was and one way or another put an end to it.

Had he ever killed a monster?

Hell yeah. Not that many Halloweens ago either. And he'd do it again if need be.

Footsteps came from behind, slow and methodical, the unmistakable sound of boot heels striking pavement.

He stopped and turned. No one followed. The wind whipped through his hair and almost tore the poster from his grip as he stared into the growing darkness for someone who wasn't there.

Shivering, he mumbled, "Just jumpy." His breath blew out in front of him, then dissipated in the wind. He shivered again. It couldn't have gotten that cold, could it? California was hardly ever like that, even in October. It almost felt preternatural. Maybe he should've bought a mask, after all. He searched the parking lot for any sign of ghostly activity. There *was* none. *Of course* there wasn't. The dead stayed dead. Ghosts didn't exist. Hunching his shoulders, he turned away and continued to his car.

Boot heels again struck pavement behind him.

He stopped and wheeled toward the sound just as the footsteps halted. A figure stood just far enough away for its face to be shrouded by the growing darkness. A faint yet familiar aroma scented the air, one he knew well but couldn't quite recognize.

"Who are you?" His breath came out as wispy ghosts, the wind drowning his voice.

The figure didn't answer.

Louder, he again asked, "Who are you?"

Still, the figure didn't answer.

He put down the framed poster and took the black case containing the easel from his shoulder. He brandished the case like a weapon. "Don't force me to take out my rifle. If I take it out, I *will* use it."

The figure began to fidget from foot to foot. Realization struck. *It must be the crazy guy from earlier...*

He took a step closer in the hope of getting a better look.

From foot to foot the figure continued, hands now wringing in rhythm with the fidgeting. "Have you ever killed a monster?"

That stopped him in his tracks. It was the same question the crazy guy had asked him. This time, however, it was unmistakably asked in his father's familiar voice—gravelly as always from too many cigars and too much whiskey.

"Have you ever killed a monster?"

He dropped the black case at his feet. He couldn't stop shivering. Gulping hard, he took a step backwards. "Who the hell are you?" The question came out with frozen breath, barely audible.

The figure didn't answer. Instead, it turned away and was swallowed by the night after only a few steps.

Even after the figure inexplicably disappeared, he stared after it. He couldn't believe what had just happened. He told himself that it must've been his imagination running wild. His father would've said it was the evils of Halloween playing tricks on him, whereas in reality, the crazy guy had to have waited and followed him out into the parking lot. Not being able to see the guy's face and the strange disappearance could be chalked up to a trick of the night. As for the voice, no way it was his father's. It couldn't have been. The stress of the moment and his own hysterical imagination had caused him to erroneously identify his father's voice when the guy spoke. That was the only possible explanation.

He inhaled deeply to calm his nerves, but when he let it out he could no longer see his breath. That alone rattled him. Then he noticed the wind had died, the October night had warmed. How could that be?

"Damn..."

The familiar yet unrecognizable aroma had also dissipated.

He reached down with trembling hands, picked up his poster and easel, then hurried off to his car. After packing the stuff in the trunk, he jumped into the car and sped off, tires squealing like a hog to the knife. He stopped off at Walmart on the way home and did something he rarely had done in the past; he bought bags of *Snickers*, *Reese's Peanut Butter Cups*, and *Milky Way* bars to give out to trick-or-treaters.

Candy was the modern-day version of soul cakes—a peace offering for hungry, malevolent spirits condemned to wander the world. Soul cakes were also used as a bribe to pay beggars on All Souls' Eve, beggars who offered in return for the cakes to say prayers for the family's departed—one cake given, one soul saved. He knew logically that it was all stupid and silly superstition yet he couldn't help but hope that his giving away of candy to trick-or-treaters would somehow appease whoever or whatever suddenly haunted him. Like with the masks, though, he could feel his dignity and sanity slipping away.

He drove the rest of the way home on autopilot, all the while his mind traversing a dark labyrinth of memories better left forgotten, memories of his father using a belt to beat him for going trick-or-treating with his friends and celebrating *the Devil's holiday*, memories of being locked in a closet for days on end with no food or water, gagging on the stench of his own piss and shit. The face of the monster he called his father haunted him, and the smell of his father's whiskey breath mixed with the stale odor of White Owl cigars that always clung to his father's clothes plagued him until he was nothing more than a trembling bag of bones. Tears streamed down his face as he pulled his car into the driveway. Once parked, he sat clutching the wheel, tussling with the past, struggling to return to the present, striving to calm his frayed nerves.

After a time, he wiped away the tears and forced his mind back to the present. Grabbing the bags of candy, he got out of the car. The October night that greeted him was cool but nowhere near as cold as in the bookstore parking lot less than an hour ago. He retrieved the poster and easel from the trunk and hurried into the house, slamming the door behind him and clicking on the porch light in anticipation of the candy beggars. He leaned the poster against a wall and dropped the easel in its case onto the floor. Next, he switched on a floor lamp that succeeded in only dimly lighting the room, leaving it in an eerie combination of light and shadow. The bags of candy he ripped open and plopped down on a table. He hoped at the very least the giving away of candy would appease his inner demons even if no others.

That's when he caught the subtle whiff of White Owl cigars. He shivered. From where the smoke smell came he couldn't be sure. Before he could even begin to think of tracking down the source, the doorbell rang and trick-or-treaters yelled from outside his front door. He didn't readily answer the call for candy. Instead, he stood perfectly still, sniffing the air.

Was someone inside the house?

He desperately wanted to investigate but the doorbell rang again, and the kids continued their incessant calls for treats. After hesitating a moment longer, he reluctantly picked up a bag of *Snickers* and answered the door.

Little ghouls, goblins, and monsters held their Halloween bags and plastic pumpkins at the ready. He forced a smile and even managed to mutter a few pleasantries while dropping candy in each.

The last kid standing there was a boy about ten years old, dressed as Frankenstein's monster. Not a cheap plastic mask and costume like most kids wore either. This boy was in full makeup and wore authentic-looking clothes—a Mini-Me of Frankenstein's monster.

He dropped two *Snickers* into the boy's bag. With honest appreciation, he said, "Awesome costume, kid." He stepped back, ready to close the door, anxious to search the house yet dreading what he might find.

"Have you ever killed a monster?"

He stopped cold. His father's gravelly voice had come out of the boy's mouth. "What the…" His breath came out frosty when he spoke. He shivered while taking an instinctual step or two backwards in retreat.

Frankenstein's monster stepped closer. His stare was blank, face slack. "Have you ever killed a monster?"

That voice…that damn voice…

Frank's eyes narrowed. Blood pounded in his ears. Outrage slowly replaced the fear he'd felt just a moment ago. He grabbed a handful of the monster's shirt, hefted the thing into the air, and shook it.

The monster flailed and kicked, all the while screaming as it struggled to break free. Suddenly the air warmed and the monster's voice again became that of a child's.

"Let me go," the boy screamed at the top of his lungs. "Let me go."

Frank blinked and shook his head as if coming out of a dissociative fugue. He dropped the boy, who crumpled at his feet.

Heart pounding, breathing hard, he stared down in disbelief at the crying ten-year-old, suddenly seeing his past self in the costumed boy. God, no. That meant in a complete role reversal he currently embodied his father. He reached down to help the boy up. "I'm so sorry." His voice creaked in his dry throat. "Let me help you."

"No," the boy cried, scooting away on hands, feet, and butt. Tears dampened and smudged the makeup on his face.

"I only want to help you," Frank insisted. He again reached for the boy.

"No." The boy scrambled to his feet. He ran off screaming, disappearing into the night.

Frank stared after the boy, then peered into the night to see if anyone had been watching. Seeing no witnesses, he backed through the doorway, closed the door, and clicked off the porch lights. No more trick-or-treaters. He couldn't take the chance of another similar incident. This one alone had shaken him to his core. What the hell had happened anyway? He couldn't understand how he'd thought the boy had spoken in his father's voice. Had guilt over his father finally driven him mad? After the incident in the bookstore parking lot and now this one, he certainly thought it was a possibility.

Then he remembered the cigar scent he smelled just as the trick-or-treaters had yelled out. He never got the chance to investigate. He sniffed the air. The White Owl aroma was gone. Stumbling across the room, he sat down hard in his favorite recliner. Maybe it was never there at all. He leaned back in the chair, closing his eyes. Maybe he *was* going mad. He needed to rest. He didn't think he'd be able to sleep, but closing his eyes and taking a minute to collect his thoughts certainly couldn't hurt.

The next thing he knew, he woke to something soft being pressed against his face. He couldn't see, couldn't breathe. He grabbed at the thing smothering him and tried to tear it away. But someone was on top of him, holding it in place. He kicked his feet out, hoping to buck whoever it was off, though to no avail. He swung a roundhouse punch but hit only air. He swung again, this time with his other fist, and still hit nothing but air, as if no one was there at all. But that couldn't be. He could feel the weight of the person on top of him and pressing down on whatever covered his face. Panic swelled in his chest as he continued to struggle, grabbing at the suffocating weapon and trying to wrench it free, all the while kicking and flailing his legs. His lungs burned from lack of air. His muffled screams fought to free themselves, to give voice to his rising terror. But the fight was quickly going out of him. His legs now barely moved. His grasp on the thing smothering him loosened. Spots formed behind his closed eyelids, followed by total blackness. His lungs formed almost a perfect vacuum as consciousness slipped away, and he found himself spiraling towards death. But before death could fully claim him, the mysterious weight on top of him and the pressure on whatever covered his face was just as inexplicably released. Air crept through to his lungs, slowly filling the void that had been there mere seconds ago. Spots returned to the vision under his eyelids. Consciousness and life reclaimed him.

    He sat up, throwing the goddamn thing off his face. He gasped, but instead of sweet, precious air his lungs sucked in a suffocating smoke. He coughed and gagged uncontrollably as he searched for the source. On the table next to him sat a glass ashtray with a burning cigar, the smoke wafting up into his face. A glass of what could only be whiskey was present next to it. He swatted them away with the back of his hand—ashtray and cigar, glass and whiskey, flying through the air, both shattering upon landing.

Wiping away tears from his burning eyes and coughing out the last of the cigar smoke from his lungs, he stared in disbelief at the pillow lying at his feet. Whereas the cigar and whiskey angered him, the pillow left him horror stricken, for he recognized it. It was the murder weapon he had used to smother his father only a handful of Halloweens ago. He hadn't disposed of it. There was no need. No one questioned an old man dying in his sleep. No autopsy was done. No alibi was needed. He had simply cleaned the pillow and put it back on the bed. Now it lay at his feet, having been used in an attempt on his own life. Someone could easily find out that his father enjoyed White Owls and whiskey, but only he knew about the pillow.

Shit, shit, shit…

Then a worse thought occurred to him. The only other person that might know about the pillow would be the victim himself. Had his father found a way back from the dead? No, that was crazy. Still, crazy things had been happening all day. It was, after all, Halloween—a night when supposedly the boundary between the worlds of the living and the dead became blurred, a night when it was believed that the ghosts of the dead returned to earth. If anyone could find a way back, it would be his father, spurred on by pure meanness, spite, and revenge, and the perfect night for it would be *the Devil's holiday*.

What the hell was he thinking? Halloween or not, he didn't really believe someone could come back from the dead, did he?

"Ghosts don't exist," he mumbled.

But the pillow at his feet told a different story.

"No. Ghosts don't exist."

"Maybe not, but do you believe in monsters?"

Frank gasped. It was without question his father's evil voice. He sat up straight, his gaze darting around the room in search of whomever or whatever spoke those words.

A figure stood in the far corner of the room, half hidden in the shadows. It took a step closer but remained there, identity still concealed.

"Do you? Do you believe in monsters?"

The crazy guy from the bookstore moved out of the shadows, stopping only a few feet away.

Frank stood. "*You...*" Frozen breath came out with that one word. A deathly cold crept into his bones. "I should've known."

The crazy guy wrung his hands together and grinned. "Have you ever killed a monster?"

Frank stiffened, both at the question and at hearing that damn voice. How could it be? His own hands fisted at his sides. Maybe this guy wasn't a pretender, after all. Maybe his father found a way to possess the innocent—the Mini-Me Frankenstein monster and this hapless guy. That had to be it. Possession was the only possible explanation, no matter how totally insane it sounded.

Shivering, he took one step closer to the possessed guy. "I do believe in monsters." His fists were now so tight that his fingernails drew blood.

The guy did the same duet with his hands and feet as he had in the bookstore earlier. The grin on his face looked maniacal. "Have you ever killed a monster?"

Frank stood as tall and as threatening as he could in attempt to show no doubt, no fear. "I have, and if need be, I won't hesitate to kill that monster again."

A siren wailed in the distance.

The guy laughed like the *Joker*. "Better hurry. They're on their way."

Without fully understanding the implications of the approaching siren or those words spoken to him and without thinking of the consequences, Frank pounced. His hands immediately went around the guy's throat. The momentum of his charge sent them both spinning in circles as if doing a macabre dance. Stumbling, they hit the floor with a thud. After one roll, Frank came out on top, straddling his adversary's chest, knees on arms, pinning the guy to the floor.

The distant siren continued its wail, getting closer.

The possessed guy glared. "Better kill me now, quick."

Frank complied, as if he had no other choice. He grabbed the discarded pillow and pressed it against the guy's face.

Outside, tires screeched. The siren died.

He continued to press down on the pillow. His adversary didn't even try to fight back but only jerked slightly underneath him as the air and life apparently drained away.

Quick footsteps thumped across the porch. The front door burst open with a bang.

He looked up in time to see a cop draw his revolver.

"Freeze!"

He did. Not because he was told to but because his father's voice now came from the cop's mouth.

The cop grinned. "Put your hands up."

Frank did as he was told. The guy under him was dead anyway. And the monster had apparently found a new home.

"Now get off him…slowly."

Except for uncontrollable shivers, he didn't move. Instead, for the first time, he thought about his circumstances. It seemed way too convenient for the cops to show up now. Who called them? It was a setup. It had to be. And his father had to have orchestrated the whole damn thing.

He thought about his next move. Did he even have one?

"Don't think about going for that rifle." The cop's grin widened as his gaze drifted to the easel in the black case.

Frank eyed the case too. It rested on the floor within reaching distance. He swallowed hard, throat dry. "That's not a rifle." Frozen breath escaped his mouth with each word. "It's only an easel. But then you already know that, don't you…*Father*?"

The cop continued to grin, a deranged glint in his eye. "I'm warning you, don't reach for that rifle."

Frank choked back burning bile. The monster's voice sickened him. The realization of what was to come sickened him. Still, he wasn't about to go out on his knees and without a fight.

"Fuck you." He pushed up off the dead man beneath him and lunged at his lifelong enemy.

A shot rang out.

And the monster had his revenge.

Fred Wiehe

Penny's Song

Evil lurks in shadows
It lingers in hallways
Hides in corners
Awaits at the threshold
Pounds at the door

The key is all it needs
Once the door opens
It's ready to pounce
Eager to run amok
Fervent to kill

And only the key
That set evil loose
Upon the world
Can lock it away again
Ending the terror

A Whistle and a Tap, Tap, Tap

An eight-year-old boy came to visit his grandpa for the weekend. That night, he hopped into bed and slid under the covers, pulling them up to his chin.

Grandpa sat down next to the boy. "Colin, I'm so glad you're here with me," he said.

"Me too, Grandpa."

Grandpa fussed with the covers, pulling them tight around his grandson and tucking them in. "There are some things I have to tell you before you go to sleep."

Colin swallowed hard. There was a sudden seriousness in grandpa's voice that scared him. "Yes, Grandpa?"

Grandpa got a far-off look in his eyes. "This is an old house, son. Very old. And because it's so old, it makes a lot of noises that may sound strange and scary at night."

The boy again swallowed hard. "What kind of noises, Grandpa?"

"The plumbing is old. Sometimes the pipes get air in them, and they make a gurgling or whispering sound. But it's nothing to worry about. And when the furnace comes on, it might make a bang or a thump. And the floors and walls creak. The wind might whistle through the eaves and bang the shutters against the wall." Grandpa focused again on the boy. He smiled. "But it's nothing to worry about."

Despite Grandpa's assurances, Colin was worried. He shivered under the covers.

"The important thing to remember," Grandpa continued, "is to never get out of bed and never go looking for the source of the noises. Do you understand?"

Colin nodded.

"Promise me."

"I-I…promise."

Grandpa leaned over and kissed Colin on the cheek. "Good." He stood. "Good." He paused there a moment, lost in thought. "Chances are," he continued, "you'll never hear a thing."

That scared Colin more than the noises themselves.

Grandpa smiled. He turned away and walked to the door. "Good night." He turned off the light and left.

As soon as the light went out, Colin had the sudden urge to pee, but he dared not get out of bed. Instead, he scrunched his eyes shut and tried not to listen for noises. But he couldn't help himself. Still, the house remained silent, and soon he began to relax and thought of getting up and going to the bathroom.

That's when he heard it. A *whistle*, and a *tap, tap, tap*.

He gasped. Remaining still, he listened.

Whistle, tap, tap, tap.

He pulled the covers over his head. That didn't sound like pipes or a furnace or creaking floors.

Whistle, tap, tap, tap.

What was it?

He wanted to jump out of bed and run from the room, but he remembered his promise to Grandpa, so he remained under the covers, cowering and shivering.

Whistle, tap, tap, tap.

Louder this time, more insistent.

Under the covers, he curled into a ball. A squirt of pee escaped, dampening his pajama bottoms. Somehow, he kept the rest at bay, but he didn't think he could hold it all night. What was he going to do? He thought about yelling for Grandpa, but he didn't want to call attention to where he hid. Maybe whatever or whoever was making the noises would go away.

Whistle, tap, tap, tap.

Maybe.

Whistle, tap, tap, tap.

He again scrunched his eyes closed, tried not to think of peeing, and prayed the noises would stop.

They did.

He began to relax and again thought about getting up and going to the bathroom, but before he could move, new noises sounded.

Scratch, scratch, squeal, scratch, squeal, scratch, scratch.

He gasped. Held his breath. Crossed his legs.

Scratch, scratch, squeal, scratch.

Silence. Then...

Scratch, squeal, scratch, scratch, squeal, scratch.

When he couldn't hold his breath any longer, he slowly blew it out. Still, he held the pee.

Silence again. Time passed. No new noises sounded. Everything remained deathly quiet.

After some time, he began to feel sleepy, eyes heavy, and without even realizing it, he drifted off.

In the morning, he woke to the sun streaming through the window. The only sounds were the singing birds in the tree outside his bedroom. There was no whistle, no tap, no scratching or squealing. He climbed out of bed, proud that he hadn't wet it and eager to visit the bathroom.

That's when he saw it. It was scrawled on the windowpane. In blood.

Came for a visit
Couldn't wake you
Be back tomorrow night

His mouth dropped open, and his breath caught in his throat. He couldn't move, speak, or even scream. Pee ran down his leg, puddling at his bare feet.

Fred Wiehe

NIGHTMARES

Stories haunt my mind like
Nightmares in my sleep
Creeping all the time
Depriving me of sleep
What I have found
Is I'll never get to sleep
Until I write them down
And make them mine to keep
Then and only then
Will I ever get to sleep

IT KNOCKED AT MY DOOR

The knock at the door came swift and hard.

I stirred. Lifted my head.

"Shit."

I lay on my stomach. Spittle hung from my mouth to the cushion.

The knock came again.

I pushed myself up from the sofa, into a sitting position. My face felt smooshed, pushed out of place like so much clay. I swiped the spittle from my chin then rubbed the numbness from my face.

Another knock.

"Yeah, yeah," I mumbled, "I hear you." I ran a hand through my sweat-soaked hair, un-plastering it from my forehead and scalp. "Shit, I hear you."

The television cast an eerie glow across the room. It was on but no program played. Only a blank, white screen stared back. No sound either.

"Cable must be out," I mumbled.

Two more knocks, in rapid succession.

My cell lay on the table next to the sofa. I picked it up and checked the clock. "Shit. Three fucking a.m. Who the hell...?"

Three rapid knocks.

I struggled off the sofa, adjusted my jeans and T-shirt to look somewhat presentable, and stumbled for the front door, barefoot. Somebody better be dying or dead. Anything short of a real emergency this time-a-night would get this visitor nothing short of a *fuck you* and a slammed door right in the face.

One more knock urged me to the door.

I turned the porch light on. Flipped the bolt lock. Threw the door open. Ready to rip whoever was there a new one.

The porch was empty.

I squinted past the glow of the porch light, into the dark. "Hello." My eyebrows knitted together. "What the...?" I scratched at the stubble on my chin. "Hello." I stepped across the threshold. Stood within the porch light's glow. Looked around.

No one.

"Fuck you," I yelled into the solitude of the night.

A swirling breeze answered my challenge. It shook the surrounding trees. Embraced me with invisible arms. A chill raced up my spine. Gooseflesh tightened my scalp. "Damn..." I shivered.

Where had that come from?

I hugged myself against the sudden cold. Looked around one last time. "Fuck you," I mumbled, turned around, crossed back over the threshold, and closed the door.

I shivered again. The cold had followed me inside. It caressed my bare feet and blew frozen kisses against my neck.

I checked the thermostat. Supposedly, it was seventy degrees. Damn thing had to be broken. But it shouldn't feel this cold even outside, not this time of year, not in California.

Maybe I was coming down with something.

I shivered.

Time to go to bed. Hide under the covers.

As I climbed the stairs to my bedroom, the frigid air held my right hand like a lover on a romantic walk. My fingers went numb, to the point of pins and needles in the fingertips. At the top of the stairs, I made a fist and blew my warm breath into it. Didn't help.

The swirling breeze that had been outside was now in the house. It enveloped me, embraced me.

I shivered. Teeth chattered. My breath now came out in frosty plumes.

Bed. I needed to get to bed.

I stumbled down the hallway and into my bedroom, the swirling, cold air walking with me, still holding my hand. I undressed. Climbed into bed. Lay on my back. Pulled the heavy covers up to my chin.

It didn't help. It felt as though I lay with a block of ice next to me. Only this ice had arms that embraced me, legs that entwined me.

I pulled the covers tighter around me. Hugged myself with them. Still, I shivered uncontrollably. Gooseflesh played across my body and gripped my scalp. My heartbeat slowed to an almost nonexistent beat. My shallow breath came out in wisps that lingered in the frozen air. Yet, despite the cold or maybe because of it, my eyes closed, and I spiraled into unconsciousness.

I opened my eyes to a woman lying next to me. She was as beautiful a woman as I had ever seen. Her hair the color of snow. Her skin a combination of translucent and opaque, like ice. Gray eyes stared at me, her biting gaze penetrating mine. Long slender fingers touched my face, traced lines across my cheeks like sled tracks in the snow.

Wisps escaped my mouth with every breath. "Who—?"

Her icy fingers touched my lips, stopping me before I could finish my question. Already under the covers with me, she snuggled closer, one leg over mine, breasts caressing me, nose nuzzling into the crook of my neck. Her naked body pressed into mine did nothing to warm me.

I trembled within her embrace. I could barely feel my extremities any longer, and my teeth clanked together like windup, toy dentures.

Still, I didn't pull away from her. I reveled in her frigid embrace, the feel of her frosty nipples pressing into me. I pulled her tighter against me, sliding my hands along the slippery skin of her back, grinding my frozen hard-on into her pelvis.

She cooed in my ear as she rolled onto her back, pulling me along with her. I slid on top of her, almost slipping off as if she really were made of ice. She didn't let me, though, grabbing on tight and keeping me in place.

"Who are you?" I whispered.

Rather than answer, she kissed me. Hard. Cold. Her ice-laced tongue danced across mine.

I trembled not only from the cold delight of her kiss but from her icy hand sliding down between us to grab my hard-on. She stroked me within her slippery grasp several times. I gasped and shuddered as she slid me into the tight, wintry confines between her legs.

At first, I just remained still within her, trying to adjust to the subzero landscape surrounding me, almost afraid to move for fear that my frozen member might break clean off. But as she began to moan and move underneath me, I began moving, as well. Slow and easy at first, slipping and sliding in and out of her. Soon, though, she began to thrust her hips upward, grinding into me harder, faster. I followed her pace, plunging deeper. I no longer cared about anything but giving her what she so desperately wanted, and the more I gave her, the more I wanted it as well. The freezing touch of her engulfed me until it no longer felt cold but instead burned. We were now at a frenzied pace. I gasped. My breath still blew out in white wisps, but my lungs were afire. Despite the frozen tundra of her body, she ignited a red-hot passion in me I couldn't control.

Finally, she screamed. Her fingernails dug into my back as she writhed underneath me.

I continued thrusting into her until a deep groan escaped my lips. My climax hurt, as if icicles of semen shot out of me. I didn't care. Once I had emptied myself into her, I wished I had more to give her. I groaned again with agonizing pleasure.

She kissed me hard, plunging her tongue into my mouth. Our tongues and lips stuck together slightly as our kiss broke apart.

I stared down into the biting gaze of her gray eyes. I worked at catching my gasping breath, noticing I could no longer see it escape my mouth. "Who are you?" I asked again.

She smiled but still didn't answer. Instead, she gave me a nudge, suggesting I roll from on top of her.

I followed that suggestion, sliding off.

She climbed out of bed. Extended her hand to me.

I took it. Climbed to my feet and stood next to her.

She turned to leave. Still grasping my hand.

She no longer needed to answer my question. Somehow, I knew who she was, what she was. I didn't care. I went with her willingly anyway. Hand in freezing hand.

As we left this world, I glanced back one last time at myself lying in bed.

Dead.

N⊕T DEAD

Pain burrows through every part of me
Broken ribs slicing me like a knife with every breath
Fractured wrist and injured thumb aching
Concussed head throbbing but empty of recent memory
Like a blank slate
The pain is always a part of me
Never gone
From it I am never free

Depression lives deep inside
Broken spirit slicing me like a knife with every breath
Fractured psyche and injured heart aching
Darkness harboring within my mind, within my soul, from it I cannot fly
Like a bird with broken wings
The depression is always mine
Never gone
But for the life of me I don't know why

Just be happy you're alive, Fred
Be happy your injuries were not fatal
Be happy you just survived, Fred
That's what's expected
That's what people have said
But that's not what I feel
I don't feel the happiness of being alive
Or of having just survived
I'm only happy I'm not dead

There's a difference

Fred Wiehe

THE COLLECTION

The fat man was on his knees. Dressed in red pajamas. Hands bound behind his back. A sock stuffed into his mouth with a piece of black duct tape slapped across his lips. Sweat beaded on his face and plastered thinning, brown hair to his scalp. The breath blowing in and out of his nose was rapid and shallow. His heart was a steady thud. Tremors shook his large frame until he looked like a quivering mass of red *Jello*.

Standing in the fat man's living room, Jamison understood the guy's fear. After all, he himself stood over the trembling lump, a Glock 23 pressed against his quarry's temple.

The fat man struggled against his restraints.

Jamison grinned. This was the part he loved the best. Not the collection itself. Yeah, that was the end game. But the fear before is what excited him most. The sight of it. The sour smell of it. Sometimes, like now, the fear was almost palpable.

The fat man blew air out his nose and struggled to speak. But with the balled-up sock firmly in his mouth and duct tape sealing the deal, all he could manage were muffled pleas.

Jamison took the pistol away from the guy's head. He hunkered down, so they were eye to eye. "You got something to say?" he asked, still grinning.

The fat man's face reddened from exertion. Tears welled in deep-set eyes, streamed down chubby cheeks. His muffled cries intensified.

"You want to plead for your life, Mr. Applebee?" Jamison asked.

The fat man stopped struggling, stopped trying to talk. He just sat there, bugged-eyed, face tear-soaked, snot hanging from his nose.

"That's right," Jamison said. "I know your name. I know who you are."

Applebee's breath raced. His bulk trembled.

"What?" Jamison asked. "Did you think this was just a random act? And you were just a poor victimized sap?" He shook his head.

Applebee's fear had reached new heights. He looked as though he was about ready to piss his pants. From the smell, maybe he already had.

This was getting fun.

"So maybe I should let you plead for your life, huh?" Jamison asked, toying with the guy.

"You going to tell me how you never hurt nobody? That you're a good guy? And you don't deserve this?" He shook his head again, the grin never leaving his face. "That what you going to tell me if I take that gag out?"

Applebee's muffled sobs answered.

Jamison nodded. "Okay, I'll give you a chance," he said. "But you better not disappoint me." He reached up and stripped the snot-soaked duct tape away with one quick swipe.

Applebee let out a muffled cry of pain.

What a wuss.

Jamison shook his head and chuckled. With two fingers, he pulled the sock out of the guy's mouth. Then he tossed it aside.

Applebee coughed and gagged. Worked his tongue around his mouth. Licked his lips. "Bastard," he croaked with false bravado. For his still quivering bulk and the wet stain on the crotch of his pajamas gave him away. "Fucking, bastard." This time the curse came out more like a whimper. "Bastard..."

Jamison shrugged off the obscenities. "You're not really helping your case," he said. Standing, he circled the fat man like a vulture. "You see, Mr. Applebee, my employer demands that I collect one soul by tonight. After some consideration, I've carefully chosen you." He stopped in front of the kneeling fat man. "Why should I go to all the trouble of changing my mind?"

Applebee gathered himself. He choked back his sobs, sniffed snot back up his nose, and took a deep, hitched breath. "What have I ever done to deserve this?" he asked. "I've never done anything to you or your employer. I've never even *seen* you before, you son of a bitch." He coughed, dry and raspy. "Far as I know, I don't even know your goddamn employer." He worked his tongue around his mouth, across his dried lips. "I'm a good man." Tears again formed in his sunken, dark-rimmed eyes. A sob strangled his voice. "I've never hurt anyone."

"You're a good man," Jamison mumbled. "You never hurt anyone." He thought for a moment while he twirled the Glock around his finger like a Western gunslinger. "Hmm, if this were a black and white world then that may be true. As bad men go, you certainly aren't the worst. At least, not yet." He stopped twirling the pistol. Pointed it at the fat man's head. "But this ole' world is grey, shades of grey, Mr. Applebee. And you've operated in the darkest shades of this grey world most of your life. You've worked in the shadows. Behind the scenes. Stabbing people in the back. Or stepping on them and squashing them like worthless bugs. All to your advantage. All the while working your way to the top."

"I'm a fucking businessman," Applebee sniveled, as if that were a defense. "Like any other."

"Like any other," Jamison repeated with a nod. "That may be true."

"Certainly, it is," Applebee said, sniffing back snot, trying not to whimper, trying to show courage.

"What about your employees?" Jamison asked. He went back to twirling the pistol. "You treat them like dirt, don't you? Pay them next to nothing? Steal their ideas? Pass them off as your own? Profit from them?"

Applebee shook his head in apparent disbelief. "Again, you're going to fucking kill me because I'm a shrewd businessman? That's not a crime."

Jamison stopped twirling the Glock. He pointed it at the kneeling fat man. "Kill?" Now he shook his head. "My employer and I prefer to think of it as collecting a soul."

"However, you think of it," Applebee bemoaned, "it's still goddamn murder. Plain and simple."

Jamison stepped forward. He pressed the barrel of the Glock against the fat man's temple. He cocked the hammer.

Applebee shuddered at the loud click of the pistol. He shut tight his tear-soaked eyes. Braced his bulk for the inevitable.

But it didn't come.

Instead, Jamison took the pistol away. He asked, "And what about your wife?"

Applebee opened his eyes. "What about her?"

"You cheated on her, didn't you?"

Applebee squinted. His jowls set firm. "Is she..." He gulped hard. "Is she...your employer?"

Jamison grinned. "Did you cheat on her?"

Applebee's face turned hard as stone. "She cheated on me too," he spat. "That bitch is no angel."

"Didn't she only cheat to get back at you for screwing your secretary?" Jamison paused. "Excuse me, administrative assistant."

Applebee didn't answer.

"And didn't you hit her after you found out? Gave her a black eye, didn't you?"

The fat man looked away. "She shouldn't have cheated on me," he muttered.

"Shouldn't have cheated on you," Jamison repeated the fat man's words. He shook his head in disbelief at the logic. "Didn't you cheat on her first?" He didn't wait for an answer he knew wasn't coming anyway. "Don't you cheat on your taxes? And didn't you cheat your first business partner all those years ago, leaving him broken and penniless? In fact, Mr. Applebee, don't you cheat on everything and everyone?"

Applebee didn't respond.

"Nothing to say?" Jamison asked. "Run out of excuses?" He chuckled. "Really, Mr. Applebee, I expected you to plead for your soul better than this."

Applebee shook his head. "I love my wife..."

Now Jamison outright laughed. "You do?"

"She just made me mad is all. Shouldn't have cheated on me." Applebee hung his head. "As for the rest," he muttered, "I'm just a businessman."

"Not much of a defense, is it?" Jamison asked.

Applebee raised his head. A look of inspiration passed across his jowly face. "Wait, I'm a businessman. You're a businessman. Let's strike a bargain."

"No deals," Jamison said. He pressed the pistol against the fat man's head. "My employer demands a soul collected. Tonight. I spent days setting you up. There's no time to find another. And even if I could, why should I bother? The trouble just wouldn't be worth it to me."

Applebee's large frame trembled anew. Gulping hard, he said, "Wait. I can make it worth your while. And it would be easy. Uncomplicated. No bother to you. I could serve up a...*soul*...to you on a silver platter."

There it was.

Jamison grinned.

What he'd been waiting for.

"How?" Jamison asked.

"There's another soul besides me right here for the taking," Applebee insisted. "Ripe for the taking."

Jamison removed the pistol from the fat man's head. "Your wife?"

"I'll pay you three times more than she's paying you."

"I never said she was my employer."

Applebee squirmed. "I'll pay you anything you want!"

"Interesting," Jamison said. He began circling his prey. "A soul for a soul."

"That's right," Applebee confirmed. "Does the soul have to be me? Can't it be her?" His voice was almost a sob as he continued, "There'd be no further bother or work on your part. She's right here. No fuss, no muss." Fresh tears of desperation ran down chubby cheeks. "And you'd profit from it threefold to boot."

Jamison nodded. "Love your wife, do you?"

Applebee didn't answer. Instead he asked, "Do we have a deal?"

Jamison gave the Glock one twirl around his finger. Caught it. Then aimed it at the fat man's head. "And you'd have no qualms in *serving up her soul?*"

"No," Applebee blubbered. "Let the bitch die. Not me."

"How will you explain it to the authorities?"

"Home invasion," Applebee explained. "Leave me bound. The description of the *perpetrators* will be anything but accurate on my part. Trust me."

"Trust you..." Jamison grinned. "Trust you…" He chuckled. Twirled the Glock. "And the money?"

"In my safe," Applebee answered. "Through that doorway." With his head, he motioned toward a doorway off the living room. "Down the hallway, in the den. The safe's in the floor, under the desk."

"Combination?"

"Twenty-five, right. Thirty-two, left. Nineteen, right."

Jamison continued twirling the Glock. "Call her down here," he said.

Now Applebee grinned. "What about the money?"

"Later," Jamison said. "Call her down here."

"We have an agreement then?" Applebee pressed.

Jamison stopped twirling the pistol. Instead, he again aimed it at the fat man's head. "Call her down," he hissed.

Applebee gulped. "Maggie," he called, voice cracking. He cleared his throat. Again, he called, "Maggie!"

At the top of the stairs, a hallway light went on. Footsteps padded down that hallway.

"Albert?" Maggie called back. "Is that you?"

"Yes, *dear*," Applebee answered. His jowly face contorted into a villainous mask. "Down here, dear, in the living room."

"What is it?" Maggie asked from the top of the stairs.

"Come downstairs," Applebee instructed. Under his breath, he added, "Bitch."

Jamison's gaze never left Applebee's. He had chosen well.

Maggie started down the stairs. Halfway down, she stopped, let out a strangled gasp, and then screamed.

Jamison never let his gaze stray from the fat man. Still, he swung the Glock around and, without aiming or even looking, fired once.

The gunfire echoed. Maggie's scream instantly silenced. Her body thumped down the stairs.

In the fat man's eyes, Jamison saw it. What he knew was there all along. Evil. Madness. He had indeed chosen well.

He turned away and looked at Maggie for the first time. The woman's body lay at the foot of the staircase, head blown apart. Blood pooled there. More blood, as well as chunks of brain and flesh and hair splattered the wall behind where the woman had been descending the stairs.

"Well, you did it, Mr. Businessman," Jamison said. "You stepped out of the grey, out of the shadows you've been operating within for years. You stepped into blackness."

He looked back at the fat man who stared at his wife's dead body with what could only be described as delight.

"*We* did it," Applebee acknowledged. Grinning, he looked back at his assailant.

"Your employer should be happy now. You collected your soul."

Jamison nodded. "I did indeed." He twirled the Glock one last time before holstering it underneath his jacket. "And I'll be back for that soul when the time comes to take possession."

The fat man's grin faded. "What? What do you mean?" Confusion crept across the features of his round face like a lunar eclipse. "You took possession of my wife's soul just now. I saw it with my own eyes."

Jamison looked back at the dead woman. "Oh, your wife's soul was just set free." He turned back to the fat man. "Yours, on the other hand…" He shrugged.

Applebee's face turned red. Tremors racked his bulk. He squinted at Jamison. "What are you talking about? We had a deal."

Sirens wailed in the distance. Someone must have heard the shot and called the cops.

Jamison grinned. "Did we?"

"I paid you, you bastard," Applebee growled. But the expression on his face was more like a beaten dog rather than a rabid wolf. "I paid you…"

Jamison walked to the front door, forgetting the money. "Did you?" He didn't care about the money. Never worked for money. For him, it was all about the collection.

"I don't understand," Applebee bemoaned.

After opening the door, Jamison turned back toward the fat man. "My employer only demanded the collection of the soul by tonight," he explained. "He's a patient man. Once he has it, he's willing to wait to take possession." He shrugged. "My employer will always be there, Mr. Applebee. Hell will always be there. Waiting. They are eternal."

"What are you raving about?"

"Why, your soul, Mr. Applebee." Jamison winked. "You gave it up willingly." He paused. "I'll be back to take possession. When it's time."

Sirens wailed. Getting closer.

Jamison hurried away. Into the night.

The fat man screamed.

SHADOW PAIN

Pain is my shadow
It goes where I go
It stalks me during the day
It lies with me at night
There's no getting away
I can't run
Can't take flight
It's with me always
No matter where I go
No matter what I do
Pain is my shadow

Under the Protection of Witches

A Novella
(Based on the feature-length script *The Uglies*
by Fred Wiehe)

Chapter I

Ellie Evans strolled through the streets of Solemn, Indiana. *Dread*—strange and inexplicable—walked with her like an old yet unwanted companion as she passed well-kept bungalows. She shuddered with a chill despite the unseasonable weather. It was almost Halloween, but still the sun wrapped the neighborhood in a cocoon of warmth. If not for the slight breeze that skipped dried leaves past her feet and ruffled her auburn hair, she wouldn't have needed a jacket at all. Still, she marveled at the laughing and squealing children who ran through the streets and surrounding yards, some wearing nothing more than shorts and T-shirts as if it were August rather than late October. Even their parents out puttering in their yards and raking leaves dressed as if autumn were nothing but a distant memory. Despite this Indian summer, however, the leaves in the surrounding oak and maple trees had turned to bright orange, yellow, and red as they were supposed to this time of year, as if not at all fooled and somehow possessing full knowledge that the death of winter lurked just around the corner.

Shuddering again, she knew it wasn't the slight breeze that sent the chill racing up her spine to her scalp. It was her invisible companion. A companion she couldn't seem to shake whenever she visited her hometown. She had arrived back from college a week ago, only to find that *dread* had not forgotten her and had been waiting for her to return.

She stopped in front of her grandmother's house, hesitating outside the picket fence at the wooden gate. Gran's house was different than all the rest in town. It was in disrepair and desperately needed a fresh coat of paint. The yard had no lawn. Instead it was an overgrown patchwork of herbs, spices, vegetables, and squash. The grotesque faces of gargoyles peeked out of that patchwork, keeping watch. A countless variety of wind chimes hung in trees and all around the porch, tinkling and ringing in the breeze, a warning for anything wicked to keep out.

She took it all in. If not for Gran and the refuge of this house, she would never return to Solemn again. She loved that old woman. Well, there *was* Jim. She was unsure how she truly felt about him, but she might return for Jim too.

She opened the gate. Before stepping through, she whispered, "You stay here." Once through the gate and up the walk to the porch, she had left *dread* behind, waiting at the sidewalk. She could still feel *dread's* eyes on her, though, and a chill again shot through her. Once through the front door, across the threshold, with the door closed behind her, she finally felt completely at ease.

The inside of Gran's house was in as much disrepair and in need of paint as the outside. The furniture was old and careworn. The living room she now navigated was cluttered and full of occult-like oddities, such as the antique book of spells on the coffee table, the collection of crystals on the mantle, and more gargoyles dispersed throughout the room. She found Gran where she thought she would—in the kitchen.

The walls in the kitchen were faded and dirty and the curtains soiled from the countless meals cooked there. Wire baskets hung from the ceiling, filled with herbs, spices, fruits, and vegetables.

Gran stood at the kitchen counter, her back to the room, facing the window that looked out onto the backyard. She chopped and sliced, fruit and chunks of cut-up pumpkin strewn about the counter all around her.

Ellie sat down on a bar stool. Resting her elbows on the round table, she watched with bemusement and in awe as the old woman bustled about the kitchen. Despite her age, Gran was still sprite and energetic, clanking and banging utensils and bottles as she prepared one of her concoctions.

"Gran, what kind of potion are you mixing up now?"

Gran scooped up sliced fruit and pumpkin, depositing both in a blender, along with the ice already there. "Hi, dear, how's Jim?"

Ellie stiffened. Looking away, she shifted in her stool.

Next, Gran poured various liquids from un-labeled bottles into the blender. Then she turned her head and looked over her shoulder at her granddaughter. Now she had the bemused look. "You've only been home from school for a few days and you've been out together every night. I only assumed..." She shrugged.

"We're taking it slow."

"Are you?" Gran slapped the lid on the blender. "And practicing safe sex, I hope."

Ellie's jaw dropped. "Gran—"

The old woman flipped the blender's switch. A high whine drowned out her granddaughter's protestations.

Ellie could feel the heat of embarrassment burning her face. Still, she couldn't help but smile, in spite of herself.

Gran flipped the blender off. She poured two tall glasses of orange, frothy drinks. Turning toward Ellie, she gave her granddaughter a wry grin.

Ellie giggled and shook her head. "Gran, you *are* a wicked, old witch."

The old woman cackled. "Never claimed otherwise, dear." She handed over one of the glasses.

Ellie took the drink. Examined it. "And just what kind of witch's brew is this?"

"I call it *pumpkin colada*."

Ellie giggled. She took a sip. "Whoa! That's strong. Definitely more colada than pumpkin."

Gran took a large gulp and smacked her lips. "Just the way a wicked witch likes it."

Both women burst out laughing.

Ellie took another sip. "I love you, Gran."

"It's good to have you home, dear." After taking another drink, the old woman scrutinized her granddaughter.

Ellie recognized that look. It put her on edge because she knew what was coming next.

"You know, dear, it's time for you to—"

"Not now, Gran." Ellie cut her grandmother off. She shifted on her stool and stared at her drink. "Please. We'll talk about it later."

"Promise?"

Ellie forced a smile. "Promise."

Gran smiled back. She lifted her glass in toast. "Happy Halloween, dear."

Ellie lifted her glass in return.

Before either of them could take a drink, a thud at the front door startled them.

Ellie jumped off her stool. Her glass slipped from her hand, smashing against the linoleum floor. Orange concoction splattered everywhere.

Another thud quickly followed on the heels of the first, this time, though, hitting glass.

"It's started," Ellie mumbled. The Halloween tradition she hated most had just begun, and it wasn't even dusk yet. Maybe she shouldn't have come home, after all, no matter how much she loved her grandmother.

Another thud confirmed what she feared. A chorus of catcalls bombarded the house next:

"Witch! Witch! Witch!"

Gran rushed from the kitchen.

Ellie followed, hot on her grandmother's heels.

Another thud resounded.

Yellow and white carnage defiled the large picture window in the front room. Children stood in the yard and on the sidewalk. Ellie could see the kids through the tainted glass. They threw more eggs.

Thud! Thud! Thud!

"Witch! Witch! Witch!"

Gran hurried to the front door, hand poised on the doorknob as another egg smashed against the other side.

Ellie rushed forward, her pretty, pale face set into grim determination as if chiseled into place by a tormented sculptor. She pushed herself between her grandmother and the door. "Wait, Gran."

"Stand aside," Gran ordered.

"What if they still have eggs?"

An egg thumped against the other side as if punctuating the warning.

The old woman smiled but without humor. "It wouldn't be the first time I've been pelted with eggs...or worse." Loose strands of gray hair had escaped from the tight bun atop her head. She pushed them aside, revealing steely-blue eyes. "I must put a stop to this, Ellie. I must remind everyone that we should be celebrated and not scorned, that we are all that stands between them and destruction. They *are* under our protection."

"But they're just kids."

Gran nodded. "Kids repeating what they've heard at home." Her careworn face hardened. "Their parents and their grandparents have forgotten. They need reminding. Everyone needs reminding."

Ellie reluctantly moved aside. Deep down she couldn't help feeling this was a mistake, but she resigned herself to her grandmother's strong will.

Without further argument, Gran flung open the door. She stepped across the threshold and into the fray, undaunted by the taunts of the children and the eggs that splattered about her.

Ellie remained framed in the doorway, unwilling to cross the threshold, unable to step into harm's way.

Gran waved her frail arm as if it were a magic wand and cried, "Be gone."

The children scattered like autumn leaves in a bitter wind, accusations of witchery still on their lips but quickly dying with retreat.

The old woman charged across the porch as if to give chase but stopped short at the top of the steps. A groan escaped her lips. She clutched her left arm.

Black clouds formed on the horizon. A flash of light illuminated the oncoming blackness.

Gran toppled down the steps, landing at the bottom in a broken heap.

Distant thunder rumbled.

Ellie screamed. She took out her cell phone, dialing 911 as she rushed outside, across the porch, and down the steps. "I need an ambulance," she screeched into the phone when the dispatcher picked up. She knelt next to Gran, checking her vitals. "99 Ravenswood Lane. Hurry, it's my grandmother."

Gran reached out and dug her long fingernails into her granddaughter's arm. "It's up to you now," she croaked, an edge of agony to her rusty voice. She stared at the heavens above. "If only your mother was still here."

"Gran," Ellie begged. She dropped her phone. "Don't leave me."

Sirens wailed in the distance. Getting closer.

"It's up to you," Gran repeated. Her eyes went blank as she released her grip, hand flopping onto the ground.

"Gran," Ellie cried, tears bursting forth.

Suddenly *dread* knelt next to her, emboldened by current events, having never crossed the gate's threshold before.

"Don't leave me," she again begged, unable to fathom facing the world alone. She buried her face in her grandmother's bosom. "Don't leave me..." Her muffled pleas, however, did no good.

And with Gran's dying breath, *dread* pressed closer and the storm above gathered.

Chapter 2

Dusk loomed overhead as an old Ford Mustang drove slowly through the secluded woods on the outskirts of town. It pulled into a small clearing, parked, and darkened its headlights.

An ancient, mammoth tree stood nearby like a sentinel through time. Its long, heavy branches reached out in all directions— leafless, gnarled and withered, bark peeling. An ugly, jagged scar marked the thick, twisted trunk where long ago there had once been a gaping wound. A small iron box was mysteriously embedded within that scar.

Inside the car, Luke made his move.

Maggie pushed him away. "Dude, why'd you bring me *here*?"

He shrugged. "Like you don't know."

The girl hooked her long, blond hair behind her ear and stared out her window. "That tree creeps me out." She shivered.

"Forget the fucking tree." Luke reached for her.

She again pushed him away. "Dude!"

"What?"

"That tree…I've heard stories about it."

Luke shrugged again. "We all have. When I was a kid, we told them around the campfire late at night. But they're just stories."

Lightning flashed over the treetops.

Maggie flinched.

Distant thunder rumbled.

The two moved closer. Luke snuck his arm around Maggie, pulling her close. This time she didn't protest or push away.

"I heard that the family of witches in town put a curse on the tree," Maggie whispered, "on this place." She snuggled in closer to Luke, but her gaze never left the tree outside her window. "The secret of the curse is supposed to be hidden in the metal box that's stuck in the trunk." She bit her lower lip, deep in thought. "How do you suppose the box got there? Magic?"

"Don't know and don't care." Luke pushed her blond hair aside and caressed her cheek. Gently, he turned her face, so she was looking at him rather than the tree outside the window. "Hey, I thought we were going to neck."

Maggie sighed. "Well, as long as we're here."

Luke grinned. He leaned in for their first kiss.

Maggie obliged, kissing him back, even giving him a little tongue.

Soon the two were lost in teenage lust and fogged windows, oblivious to dusk giving way to a densely black night, the flashes of light periodically brightening the treetops, and the far-off peel of thunder.

A bolt of lightning ripped a hole through the blackness outside their windows. It rammed the iron box held captive within the tree. The thunderous boom that followed in hot pursuit shook the Mustang.

Luke jerked away and cried out—high and shrill.

Maggie sat up straight, wide-eyed and breathless. "Dude, what was that?" She fumbled with the buttons of her blouse. "It sounded like a bomb."

Luke squirmed in pain. "You fucking bit me," he squealed.

"Stop being such a baby."

"You could've bitten it clean off." He struggled with his pants and surreptitiously wiped away a few tears. "Then where would I be?"

Maggie rolled her eyes. "The same dickless jerk you are now."

"You didn't think I was a dickless jerk a few seconds ago."

"Well, I think so now. Zip up and shut up."

Luke fumbled with his zipper and kept his mouth shut.

Maggie used the palm of her hand to clear the fogged window. The squeal of her hand on glass raised the hackles on the back of her neck, but she continued until she could at least somewhat see. She pressed her face to the window.

"What the hell's out there anyway?" Luke leaned over her, face pressed to the window.

"I can't see anything. It's too dark."

Lightning flashed overhead, illuminating the clearing and the tree for a split second.

"Jesus Christ," Luke exclaimed, "did you see that? Lightning must've hit the tree."

Thunder rumbled.

"I didn't get a good look," Maggie complained. "Turn on the headlights."

He did as he was told. The car, however, was parked parallel to the tree, and the headlights shot past it instead of onto it. Still, the headlights helped illuminate the clearing, if not the tree directly.

Maggie wiped away the returning fog, palm squealing against glass. She and Luke peered through the window.

The tree looked as if it had a gaping hole where the scar had been just moments before. Sporadic tongues of flames still ignited the scorched edges. Smoke lingered in the heavy air. The iron box lay open a few feet from the base of the tree, blackened and smoldering, the secrets that had been hidden inside apparently lost forever.

"I told you this place was cursed," Maggie muttered.

"What's that?" Luke asked.

"What's what?"

A small, dark figure, not more than four feet tall, staggered through the lingering smoke and darkness, just beyond the edge of the headlights.

"That."

"Someone's out there," Maggie exclaimed. "I think that's a kid."

"It can't be a kid. What would a damn kid be doing out here all alone?"

Maggie's palm squealed across the glass. "I tell you it's a kid." She pounded Luke's shoulder with her fist. "We've gotta help him.

Get out of the car." She pounded him again. "We've gotta help him."

Luke shot her an indignant look and rubbed his arm. "Okay…okay, stop hitting me." He opened his door. "A guy can take just so much abuse."

"Get out of the car."

Luke stopped. "It's starting to rain."

Maggie pushed him from behind. "Get out."

"Okay…okay…" Luke climbed out.

Maggie scooted across the seat, scrambling out the same door, right behind.

Luke stumbled out of her way. "I would've never asked you out if I knew you were like this."

She punched him again. "Shut up."

Luke rubbed his arm but complied.

Once outside the car, they both stopped short. A light drizzle greeted them. A pungent odor of ozone hung in the still, heavy air. Lightning flashed overhead, electricity igniting the night. Their hair stood on end. Thunder rumbled as they held onto each other, neither of them sure now that getting out of the car was such a good idea.

The small, dark figure staggered toward them.

"We gotta help him," Maggie muttered.

Still holding onto each other, they crept forward. Maggie reached out a hand. "Don't be scared," she said. "We'll help you."

The figure answered with strange chittering sounds.

They both stopped. "We'll help you," Maggie repeated. "Don't be scared."

The figure continued its strange noises.

Luke gulped hard. He took a step backwards. "Maggie, let's get back inside the damn car."

With that declaration, a second figure, just as small and just as dark, staggered out of the lingering smoke and darkness. Another followed it, then another and another, more and more of them escaping through the gaping hole in the tree.

Chitter…chitter…chitter…

"Back inside the car," Luke repeated.

Still holding onto each other, they stepped backwards, unwilling to turn their backs on these things.

The chittering grew louder and more rapid. Beady, red eyes blinked from out of the darkness. The leader exposed razor-sharp teeth and spread large, bat-like wings. The others followed suit.

Maggie screamed.

They turned as one and took off for the car.

Luke tripped and fell after just a few feet. "Maggie, help."

The horde shrieked in unison.

"Maggie, fucking help me."

She never looked back. She kept moving as fast as she could for the refuge of the Mustang.

The horde took flight, pouncing on their helpless prey.

When Luke squealed like a pig being slaughtered, Maggie stopped and turned. She knew she should keep going, but she could no longer bring herself to leave her friend behind.

From under the pile of attacking beasts, Luke kicked his legs and flailed his arms to no avail. There were too many. The things tore into him. Soon his legs and arms only moved with involuntary spasms. His squeals died and all that could be heard were the horrible sounds of the things ripping flesh and sucking blood. He was beyond helping.

Maggie screeched in horror. She turned on her heels, continuing her flight to the car, climbing in and slamming the door behind her. She screeched again as she witnessed the final carnage through fogged glass.

When one of the large, bat-like creatures pounced on the car, she quickly locked the doors. More of the horrid things followed suit. They skittered across the hood, roof, and trunk, searching for a way inside. Ugly, rodent-like faces pressed against the glass, peering in from all sides with their beady, red eyes.

The constant chittering, the sounds of claws and wings scraping along the car, wracked her nerves. She had to get out of there, before those things got to her. Grabbing for the keys in the ignition, her breath strangled in her throat. They weren't there. Frantically, she looked on the seat next to her, felt on the seat under her, and searched the floor.

Nothing.

Luke must've taken them with him.

She swallowed back burning bile and considered her options. Without much thought, she leaned on the horn. It blared into the night, almost mournful.

The creatures took flight, suddenly gone.

She tried to catch her racing breath.

Were they really gone?

She scanned the landscape and the sky the best she could through fogged glass, drizzle, and darkness.

There was no sign of her attackers.

Lightning flashed.

What she could see was Luke lying motionless on the ground.

Thunder rumbled.

She bit her lower lip.

He had to have the keys, probably in the pocket of his jeans.

Once more, she scanned the landscape outside her window. Still no sign of the beasts. It was now or never. Steeling herself, she reached for the door handle.

Before she could make her move, something rammed the car.

The Mustang rocked on its shocks. She screamed, piercing and shrill. She held on for dear life as time and again large, winged creatures dive-bombed her sanctuary, rocking it, denting it, cracking glass, until finally the windshield shattered and the beasts were on her.

Screams filled the night. Blood splattered the windows.

The beastly chitters turned into feeding-frenzy growls.

Chapter 3

Deep shadows loomed across Gran's gloomy living room. Outside the egg-defiled picture window, far-off lightning occasionally illuminated the darkening sky. A rumbling thunder travelled with the lightning, a few brief seconds behind. Flashing red and blue lights rhythmically splashed across the house, through the window, and into the living room.

Ellie sat on a threadbare, faded sofa. Tears and anguish marred her pretty face. Sobs choked her throat. Her hands fought with balled-up wads of Kleenex. *Dread* no longer shadowed her, no longer followed her as a companion, but instead lived within her. She could no longer hide from it or leave it behind. It was now as much a part of her as her soul.

Deputy-Sheriff James Steady stood at the window, watching the Medical Examiner drive off with Gran's body. "They've taken her," he said. He left the window and sat down on the sofa.

Ellie remained mute, staring at nothing, trembling hands wrestling with the tissue.

"I'm sorry, El. Those kids, they had no right taunting her the way they did, calling her a witch."

Ellie turned and eyed the man sitting next to her as if he were a stranger. He was no stranger, however. The sight of his handsome face, brown eyes, and dark, wavy hair still made her heart jump just like when they dated in high school.

She pushed strands of auburn curls from her face, wiped away some tears, and choked back a sob. "Jimmy, those kids had no right taunting her for what she was, but Gran *was* a witch."

Jim shook his head. "What are you telling me, El?" He snickered but without humor. "Ding-dong, the witch is dead?" He paused. "I don't think so."

Ellie smacked him on the shoulder. "No jokes. Not now." She wiped away more tears. "Not about this."

He looked down at his hands. "I'm sorry, El. I just meant…" He looked up into Ellie's eyes. "Your grandmother was a sweet, old lady, nothing more."

She squared her shoulders and gave the deputy a hard look. "Jim Steady, you know better." She could hardly believe what she had just heard. Maybe her old boyfriend was a stranger, after all? "You didn't want to admit it to yourself when we dated in high school and apparently you still don't."

Jim looked away.

"It was the rumors that broke us up. You didn't say so, but I knew it was true."

"El, I didn't—"

"It's okay," she interrupted. "I understood...sort of." She shrugged. "But when you asked me out again, I assumed you'd come to terms with it." Now she looked away, staring at the wadded-up Kleenex in her hands. "I guess we should've talked about it before we made..." Her voice trailed off.

Jim reached for her hand.

Ellie pulled away.

"I hope you're not sorry," he whispered, "because I'm not."

Ellie studied her boyfriend's face. Could she call him her boyfriend, having just started dating again? She wasn't sure. But there was a far more important question to answer, and only he could answer it, so finally pointblank she asked, "You're not sorry you had sex with a witch?"

"I'm not sorry we made love, if that's what you mean." Jim again reached for her hand.

This time she didn't pull away.

A sly grin played across Jim's face. "And just for the record, we didn't break up because you were witchy. We broke up because you were bitchy."

"Jim!" She smacked Jim on the arm but suddenly found herself grinning through the tears. "You're a jerk."

He grinned from ear to ear. "Got you to smile, didn't I? Even if it was for just a second."

A flash of light hit the picture window and lit up the entire room for a split second. A sonic boom followed.

They both jumped to their feet, rushed to the window, and peered into the cloud-infested sky.

"It's started," Ellie choked out.

Dread strangled her from within.

"What's started?" Jim pressed his face to the glass, straining to see. "World War III?"

She closed her eyes and concentrated, willing *dread* to release its stranglehold. Finally, she managed to mutter, "Might as well be." She had hoped beyond hope that Gran's death would not set into motion events that she felt ill-equipped to handle and to stop.

"What?"

She opened her eyes and stared into Jim's confused face. "Take me to the tree," was all she said.

Chapter 4

The rain had died. Lightning and thunder were nothing more than ghosts and echoes. Damp air and puddles and mud were the only remnants left of the passing storm.

Headlights on bright, spotlight lit, the police cruiser pulled up behind a Ford Mustang already parked in the clearing.

Ellie gasped at the sight. She shook her head in disbelief and despair.

The Mustang sat dead, dark, and lifeless on four flat tires. Its windshield and windows were shattered. Its roof was concave, and its body looked as though it had been slammed repeatedly with a sledgehammer.

"Shit, El, what could've happened?"

She had no ready answer, at least not one she was willing to share now. Instead of answering the question, she said, "Jimmy, move the spotlight onto the tree."

Jim complied.

The spotlight cut through the night, throwing a harsh light across the clearing. The tree had been split open, edges burned and still smoking. A few feet away lay the iron box. Blackened, opened, and empty.

Her gaze riveted to the box. This confirmed her deepest fears. The death of her grandmother had broken the spell. "They're free." She bit her lower lip until it bled. Her trembling hand wiped away tears. "They're free."

"Look," Jim said, as if he hadn't heard those dreaded words. "I guess we know what happened to the owner of the Mustang." He shifted the spotlight slightly. Not far from the box, a dark figure in ripped clothes was sprawled on the ground, looking like a discarded scarecrow, the stuffing stomped out of it.

Ellie again gasped.

"I need to get out and investigate. El, I want you to stay put."

She wiped away the remaining tears. Going out there was the last thing in the world she wanted to do. Still, she gathered herself, steeled her nerves. "Not on your life." Without further hesitation, she opened her door and climbed out.

Jim sighed. "Like I said, we broke up because you were bitchy, not witchy." He opened his door and followed.

"I heard that." She looked at Jim over the roof of the cruiser.

He grinned at her. "Meant for you to."

"You really *are* a jerk, James Steady," she retorted. She couldn't stop herself from smiling back. Verbally jousting with Jim created the illusion of normalcy. But she knew everything was anything but normal.

The two stood on either side of the cruiser for a moment, taking in the night. A slight breeze ruffled the leaves of the surrounding trees, which in turn encouraged raindrops to shake loose of the leaves and plunk to the soggy ground. A nearby night bird sang a cheery melody. Cicadas chimed in. Small, nocturnal animals scurried in the brush at the edge of the clearing.

Again, the illusion of normalcy pervaded the night. In fact, under other circumstances the setting could be considered romantic.

Ellie glanced at Jim, then turned her attention away, and eyed the gaping wound in the trunk of the ancient tree. Next, she turned toward the dark figure lying on the ground not far away.

Unfortunately, though, romance was not in the cards, and she knew nothing would ever be normal again.

Suddenly, Jim was at her side.

"You can stay here. There's no need for you to get any closer."

She shook her head. "I have to see for myself."

He nodded in resignation.

Together, the two inched toward the *stomped scarecrow*. The biting odor of death and the incessant buzzing of flies, however, warned them that they wouldn't find remnants of straw.

Standing over the body, Jim used the toe of his boot to flip what was left of it over onto its back.

Ellie had to stifle a cry. She held a hand over her mouth and nose.

The spotlight revealed every gory detail of the ravaged corpse, of the dismembered limbs, of the blood that soaked the ground, of the flies and other bugs that feasted on what little flesh remained.

Even the normally tough deputy-sheriff gagged at the sight.

"Who do you think it…*was*?" Ellie choked out from behind her hand.

"Who could tell?" Jim regained his composure. "He might as well have the golden arches over him with a sign that reads, *Billions of Animals and Insects Served*."

Ellie smacked him on the arm but said nothing. Instead, she scanned the clearing like a frightened mouse.

"Sorry." He rubbed his arm. "But seriously, El, the M.E. is going to have a hard time figuring out cause of death vs. injuries postmortem." He hunkered down and inspected the corpse closer. "It looks like he's been out here for days, if it is a *he*…who could tell? But what's really weird is no one's recently filed a missing person's report. You'd think someone would've by now."

"You'd think…" She continued to scan her surroundings, fighting the instinctual urge to flee. She didn't need a medical examiner to tell her cause of death. Animals hadn't done this to the body postmortem, and she was sure it hadn't been out there for days. This had to have happened less than an hour ago, right after they heard the sonic boom, right after the lightning hit the tree. She thought of warning her companion but decided he'd never believe her, not without evidence. For the time being, she kept quiet but alert.

Jim stood. "I'm going to take a look inside the car. You okay?"

She nodded, despite wanting to run and scream.

At the Mustang, the deputy-sheriff inspected the beaten car inside and out. "There's no one inside," he called, "but there's blood and lots of it. And I bet it's not *his* either." He looked around the clearing from where he stood. "This has always been a place kids come to be...uh...you know...*alone.* Considering that, and with the amount of blood in the car, there must be another victim here somewhere." He moved to the back of the car. "I better run the plates." He looked at Ellie. "You still okay?"

She hadn't moved. Again, she nodded.

Jim walked back to the police cruiser to use its computer.

While he did that, Ellie stumbled to the tree, legs wobbly underneath her, acutely aware that one or more of the escapees from Hell could be hiding somewhere close. Still, she found the courage to go on. She had to see for herself. Glancing around nervously, she examined the cavernous hole in the twisted trunk. It seemed impossible, but the hole looked to go on forever—back and then down, as if it were a tunnel leading to perdition.

And maybe it was, she thought, *for the things now loose upon the world were certainly born of Hell.*

Shivering, gooseflesh scampering across her skin like bugs on that corpse, she turned away and tiptoed around the dead man to the blackened and damaged iron box. It lay at her feet, opened and empty. She bent over to pick it up but a strange noise brought her up short.

Chitter…chitter…

She straightened, cocked her head, and strained to hear. Turning in circles, she searched for the source of the noise. Nothing lurked within the clearing lit by the cruiser's spotlight. Only blackness lay outside the harsh light's perimeter. The noise stopped, but still she remained alert—watching, listening.

The night and the once active nocturnal wildlife had suddenly and strangely gone deathly silent. The air hung heavy and still.

Chitter...chitter...

Her breath caught in her throat. "This isn't good." Her heart slammed against her ribcage. She felt sure at least one of the things had remained behind and now stalked her. She glanced toward the police cruiser. The driver's door was open, but Jim sat inside the car, safe.

Remaining ever vigilant, she hunkered down and blindly picked up the iron box, clutching it to her breast as she stood. Trying to remain at least outwardly calm, she crept toward the safety and protection of the police cruiser.

Chitter...chitter...chitter...

A shadow from above moved across the lighted area.

She dared not look skyward but could no longer pretend ignorance, could no longer maintain false bravado. A scream escaped her lips as she fled full speed toward Jim and the car.

Within only a few frantic steps, her stalker dropped out of the sky. It pounced on her as a hawk would spring on a field mouse. Wings beat against the night air. Pain seized her neck and shoulder. Sharp claws dug into her flesh.

She crashed to the ground, face first. A mouthful of dirt stifled her screams. She kicked and flailed as the thing dragged her along the ground. Once outside the lighted area, it collapsed on top of her, folding its membranous wings and wrapping them around her like a protective cocoon. However, it offered no protection, only pain and death as its dagger-like teeth ripped through her shirt and struck flesh. In her mind, she screamed and fought back, but in reality, she couldn't move or make a sound, pinned within the prison of the wings.

Muffled gunfire struck the night. The thing convulsed around her. Its teeth mercifully released her flesh. A shriek shattered her hearing. Wings released their grip. Another round of gunfire followed. The thing rolled away, its shrieks turning to wails.

She raised her head, spitting and coughing up dirt, blinking dirt and sweat from her eyes. Jim stood a few feet away. The thing squirmed in pain on the ground at his feet. It struggled to get up, bared sharp fangs, and hissed.

He aimed his revolver. "You feel lucky, punk?" He fired one last time, a clean shot to the horrid thing's head. It collapsed onto the ground, surrounded by splattered blood, bone fragments, and brain tissue.

He lowered his revolver. "Take that, you ugly piece of shit."

That was the last thing Ellie saw or heard before everything turned pitch black.

CHAPTER 5

The threatening storm had passed with the coming of night. The town of Solemn began celebrating Halloween. Homes all over town now impersonated haunted houses. Yards became fake cemeteries complete with headstones and grave markers, plastic body parts and severed heads strewn about them. Store-bought and homemade ghosts and monsters peeked out of shrubs, hung in trees, and lurked around corners. Strobe lights and imitation fog blinded trick-or-treaters in the already pitch-black night. Scary music and phony, recorded screams filled the damp air. Costumed teenagers and children crowded the streets. Parents accompanied the smaller trick-or-treaters, but most of the little ghouls, goblins, vampires, and assorted other monsters ran rampant from house to house. They splashed through puddles and tore up muddy yards as they yelled trick or treat, screamed, and laughed, collecting their candy.

Hidden in plain sight within this pandemonium, blending seamlessly into the crowd of counterfeit monsters, were hideous, dark creatures. Their incessant *chitters* were drowned out by the ensuing noise. They wrapped their wings close around their four-foot frames and toddled along with everyone else as if they too were nothing more than trick-or-treaters.

In a sense, these creatures were trick or treating. The townspeople of Solemn just didn't know that they were the treats.

Chapter 6

Three dark figures hurried along a crowded street of trick-or-treaters. They each wore dark hoodies and monstrous rubber masks. Carrying pillowcases laden with candy, they ducked into a back alley, stopping halfway down. Buildings surrounded them on three sides. The only way out was the way they had come.

All three simultaneously took down their hoods and pulled off their masks.

John tried not to stare, but he couldn't tear his gaze from Leslie. Her red hair hung sweaty and tangled to her shoulders. Her freckled face shined with perspiration. He should've thought her a bit disgusting but instead he thought she never looked hotter.

"These things are hot," Leslie said.

That jolted John from his thoughts. "Huh…what…?" he stammered. Had she been reading his thoughts?

She gave him a weird look. "The masks, they're hot."

"Oh yeah," he quickly agreed. "The masks are hot."

Lincoln gave John a friendly shove. "What else is hot, John-boy?"

John shot daggers at his friend. The asshole knew. Somehow, he knew.

Lincoln laughed. "Go ahead, John-boy, tell her."

John hated it when anyone called him that. And he hated that Lincoln knew his secret, and right now he just plain hated Lincoln. He hated himself too, though. The three of them had been best friends, inseparable, since first grade. Now, ten years later, he suddenly started looking at Leslie differently, feeling all weird around her. He dreamt about her sometimes, waking in a sweaty and sticky mess. It was embarrassing, even though nobody but him knew. And he hated himself for it. He'd probably ruin their friendship over it. He didn't want that.

Leslie scrunched her face. She pointed at Lincoln. "I think that mask fried what little brain you had left." She looked from one friend to the other and back again. "Wow, you guys are a mess." She giggled and tried to fix her hair. "I hope I don't look as bad."

"You look worse…so much worse." Lincoln winked. "Tell her, John-boy. She looks fucking hideous."

John could feel the heat in his cheeks. He wanted to punch his so-called friend.

Somehow, he managed a smile. "You look…*hideous*."

"Shut up," Leslie shouted, fussing with her hair in earnest.

Lincoln shook his pillowcase. "Hey, are we eatin' candy or not?" Now he gave Leslie a friendly shove. "Unless you wanna give me a different kind of sugar." He puckered his lips and kissed the air.

She scrunched her face anew. "Yuck, you're disgusting."

"So are you, but I'm willing to look past it."

"Jerk!"

Lincoln winked again. "Maybe you'd rather give your sugar to John then."

Leslie glanced at John and blushed. She then looked at her shoes, but said nothing.

"You're a shit," John said. The urge to punch the guy was stronger than ever. He was really pushing it.

Lincoln unwrapped a *Snickers* bar, shoving the entire thing into his mouth. "Just tryin' to bring you two nerds together," he said around the wad of candy.

John's mouth dropped. He looked at the girl he secretly loved. She still studied her shoes. Why hadn't she protested a kiss for him? Why wouldn't she look at him now? He shot his friend a look. What exactly did Lincoln know?

He didn't have time to contemplate those questions further. Behind him, something made a noise, like a *chitter*. Then came a *tapping* sound, like a dog's toenails on pavement. He turned in time to see a shadow enter the alley and disappear behind a dumpster. "What was that?"

Lincoln swallowed the last of the candy bar. "What was what?" He unwrapped a *Milky Way* and shoved that into his mouth.

"I heard something. Then I saw a shadow. It ducked behind that dumpster."

Leslie looked up. Her expression suggested gratitude for a change of subject. She shrugged. "Probably was just a dog."

Lincoln swallowed. "Or a goddamn rat."

"Eww!" The girl shivered.

John looked nervously around the dark alley. "I guess."

From the back of the alley came a flapping of wings. More toenails on pavement followed.

Leslie gasped. "That wasn't a dog or a rat."

Lincoln glanced behind him. "Bat." He shoved in another candy bar. With a shrug, he said, "Basically just a fucking rat with wings."

John wasn't convinced. He squinted, straining to see. Night, however, engulfed the alley, making it impossible. Then Leslie moved closer, shoulder to shoulder, and he lost all thought other than the slight feel of her next to him.

A metal garbage can at the back of the alley crashed to the pavement. It rolled across concrete, banging against a wall.

All three teenagers startled. John gasped. Leslie let out a tiny squeal and grabbed his arm. Lincoln just fell silent. All three stared back into the darkness.

"Let's get the hell out of here," John suggested.

Lincoln nodded. "For once, John-boy, we're in agreement."

With his love still clutching his arm, John began retreating toward the alley entrance.

Lincoln started to follow, but a flapping noise stopped him in his tracks. Before he could turn around, a winged creature swooped out of the darkness. Its shriek sounded demonic as it pounced onto his back. Wings flapped at the air. Talons ripped through the hoodie and dug into flesh. Fangs sank into his throat, stifling the beginnings of a scream.

Leslie screamed for her friend—piercing and shrill. Her fingernails dug into John, who was frozen in time, unable to react, unable to think.

Blood spurted everywhere as the horrible thing brought Lincoln down. It collapsed on top of the boy, wrapping its wings around its prey, growling as it hungrily fed.

Wide-eyed, splattered in his friend's blood, John watched the grisly scene. He heard Leslie's screams and felt her pulling on his arm, but lost within himself, he did nothing to move. Even when another winged monster dropped out of the night, he couldn't react. The thing landed on Leslie's head, grabbed her by the hair, ripped her from him, and flew off. Her legs kicked at the air. Her screams echoed through the night, even as she disappeared.

Still, he did nothing. His mouth opened as if to scream, but no sound came out. A warm wetness spread from his crotch and down his trembling leg. He never even saw his attacker until the thing was upon him.

By then it was too late.

Chapter 7

Kathy held Mama's hand as they walked down the sidewalk. She looked longingly at all the costumed kids running the streets, carrying their bags full of treats, smiling and laughing, celebrating Halloween. Something she had never been able to do. Something she fantasized doing.

Her mother brought them to a stop. Jolted from her thoughts and fantasies, the ten-year-old looked up at the mammoth church before them. Stone steps led up to heavy-looking, wooden doors. Stained glass windows looked like large, kaleidoscope eyes in the stone walls. A lighted clock tower with a cross on top reached up to the heavens.

"Let's go inside, child," Mama said.

Just as they started up the steps, a huge bird-like shadow passed across the front of the clock tower.

Kathy halted, breath caught in her throat.

Her mother stopped a step ahead. She looked down at the girl and tugged her hand. "Come, child. Don't dally."

Kathy looked back up at the clock tower. No sign of the bird shadow. It must've been her imagination running wild again. The evils of Halloween, Mama would say, playing tricks on her. She stepped up next to her mother and continued up the steps to the double doors. The two crossed the threshold together, the big wooden doors closing the evil world out behind them.

Inside, the lingering smell of incense tickled the girl's nostrils, forcing her to stifle a sneeze. Tall, white candles in golden candlesticks lit the entryway. The celebratory sounds of kids outside could still be heard as they tiptoed to the threshold that led to the main body of the church. Before crossing that threshold, they stopped at the fonts of holy water flanking each side. Both dipped in two fingers and then made the sign of the Cross before crossing the threshold and continuing down the wide aisle. Their footsteps echoed in the high-domed church as they passed row upon row of empty wooden pews.

All the while, dread brewed in the cauldron of Kathy's stomach.

It wasn't the grand altar awaiting them beyond the sanctuary railing that slowed her pace with misdoubt or the crucifix towering over it or the statues of Jesus, the Virgin Mary, and various saints surrounding it. It wasn't the confessionals flanking the railing, where sins were told to priests that stirred the brew in her stomach. It was the prayer station that gave life to her dread, a place where people prayed and lit candles in crimson-glass cups for the dead.

At the end of the aisle, Mama crossed herself and genuflected before the altar. When the girl didn't follow suit, Mama simply said, "Child?"

Kathy crossed herself and went down on one knee as was expected.

Afterward, her mother led the way to the prayer station. They both knelt at the sanctuary railing in front of the station. Mama lit a votive candle and made the sign of the Cross. "That was for Daddy." Even though she whispered, her voice echoed in the vacant church.

Kathy looked down at her folded hands. Her stomach churned. She knew it was for Daddy. Every week, she and her mother lit a candle and said a prayer for Daddy's soul, a constant reminder that *he* was dead.

She looked up from her hands, over her shoulder, and down the long aisle, toward the large double doors and escape. The faint sound of other kids celebrating Halloween continued outside, calling to her.

"There's nothing out there for you, child," Mama said, glancing down. "We don't celebrate the Devil's holiday."

Gasping at being caught, Kathy quickly turned back around, again staring at her folded hands. She wanted to protest but bit her lower lip instead.

"Those people will regret their ways, child. They brought the Devil down on us once before, many years ago. My own Mama told me the story."

The girl nodded. She had heard the warning before.

"They'll bring the devil again, child. Mark my words." Mama crossed herself. "And we don't want to be a part of it now, do we?"

Sounds of the *Devil's holiday* again drifted through the church from outside.

Even after her mother's lecture, Kathy glanced down the aisle again, toward the exit. She couldn't help herself. She longed to be free of church, to forget for at least a short while that her father was forever gone. She longed to have fun.

"It's the Devil's work out there, child," Mama scolded.

Kathy gasped. Caught again. She quickly turned her attention back to the prayer station.

"Now light a candle for Daddy and say a prayer."

Reluctantly, she reached for a wick from the supply next to the candles. She lit it from an already burning candle and used it to light another. Afterward, she blew out the wick, put it down, and dutifully made the sign of the Cross.

A crash from behind stopped her in mid-prayer.

Both girl and mother gasped, simultaneously whirling toward the sound. The older woman pulled her daughter close as they stared toward the entryway.

Another crash followed on the heels of the first. A strange skittering-clicking noise came after.

But the noises weren't coming from the entryway.

Kathy's heart thumped as her gaze drifted up toward the choir loft that extended out over the back pews. New skittering-clicking noises accelerated her heartbeat even more. The odd *chitter* that followed choked her breath.

Something that looked like the Devil hopped up onto the choir loft's railing.

She screamed even as her mother pressed her closer.

The Devil perched itself on the railing and spread large bat-like wings. Its screech boomed through the church, rivaling her own scream.

"Child, they brought the Devil," Mama shrieked. "I told you. They brought the Devil."

The Devil suddenly took flight. It swooped down from its perch, flying low along the pews. With mouth open and razor-sharp teeth exposed, the thing hit the older woman head-on. The impact sent her and the attacker crashing through the railing and into the sanctuary.

Knocked free, Kathy tumbled in the opposite direction, landing in front of the first row of pews. She scrambled to her knees in time to see the Devil's massive jaws clamp down on her mother's face. Blood splattered everywhere. She screamed again at the sight of her mother being eaten alive.

At that, the thing stopped its feast. Slowly, it turned its hideous, blood-soaked face toward the girl and hissed.

Kathy choked on her scream. On hands and knees, she clambered to the first row of pews. She scrunched underneath them. Face soaked with tears, blood pounding in her ears, she crawled from under one row of pews to the next, desperately trying to remain unseen and unheard, desperately trying to make good her escape.

Behind her, scrapes and chitters gave chase.

She quickened her pace. Something grabbed at her ankle, cutting her. She screamed.

Chapter 8

Charlie placed a bowl of candy on the small end table next to his favorite easy chair. Settling into the chair, he picked up the remote that turned on the cable box. He used another remote to turn on the wide-screen television and yet another for the sound system.

"Goddamn technology," he muttered.

He ran his hand through what little hair he had left. There was a way to set up one remote to do it all, but he couldn't for the life of him figure out how. He was an old man in a young person's world. He hated it, but there was no getting around it. His brat of a grandson once told him, "Gramps, you're like a mule with a spinning wheel. Don't know how he got it and dang if he knows how to use it." He was surprised. He thought the kid was pretty damn smart coming up with that, pretty funny too.

He grabbed a *Baby Ruth* from the bowl, unwrapped it, and took a bite.

He later found out the line was stolen from *The Simpsons*. Not surprising. He didn't think the kid could've come up with that on his own since the dad—a good-for-nothing son-in-law—wasn't exactly the brightest bulb in the package, and everyone knew an apple didn't fall far from the tree.

He finished off the candy bar, brought up the guide on the TV, and started scanning through the channels. How could he have hundreds of channels to choose from and still not be able to find anything decent to watch? He remembered the days when there were only three network stations and one local yet there was still a better chance of finding a program worth his time. He was about ready to give up when he came across one of his favorite old horror movies, *The Bat*, starring Vincent Price. He grabbed another candy bar and settled in to watch when the doorbell rang.

Outside, kids called, "Trick or treat!"

His wife yelled from the kitchen, "Get the door."

He grunted as he pushed himself up from the chair. "I'm not deaf, you old bat," he grumbled under his breath. He still wasn't used to the nagging even after forty-something years of marriage.

"What?" Agnes called.

"I got it, *dear*," he yelled back, grabbing the bowl of candy and shuffling toward the door.

The doorbell rang again. "Trick or treat! Trick or Treat!"

"Damn brats," he grumbled. "I'm coming," he yelled.

He reached the door, opening it to a group of costumed kids standing on his porch.

"Trick or treat!"

He stopped in his tracks. Annoying brats. He clutched the bowl of candy close. "You see me standing here, don't you?"

A kid dressed as Dracula stepped forward and held out his bag. "Aww, come on, mister…trick or treat."

He scowled but said nothing. No reason to get in an argument with a kid. He wasn't that crotchety yet. At least he didn't think so. He dropped a piece of candy in *Dracula's* bag. The little monster turned and ran off. One by one he dropped candy in each trick-or-treater's bag. He started to loosen up. He even smiled. "You sure are a bunch of scary monsters."

Just then a little girl in a princess costume stepped forward, bag at the ready. She gave him a defiant stare. "I'm not a monster. I'm a princess."

His smile faded as he dropped candy into the girl's bag.

The little girl stuck out her tongue then turned and ran from the porch.

He watched in annoyance as the girl ran across his yard. "Princess, my ass. Little, fucking monster is more like it."

A scream jolted him. He glanced over his shoulder, expecting…

He didn't know what he was expecting, but mercifully the scream came from the horror movie. Shaking his head and smiling at his own stupidity, he turned back to the last two remaining trick-or-treaters on his doorstep. The sight of them stole his smile and made him gasp. "What the hell?" He paused and cleared his throat. "Uh, excuse my language, *kids.*"

Chitter!

He scrutinized the two and tried to smile again but couldn't muster one. "Uh, those are hideous costumes. Are you some kind of *bats* or something?"

Chitter!

"Leave the kids alone, Charlie," his wife yelled from the kitchen. "Just give them candy."

Charlie glanced over his shoulder. "Speaking of bats," he grumbled. Candy in hand, he turned back to the two *trick-or-treaters*.

The things before him hissed and bared teeth.

"What the—?"

He staggered backwards. The plastic bowl slipped from his grasp, thumping to the floor. Candy flew into the air and scattered everywhere. He turned to run, but one of the things was on him before he knew it. He went down hard, face first, with a thud. The thing climbed onto his back. Large wings wrapped around him. Sharp teeth sank into his neck. He screamed and writhed in pain as it ripped away flesh. Blood spurted everywhere. He tried to fight back, but the weight of his attacker and the embrace of its wings made it impossible for him to move. For the first time in decades he prayed, first to be saved and then to die quickly. His prayers weren't answered. His attacker was relentless. The pain was unbearable. Blood poured from him. Soon his screams died.

On the brink of life and death, he heard Agnes' bloodcurdling screams from the kitchen.

Chapter 9

The police cruiser's spotlight still cut through the night, throwing a harsh light across the clearing.

Ellie raised her head. Groaning, she spat and coughed up more dirt. What happened? Her aching head was groggy, her memory spotty. She rolled onto her back and lay there. Looking up at the night sky, she forced herself to recall. Slowly, her mind cleared until the horror of the attack—being imprisoned within those horrid wings, not being able to breathe, and the painful bite—coalesced in her memory. Then a thought more horrible than those memories struck her. What if that thing came back? Instant panic reanimated her. She struggled to get up, but the pain shoved her back down. Clutching her neck and shoulder, her hand found blood, so much blood. She had to get up. She didn't want to die there, lying in the dirt. The pain, though, was too unbearable, her head still too groggy.

"El," Jim hollered. He ran to Ellie and squatted beside her, pistol still in hand. "You're safe. It's dead."

She spat. Coughed up more dirt. "Are you sure?" Her own voice sounded foreign to her—like a creaky gate.

"I killed it. I'm sure."

She again tried to get up. She groaned. "Help me."

Jim holstered his pistol and helped her into a sitting position.

She groaned louder from the pain of exertion. Her hand pressed against the wound. Blood flowed freely through her fingers. The world around her blurred and spun.

Jim brushed dirt-caked hair away from her face. "That looks bad, El, real bad."

She winced. Concentrating on clearing her vision and slowing her world, she said, "James Steady, you were always one for understatement."

He grinned as he pulled out a handkerchief and placed it over the wound.

She jerked and grimaced.

"Sorry, El, I didn't mean to hurt you."

She blinked away dirt. She couldn't believe what she'd just heard. "You saved me, Jimmy."

Jim pulled the blood-soaked handkerchief away. "Not yet. We need to get you to a hospital."

"No," she said. She wasn't about to go to a hospital. There was too much to do and very little time in which to do it. Lives were at stake.

"El, you could bleed to—"

"No," she insisted. "You were a licensed EMT, right?"

"Still am. My license is current."

She shifted her weight and groaned. "And you have a first aid kit in the car?"

"Yeah, but—"

"Get it. Dress the wound and stop the bleeding."

Jim sighed. "This is why we broke up."

She coughed, grimacing with pain as she did so. "I know, bitch, not witch." Her voice trailed off. Spots of light floated in her vision, and her world spun a little faster.

"El, you okay?"

She grabbed Jim's arm and squeezed. "Get the first aid kit."

Reluctantly, he hurried off, returning with the kit moments later. Hunkering down, he dressed the wound. "Are you hanging in there?"

She flinched as he worked on her wound. "By a thread, Jimmy."

"Well, maybe we should take your mind off the pain. Tell me about that thing. What was it?"

She gave him a sidelong glance. "I guess there's no reason to keep anything from you now."

Jim didn't look up. He kept dressing the wound. "Didn't know there was any reason before."

"You wouldn't have believed me before."

He tied off the bandage.

"Ouch!"

"Sorry."

"I just bet you are."

He grinned slightly and closed the first aid kit. "So?"

Even with the proof of her claim lying dead just a few feet away, she still hesitated a moment; he might not even believe her now. Finally, she answered, "An *ugly*. At least that's what Gran called them."

Jim shook his head. "Come on, El. That's just a scary campfire story. I heard it as a kid. There's no such thing as ghosts, vampires, or *uglies*."

"Didn't get a good enough look, huh? Well, I did. Too good a look." She held out her hand. Jim was right about one thing.

Talking helped take her mind off the pain. Her vision even started to clear a bit, and her spinning world slowed. "Help me up, and we'll take another look."

Jim leaned in closer, so she could put an arm around his neck, then stood, helping her to her feet. Holding onto each other, they both stumbled toward the hideous corpse and the pool of blood that surrounded it. They stopped just a few feet away, staring down at it.

She closed her eyes a moment to regain the lost equilibrium from standing and leaned hard against Jim. Feeling slightly better, she opened her eyes and said, "There may not be ghosts or vampires, but does that look like just a story to you?"

Jim shivered at the sight of the thing and screwed up his face. "Damn, the stink's certainly real enough anyway." He paused. "Okay and it's hella ugly too."

"Hence the name."

"So, seeing it and having killed it, I guess I have to accept its existence. But where'd it come from?"

She hesitated. She knew he wasn't going to like the answer. Finally, she admitted, "I don't know. Gran didn't even know, I guess. At least she never said, and I never thought to ask." She shook her head. "I only know the story. One night, they swooped out of the sky and attacked the town. Gran was just a little girl then. It was her mother's magic that imprisoned them within the tree."

"Wait a minute," Jim interrupted. "*Them*? There's more than one?"

She nodded.

"How many?"

"I don't know."

He fidgeted, glancing around the clearing. "This isn't good."

"As I said before, James Steady, you're the master of understatement."

"Well, can you at least tell me how they escaped? What happened to the magic spell?"

She wiped away a tear from her dirt-smudged face. "Gran died."

Jim pulled her even closer. "I'm sorry, El."

She wiped away another tear. "We should've been ready."

As if he didn't hear, Jim asked, "When your grandmother's mom died, the magic spell held, right? Why not this time?"

If possible, she leaned even harder on Jim. "Gran was prepared. Her magic was strong. As her mother lay dying, she came to the tree and performed the ritual." She took a deep breath. "My mother should've been next in line to hold the magic spell in place."

"But she died when you were just a girl."

She nodded, grimacing at the pain shooting through her neck and throbbing into the back of her head. Bright spots of light attacked her vision. Somehow, though, she remained standing, conscious, and coherent. "And we were unprepared," she reluctantly admitted, wiping away tears. "*I* was unprepared."

"You can't blame yourself, El, for your grandmother dying so suddenly."

Now the tears came faster than she could wipe them away. "I should've been ready." She choked the words out. "I wasn't because college was more important to me than my craft, more important than protecting the town. Gran tried to tell me, tried to warn me." Her world spun out of control. Her knees buckled. She kept her feet only thanks to Jim's support.

"El, we've got to get you to a doctor." He held on tight. "You're getting weaker. You might have a concussion. And that bandage is almost soaked through. There must've been an anticoagulant in that thing's saliva. The bleeding's not even slowing down."

She shook her aching head. Somehow, she found the strength to steady herself. "No time. I've got to put those things back."

Even as she said those words, she doubted herself. She worried that her magic wasn't anywhere near strong enough. After all, she had barely practiced her craft over recent years. Even when younger, she had only attempted small, insignificant spells. What made her think she could pull off something as life or death as this? Was it arrogance? No. More like desperation.

"El, you can barely stand."

"I've got to do it, Jimmy." She pushed away. Yes, definitely desperation. "It's *my* responsibility."

Jim sighed. Reluctantly, he released his grip. "Okay, how? How are you going to put them back?"

She fixed her gaze on Jim. "You don't think I can do it."

He stood rock solid. "I think you can do anything you set your mind to, Ellie Evans." The look in his eyes, though, was one of worry. "That is if we can keep you alive long enough anyway."

She gave him a half smile. "I'll stay alive…long enough, anyway."

Jim held her gaze. "How are we going to do it?"

"We?"

He nodded. "I'm in this until the end. What do you need?"

A kiss and a hug, she thought. What she said, though, was, "I need the iron box."

"I'll get it. Are you going to be okay?"

She swayed but remained standing. She wished she need not involve Jim, she wished she could protect him from all of this, but she needed him, needed his strength. "I'll be okay. Get the box, Jimmy."

He hurried off.

She stumbled backward a step or two but regained her balance. Blinking away the spots of light, she concentrated on slowing her spinning world. She tried not to worry about the warm blood trickling down her arm and dripping from her fingertips. She tried not to think about the constant struggle just to remain conscious.

When he returned, Jim asked, "Now what, witchy woman?"

She focused on him and nothing else, determined to find the strength somewhere within to go on. Squaring her shoulders, she said, "Now we need salt, holy water, and dirt from consecrated ground."

Chapter 10

Far exceeding the speed limit, the police cruiser sped along the two-lane, country road. Its headlights sliced through the night, illuminating the stark countryside. Blue and red emergency lights flashed. Except for the hum of the engine, the cruiser ran silent—no siren.

Inside the car, Ellie clutched the iron box as if it were a lifeline keeping her from crossing to the other side. She needed to rest for what was to come. The pain from her wound was debilitating, her head groggy from loss of blood. Still, she couldn't relax or close her eyes. Her mind raced with the challenges ahead, and, honestly, she was afraid that if she closed her eyes she might never open them again.

Her grip on the box tightened.

For the most part, Jim kept his eyes on the road, but he periodically stole glances of her, worry shadowing his face.

"I'm fine," Ellie said.

Jim clutched the steering wheel as if *it* were his lifeline. "You don't look fine." He glanced at her. "And that bandage is soaked through again."

She didn't respond. She knew he was right. She could feel the blood trickling down her arm.

Jim concentrated on the road. Finally, he grabbed the radio's handset and attempted to contact the dispatcher. "This is Deputy-Sheriff Steady. Come in dispatch."

All he got back was static.

"Doris, come in."

Static answered.

"Dammit, Doris, answer. This is no time to be out suckin' on a cancer stick. It's an emergency, for God's sake. Come in."

Static laughed at him.

He slammed the handset back in place. His hands on the steering wheel now clutched it more in a death grip. "This isn't good."

"Master of understatement," Ellie said, groaning as she did so.

Jim sighed. "Okay, witchy woman, what's your plan?"

She shifted, grimacing. "First stop is my house."

"Why not stop at the cemetery first? We'll be passing it on our way into town."

"We'll save that for last, on the way back. There's an order to things. I want the salt first, and we're sure to find some at my house."

Jim glanced at her bloody bandage then her pain-riddled face. "Maybe Doc Ames should be our first stop."

She eyed him. "No time."

"If you die, *hope* dies with you." Jim paused. "I die too."

Her smile was thin and tight but a smile nevertheless. She took one hand off the box and gave him a loving touch on his arm. "I won't die, promise."

One corner of Jim's mouth turned up. "Break that promise and I'll never forgive you."

"I love you too, James Steady."

His half smile turned full.

She put her hand back on the iron box, leaving a bloody handprint on Jim's sleeve. Her head swam. She leaned back. Against her better judgement, she closed her eyes. She couldn't fight the urge to do so any longer. "Now drive faster, Jimmy. There's a reason you can't raise Doris on the radio, and it's not because she took a smoke break."

Jim punched the accelerator. The engine roared as the car lurched forward.

Chapter 11

The doozy of a storm had finally passed. A lightning bolt had lit up the entire sky. The crack of thunder that followed had been deafening. The grounds were still soppy from the rain, and puddles littered the cement walkways.

Joe Shepherd leaned against the red-brick wall surrounding the Solemn City Cemetery, enjoying the rain-washed night air. He had been the groundskeeper there for going on over forty years now.

He spat a wad of tobacco juice onto the ground, splattering his already stained boots.

He liked his job. He liked the dead. They never disagreed and didn't talk back.

He watched the last car of visitors pull out the gate and onto the road.

It was the living he could do without.

He pushed away from the wall. Careful not to step on anyone's grave, he trudged across the lawn, boots sinking into the wet and muddy ground as he made his way to the wrought iron, double gate. It was well past closing. He should've kicked out those last visitors and locked up right at sunset. With the storm and all, though, he had let it go. Besides, those people had just sat in their car, waiting out the storm. For once, the living was no real bother.

He closed and locked down one side of the double gate. Before he could get to the other, he noticed a police cruiser barreling down the two-lane road towards him. Its red and blue lights were running, but the siren was silent. It zoomed past him at top speed.

"What the hell's the emergency?" he grumbled. "Everyone out here's already dead." He spat a wad of tobacco juice at his feet. "Except me, anyways."

A creature swooped down out of the night sky, pouncing on him without warning and knocking him to the ground. Fangs sank into soft flesh, ripping his throat out before he could even get off the beginnings of a scream. Then the thing took flight, hauling off its fresh kill.

The wrought iron gate swung open with a rusted creak.

Chapter 12

With lights flashing and siren now wailing, the police cruiser streaked into the outskirts of town.

Solemn was under siege. Pandemonium reigned. Uglies swarmed the night sky like black thunderclouds. They swooped down, bombarding cars, crashing through roofs and breaking down doors of homes and stores, shattering windows, chasing fleeing trick-or-treaters and their parents. Screams echoed through the streets. There seemed no place to hide. No one was safe.

"Look out," Ellie cried.

Jim leaned on the horn and abruptly swerved to miss an oncoming car. "It's like driving through a war zone."

As if to emphasize that point, one car crashed through a storefront while another simultaneously ran into a light pole and burst into flames.

The guy stopped cold in his tracks, staring at the car bearing down on him, frozen like a deer in headlights.

"Move," Jim yelled, still leaning on his horn.

Right before the cruiser struck, the guy was snatched by an ugly. The cruiser sped past what would've been the point of impact as the ugly flew off with its screaming, kicking prey.

"What the—?" Jim yelled.

More and more screams mixed with the sounds of screeching tires, squealing brakes, and crashing cars as the uglies were met with little or no resistance, some flying off with their impending meals while others ripped into men, women, and children right there on the now bloody street.

Jim pounded a fist on the steering wheel. "Main Street's like one giant smorgasbord for these fuckers. We've got to do something."

Ellie closed her eyes, unable to stand the sight of the carnage outside her window any longer. "If you stop, we'll die too. Then no one will be saved." She choked back a sob and wiped tears away. "Our only hope is the ceremony. That's the only way we can stop all of them."

Jim punched the steering wheel. "You're right. I know you're right. But—"

She put a hand on Jim's arm. "Get us to Gran's house." When she took it away, blood left its mark on his sleeve.

Just before ramming two smashed cars, the police cruiser took an abrupt right. It zigzagged down the side street, running up on the sidewalk and back into the street, to avoid wrecked cars and fleeing people. After one more quick turn to the right, the cruiser crashed through Gran's picket fence, continued across the yard, smashing gargoyles and the patchwork of gardens, skidding to a sudden stop in front of the porch.

Jim grabbed the shotgun mounted on the dashboard. He pumped a round into the chamber. "I'll give you cover." Then he took the pistol from his holster and held it out to Ellie.

She eyed the pistol with revulsion.

"You remember how to use it?"

She nodded. "You taught me well." Still, she hesitated to take the pistol in hand. "Target practice is one thing, Jimmy. I never thought I'd have to kill anything."

"Remember, that's what they are, El…*things*…abominations against nature and all that's good in this world." He still held the gun out. "Take it, El."

She nodded acceptance and took the pistol, understanding she had to protect herself if they were going to succeed. But the thought of killing something—even abominations—made her stomach roil.

"Besides," Jim said, "it's not like you're going to be shooting at cute little bunnies or anything. These things are uglier than my old hound dog I had as a kid."

"Blue?" Ellie smiled at the memory in spite of herself and her situation. Jim had that way about him.

He nodded. "Blue."

"He *was* ugly," she confirmed.

"Well these things are uglier than Blue's ass."

She laughed, but it soon turned into a grimace. "Don't make me laugh, Jimmy. It hurts."

Jim eyed her wound, his face turning serious. "El, be quick. Get in, get the salt, and haul that scrumptious ass of yours back out here."

She gave Jim a flirtatious look. "You sure know how to sweet talk a girl, James Steady."

Jim smiled and gave her a wink. "You ready?"

Now it was her turn to get serious. "No."

Jim grinned. "Me neither."

They stared at one another for a heartbeat, taking in every detail as if it were the last time that either of them would ever see the other again.

"Let's do this," Jim said.

With that, they both opened their doors and vaulted into the night.

Chapter 13

Ellie hit the ground running, slipping after only a few feet and almost going down. But Adrenaline pumped through her, keeping her feet moving, her heart racing. Halfway to the porch steps, an ugly swooped down on her. Jim's shotgun boomed, blasting the thing out of the sky. It hit the ground with a thud at her feet. Not missing a beat, she leapt the dead thing then staggered up the steps and into the house, slamming the door behind her.

Outside, Jim's shotgun boomed, sounding like the thunder from earlier in the day.

Inside, she stumbled into the kitchen. Glass crunched underfoot. She slid through the spilt orange concoction that was still on the floor, catching herself from falling by grabbing the kitchen counter. Remnants of fruit and pumpkin still littered the counter. The dirty blender stared back at her.

Just a few hours earlier, Gran stood almost in this exact spot, laughing and talking, and *alive*.

She clutched the edge of the counter with one hand and the pistol in the other. Her knees almost buckled underneath her. Blood trickled down her arm, leaving droplets on the counter's surface.

In some ways, Gran's death felt an eternity ago. So much had happened since as a result.

She choked back a sob and leaned more heavily on the counter, her knees and her resolve weakening.

Yet, the ache in her heart and in her soul reminded her that barely any time at all had gone by since Gran's passing. Then she wondered if time would ever really lessen the ache anyway. Her mother had passed when she was still a child, and her heart and soul still ached from that loss. Why should the loss of Gran be any different? It wouldn't. It would be worse. She had known Gran longer and was closer to her than she had ever been to her mother.

She took a deep breath and straightened. Gran wouldn't want her to get lost in grief and despair. There was too much at stake. Too many people were dependent upon her. She had to stay strong.

Reaching up, she opened a cupboard and grabbed the large container of salt. She turned away to retrace her steps but stopped. Instead, she opened a drawer and took out an empty glass vial with a rubber cap. She stuffed the vial into the pocket of her jeans before again turning away, the container of salt in one hand and the pistol in the other.

After only a few steps, the house began to spin. Warm, wet blood streamed down her back and her arm, the bandage now soaked through. Consciousness started slipping away. But she managed to maneuver to the living room before her legs completely turned to rubber and gave way. She dropped both pistol and salt as she crashed to the floor.

Chapter 14

Outside, full-fledge war had broken out. Jim crouched behind the police cruiser. His shotgun boomed. A circling ugly dropped from the sky and thumped to the ground, joining the littered carcasses already in the garden.

More gunfire echoed through the town. Apparently other people had gotten out their hunting rifles and handguns, joining in the battle.

He pumped another round into the shotgun's chamber. It was awesome others were taking up arms, but there were too many of the foul things and not enough townspeople with guns to make a difference. At best, they might hold the creatures off for a while and thin the colony a bit. He now truly believed Ellie when she said that everyone's survival rested solely on her magic.

Where was she anyway? What was taking her so long? They needed to hurry.

He thought about going in and retrieving her just when an ugly circling overhead swooped down. It rammed him in the back, knocking him off his feet and sending him crashing face forward onto the ground, the shotgun landing next to him in the dirt. Groaning and cursing, he rolled onto his back. He wiped dirt from his face and eyes with one hand and grabbed the shotgun with the other. Frantically, he searched the sky for the predator he knew had to be there. No way it would just fly off, leaving a tasty meal behind.

The ugly passed overhead. Shrieking, it dropped from the sky, claws extended for the kill.

He brought up the barrel of the shotgun. Having no time to aim, he let loose with a blast. Luck was on his side. The thing's face exploded. Flesh, brain tissue, and blood rained down, followed by the corpse thumping on top of him. Wailing, he pushed the carcass away, and scrambled to his feet.

"Oh, man, that's fucking disgusting." Gagging on the smell, he wiped the gore from his face and clothes the best he could.

An ugly passed overhead.

He pumped the shotgun and blasted the thing. This one fell at his feet.

"Ellie, where are you!"

More uglies circled above.

He turned and ran for the front door.

"Ellie!"

Chapter 15

Ellie groaned and pushed herself into a sitting position. Blood ran freely down her arm and pooled on the floor. Sitting there, she tried to remember what had happened, what she had been doing before losing consciousness. She recognized Gran's living room. That was something. Everything else was hazy. Why was she there?

Nearby lay the container of salt and the pistol.

That was it. She was collecting what she needed for the ceremony. It was the only way to put the uglies back within the prison of the tree.

Outside, gunfire boomed.

Jim, he was waiting for her, all the while keeping the uglies at bay.

"Jimmy," she mumbled, "I'm coming."

With great effort, she pushed herself to her feet. There she swayed as if standing on a deck of a ship, sailing in rough waters.

"Gran, give me strength."

On unsteady feet, she maneuvered to the container of salt and the fallen pistol. With even more effort, she reached down and plucked the items one at a time off the floor.

Outside, more gunfire boomed.

"I'm coming Jimmy."

She used the furniture to steady herself as she stumbled to the front door, leaving a trail of blood behind her. At the door, she opened it and thrust herself through.

Jim met her on the other side of the threshold, catching her in one arm just before she collapsed.

"I was just coming for you, honey."

About that she had no doubt. She knew Jim would never leave her. Just being in his arms gave her renewed strength.

"I've got the salt, Jimmy. Get me out of here."

Holding on tight, Jim helped her across the porch, down the stairs, and back to the car. Once she was safe in the passenger seat, he slammed the door. Before he could maneuver around the car to the driver's door, an ugly swooped down, giving him a glancing blow in the back of the head and knocking him to his knees. The thing shrieked wildly as it again ascended and circled.

On his knees and groaning, he tried to gather his wits. The blow left him woozy and disoriented but he held on tight to the shotgun. He felt the back of his head. His hand came away with blood.

Ellie pounded on her window with the palm of her hand. "Jimmy," she cried, "look out!" She saw the ugly as it circled and began to swoop down for a second assault.

As the creature dropped from the sky, Jim wheeled around, brought the shotgun up, and fired. The blast hit the ugly in a wing. The thing cried out and plummeted from the sky like a damaged helicopter, hitting the ground with a thud. There, it squawked and cried, struggling with its one good wing to get airborne again. But all it succeeded in doing was rising a foot or two off the ground before dropping back to Earth.

Ellie continued to slap her window. "Jimmy, get in the car."

Ignoring her pleas, Jim climbed to his feet and staggered toward the wounded ugly. He watched the thing struggle to escape, its bleats falling on deaf ears. As he raised his shotgun and took aim, he remembered a line from *Terminator 2*. Grinning, he croaked, "Hasta la vista, baby." He fired, blasting the thing's head into flying shrapnel of flesh, skull fragments, and brain matter. With that task completed, he turned, hurried to the car, climbed behind the wheel, and slammed his door.

Ellie scowled. She slumped back in her seat. Now that the immediate danger to Jim was behind them, adrenaline seeped away and exhaustion again overtook her. "You just had to play Schwarzenegger, didn't you?"

He grinned.

"You're bleeding," she mumbled.

He again touched the back of his head. His hand still came away with blood. "Nothing too serious."

"Thank God for a hard head."

He continued to grin as he reversed the cruiser across the garden and onto the street, tires squealing as they hit pavement. The tires squealed again as the car lurched forward and rocketed down the street in a cloud of smoke.

Chapter 16

The Devil still lurked in the church.

Within the pitch-black confessional, Kathy pulled her knees to her chin. She hugged her legs in a death grip. Tears streamed down her cheeks. Her breath came out shallow and ragged as she desperately tried to control her breathing and quiet her sobs. She had made it to the confessional without the Devil catching her or seeing her. But it hadn't given up. She could hear it skittering about, looking for her amongst the pews.

Mama was dead. No one else even knew she was in the church. Who would save her? Rocking back and forth, she bit her lower lip to keep from screaming.

Sharp toenails clicked across the floor right outside the confessional. Wings scraped along the wall. The Devil chittered.

She made the sign of the cross and held her breath. She bit her lower lip so hard that she drew blood, refusing to scream.

Chapter 17

Gunfire and screams echoed through the night. Townspeople were still fighting back, but many ran blindly through the streets in their futile attempt to escape. Winged creatures swooped out of the black sky, taking down victims and feeding at will.

With red and blue lights flashing and siren wailing, the police cruiser carrying Ellie and Jim zoomed through the streets. It swerved around fleeing pedestrians and speeding cars alike, coming close to catastrophe several times, almost running over fleeing people or hitting both moving and abandoned cars. At one point, it ran up on a sidewalk, scraped against storefronts, barreled into garbage cans, ran over a newspaper stand, and sideswiped a telephone booth. In the midst of flying sparks, it came under control again and was back on the street. And despite its growing disrepair and missing body parts, the car miraculously continued to speed towards its destination.

Inside the car, Jim clutched the steering wheel in a death grip and sweated bullets as he concentrated. Next to him, Ellie slumped in her seat, seemingly unfazed by the abandoned recklessness of her ride. He glanced her way but mostly kept his attention on the job at hand, which was not crashing or running anyone over.

"You okay, El?"

She moaned. "Just drive, Jimmy. Get me to the church."

"When this is over, El, I'll get you to the church for a different reason."

She gave Jim a sidelong glance, a slight smile on her pain-riddled face. "Don't make promises in the heat of the moment...promises you can't keep later, James Steady."

He smiled back. "Oh, I can keep it, witchy woman."

A screaming woman suddenly ran out in front of the cruiser.

"Jim, stop," Ellie cried.

He slammed on the brakes. Tires squealed in protest as the car came to an abrupt stop.

The woman lunged onto the hood with a thump. She crawled up toward the windshield, eyes bulging, mouth agape. "Help," she screamed, "help me."

Before either of them could make a move to help, an ugly swooped out of nowhere. It snatched up the woman, ripping her from the car, the woman's fingernails scraping across the hood as she tried to hold on. An instant later, she was taken, caught within the clutches of the ugly's massive claws, kicking and screaming as the thing took her higher and higher.

Jim slammed a fist against the steering wheel. "Fuck!"

Ellie choked back a sob and slumped in her seat. "Get me to the church, Jimmy. Before it's too late. It's our only hope. It's *their* only hope."

With clenched jaw, he punched the gas pedal, and the cruiser took off in a cloud of smoke and peeling rubber.

Chapter 18

The police cruiser ran up onto the sidewalk, skidding to a stop just short of the church steps. With the engine still idling, Ellie blinked her eyes open and stole a peek at Jim. He was leaning over her, examining her wound. She knew it was bad. She didn't need him to tell her. The bandage was soaked through, and she could feel the blood streaming down her neck and arm.

Jim's brow furrowed. "El, you're going to bleed out if we don't get you help."

She moaned. He was probably right. But it didn't matter. She didn't matter. All that mattered was that she performed the ceremony and put those things back where they belonged before she bled out.

Jim turned away, putting the car in gear. "That does it. I'm getting you to the hospital, El."

She grunted with disapproval. She needed to take control of the situation. Reaching out, she grabbed Jim's arm with all the strength she could muster. "No. Do something, Jimmy!"

He ran a trembling hand through his hair. "There's only so much I can do, El."

Out of nowhere, an ugly dive-bombed the car, rocking it on its shocks. That got both of their attentions. Ellie sat up, peering outside her window. Then she turned to Jim. "Do *something*. Get me back on my feet, Jimmy."

He gaped. "Dammit, El, I'm not a doctor."

The ugly made another run at the car. They both gasped as a loud bang rang out, and the car rocked on its shocks.

"Jimmy, you were an EMT before joining the Sheriff's Department. Think of something."

He shook his head. "In my case, EMT stood for Emergency Medical Twit. It's why I became a deputy-sheriff."

Gunfire echoed in the distance like a mocking laugh.

She touched Jim's arm. "I believe in you, James Steady. Think of something. You can do this."

With a sigh, he nodded. Reaching under his seat, he pulled out the first aid kit.

Ellie leaned back in her seat and closed her eyes, features slack, energy completely drained. "Hurry," she moaned.

Jim removed the old bandage and threw it onto the floor. He cleaned the wound with antiseptic the best he could and redressed the wound with a more intricate and confining bandage that nevertheless left Ellie's arm free to use. But blood almost instantly began to show through as the bandage absorbed it.

"Damn, El, it won't stop bleeding. And you're losing strength too. How do you expect to keep going?"

Her eyes were completely closed now, and her head lolled to one side. "Find a way," she muttered.

He thought for a moment and then rummaged through the kit. Pulling out an EpiPen, he stared at it long and hard. Then he looked at Ellie, half conscious next to him. "Crap. El, can you hear me?"

She moaned. Jim's voice sounded as if it were coming from deep inside a cave, echoey and far away, but she could make out what he was saying. She nodded.

"El, this is epinephrine. It might stanch the blood flow. It also should inject you with enough adrenaline to get you back on your feet." He paused. "Short term anyway."

She again nodded. "Do it."

He stared at the EpiPen then at Ellie. "It could also kill you, El. Do you understand?"

An ugly rammed the windshield. The impact made a crunching noise and created a spider web of cracks.

"Fuck," he exclaimed.

Ellie didn't have the energy to react. Her eyes blinked open. "We're dead anyway if you don't."

He sighed, hesitating.

She took a shallow breath. "Do it."

He did as he was told, injecting the drug into Ellie's arm.

She gulped air, and her body spasmed and convulsed. She suddenly jerked upright, fully alert, thoughts racing as fast as her heart. "Holy crap." Her chest heaved as she tried to catch her breath, slow her mind.

"You okay?"

"My heart might burst through my chest." She gulped more air. "Otherwise, I think so."

"That's the drug taking affect."

"Should've done this a long time ago." Her breathing and heart rate slowed to a more normal pace. Her mind focused into coherent thoughts "I feel like I could tear those things apart with my bare hands."

"Yeah, you could also have a stroke or a cerebral hemorrhage any second."

Tremors wracked Ellie's bloodstained hand as she took out her pistol. She now only had one thought; get the holy water. "Then we better hurry." Every muscle in her body twitched. Even her voice quivered as she spoke. "Just like before, Jimmy. You lay down cover. I get inside and get the holy water."

"Fast," he added.

She nodded and smiled. "Light speed."

They gave each other a last look, their eyes saying everything that needed to be said.

"Let's do it," Jim said.

Simultaneously, their doors opened, and they both bolted into harm's way.

He pumped a round into the shotgun and fired at an attacking ugly, wounding it but not bringing it down. It shrieked as it flew off, limping through the air.

Moving on pure adrenaline, Ellie rushed up the church steps and yanked open the heavy door. As she rushed across the sanctified threshold, she prayed to God that this wouldn't be the last time she saw Jim...*alive.*

Chapter 19

Once inside the church, Ellie slowed her pace, giving into caution over speed. Outside, gunfire echoed, and again she prayed for Jim. She hadn't realized the breadth and scope of her love until their lives were in danger. She prayed it wasn't too late. She didn't want to lose him now. With Gran gone, he was the last person alive she truly loved.

Holding the pistol at the ready, those thoughts and feelings raced through her as she moved quietly and cautiously across the narthex to the threshold of the nave and the fonts of holy water that flanked the entryway. Pure adrenaline from the epinephrine injection was the only thing that kept her going. That and getting back safe and sound to Jim.

At the fonts, she pulled the empty, glass vial from her jeans' pocket and immersed it in holy water. Once the vial was filled, she capped it and stuffed it back into her pocket.

Gunfire continued to echo outside. With thoughts of getting back to Jim, she turned to leave. But a sudden and loud noise from the nave stopped her in her tracks. "No," she hissed and whirled toward the sound. She knew she should just ignore it and flee the church, but the thought of leaving one of those creatures alive in this holy place sickened her, if indeed it was an ugly that made the noise. Maybe it wasn't. Maybe someone was hiding here, taking sanctuary.

She took one cautious step across the threshold from narthex to nave for a better look and stopped. The wide aisle and row upon row of pews stretched out in front of her. The sanctuary railing at the end of the aisle was shattered, broken pieces strewn everywhere.

"Shit—" She cut herself short. "Don't curse in church, Ellie Evans."

She took three hesitant steps forward. That's when she saw the body lying in a pool of blood beyond the broken railing, at the foot of the high altar.

"Shit— don't curse, dammit." She sighed in frustration. "Don't curse."

But the dead body just ahead was ample reason to curse, even in church. Wasn't it? Besides, whatever killed whoever lay there might still be lurking about. Pistol still aimed and ready, she scanned the surrounding pews. She retreated a few steps but stopped. What if this *whoever* wasn't dead but just hurt and in need of help? She couldn't just leave them.

Reluctantly, she moved forward again, taking hesitant steps down the aisle, all the while scanning the rows of pews on either side of her for any sign of impending attack.

"This is stupid," she whispered, still moving forward, not heeding her own warning. "This is really stupid."

Just short of the railing, she stopped. From there, she could see the body clearly. "Dead. Definitely dead." The body was ripped apart, entrails swimming in blood on the floor. Earlier that very day the sight would've immediately made her vomit. But now? No, she had already seen and experienced too much to cause even a gag reflex now.

Slowly and cautiously, she backed away. She wanted to turn and run but was afraid to turn her back in case the thing that had mutilated this poor man or woman still lurked in the sanctuary ahead. But she was also afraid that the thing might be hiding amongst the pews or within the shadows at the very edges of the nave. It was also a possibility that the thing circled around, got behind her, and was now back at the entryway. She couldn't see everywhere at once, but she did her best, her head and gun hand swiveling from side to side and forward and backward.

A quarter of the way into her retreat, a scraping noise off to the left brought her up short. She whirled toward the sound, breathing hard, gun hand wavering. The confessional loomed before her, heavy purple drapes covering the openings to the two cubicles where people knelt and confessed their sins, the cubicle in the middle where the priest sat enclosed by a door.

A thump came from one of the cubicles. She couldn't tell which one.

"Shit...don't curse."

Pointing the pistol out in front of her, she inched down the long pew toward the confessional. At the end of the pew, she stepped out into a narrow aisle. She took a deep breath, pointed the pistol at the draped cubicle on her left, and yanked back the drape. Empty. She let out her held breath. She turned toward the draped cubicle on her right and repeated the process. To her relief, it too was empty. That left the priest's cubicle in the middle. Grasping the door handle, she took a deep breath and held it as she pulled open the door and simultaneously thrust the pistol forward, ready to fire. What she found, though, wasn't an ugly but a little girl with a tear-soaked face, curled up in a ball and rocking back and forth.

She quickly lowered her weapon and dropped to her knees. "It's okay...I won't hurt you."

The little girl immediately vaulted forward, into her arms.

Ellie held on tight. "It's okay. It's going to be okay now."

A scraping noise came from behind, followed by a shriek.

The little girl pushed back out of her arms and fell backwards into the confessional. A look of terror etched the features of her face. She let loose with a high-pitched scream that echoed throughout the church.

Ellie whirled around and blindly fired, the pistol's report echoing on the heels of the little girl's scream.

An ugly scrambled down a row of pews toward her. The blind shot hit the thing in the chest. Blood gushed from the wound. But it kept coming, baring fangs and shrieking like a wild banshee.

She fired again as she too fell backwards into the confessional, slamming the door shut behind her. The ugly hit the other side, but the door held. She fired three more times. All three bullets penetrated the door. The ugly on the other side shrieked. There was a thump, followed by scraping noises, as if the creature was in retreat.

Her breathing hard and labored, she held the little girl in a one-arm embrace, continuing to aim the pistol at the door. Gunfire boomed in the distance, but the church beyond the confessional had gone deathly silent. The little girl sobbed quietly in her embrace as they both stared at the closed door.

Was the thing dead or just playing possum, biding its time? There was no way of knowing. Only venturing out of the confessional would tell for sure.

With the little girl now under her protection, Ellie was reluctant to take the chance. Instead, she stared at the door, lost within the candlelight streaming through the three bullet holes like the tiniest rays of hope in a small world otherwise shrouded in total gloom.

Chapter 20

Sporadic gunfire echoed in the distance. Otherwise, everything was quiet. The creatures were no longer anywhere in sight. The street running past the church was empty of cars and foot traffic.

Jim crouched next to the police cruiser, back pressed against it, shotgun at the ready, waiting. "It's too quiet," he muttered. "And she's taking too long. Something's wrong."

As if in answer to Jim's disquiet, a gunshot rang out from inside the church.

"Dammit, I hate it when I'm right."

Another gunshot. Without thinking of his own safety, he pushed up from his crouch and ran for the church. He only made it as far as the steps before an ugly screeched above. He wheeled toward the sound and blindly fired into the night sky, the blast booming through the night. Shrieking, the ugly fell from the sky, landing directly on top of him. Both he and the ugly hit the pavement. The shotgun slipped from his grasp, skidding across the sidewalk. Man and monster rebounded to their feet and faced off. The winged creature hissed and bared fangs. Jim stared into that hideous face.

"Where's a witch when you need one."

When the ugly took one hop towards him, he noticed the gaping wound in its chest. He had hit it with that last wild shot.

"Got you, didn't I, you ugly motherfucker."

The creature hissed.

He took his eyes off his adversary for just a second in search of the shotgun. It rested on the sidewalk, a few feet away.

The ugly hissed again and advanced another hop.

"Want more, do you?" He turned his attention back to the menacing thing.

The ugly hissed.

"Come and get it."

He made his move, diving for the shotgun. Even wounded, the creature moved quickly and was on top of him. They scuffled on the ground, rolling along the pavement, a mass of kicking legs, flapping wings, swinging arms, and gnashing teeth. Jim yelled and cursed. The ugly shrieked.

They broke apart. Jim rolled free, snatching up the shotgun. As he bounded to his feet, he pumped the shotgun, aimed, and pulled the trigger. But the hammer clicked on an empty chamber.

"Oh shit!"

The ugly shrieked and attacked.

He turned the shotgun into a club and swung it like a baseball player swinging for the fences, smashing the thing in the face. The ugly cried out as it hit the pavement. With the thing down, he took advantage, using the shotgun stock to crack its face again and again and again, until finally it barely moved and mewed pitifully.

Scraped, scratched, bloodied, and breathing hard, he stared down at the dying thing at his feet. "Didn't think you could get any uglier. I was wrong."

Giving the ugly one last crack with the shotgun's stock, he killed it.

Chapter 21

Ellie huddled with the little girl in the gloom of the confessional. She aimed the pistol at the door, waiting, listening. The church beyond the confessional was deathly quiet. Still, she was reluctant to venture out and put the girl's life at further risk.

But they couldn't stay there forever. She still needed to collect dirt from consecrated ground. She still needed to perform the ceremony and send these creatures back to their prison within the tree.

The girl no longer cried, but her breathing was littered with periodic, hitched sobs. "Maybe it's gone," she whispered between sobs.

"Maybe," Ellie whispered. "Or maybe it's dead."

The girl choked back a sob. "Hope so."

A hint of a smile crept across Ellie's face. "What's your name, sweetheart?"

"Kathy."

"Hi, Kathy. I'm Ellie. You're quite the brave, little girl."

The little girl choked back a sob and wiped her face dry with the palm of one hand. She shook her head in disagreement. "Mama's dead because of me. I-I didn't help her. I ran." New tears streamed down her face.

Ellie pulled the girl closer, hugged her tighter. "There's nothing you could've done to help your Mama, sweetheart. I'm sure of it."

Sobs now racked Kathy.

"You did what you had to do to survive. I'm proud of you for that. I know your Mama would be too."

Kathy wiped away tears, fighting to get herself under control.

"Kathy, you're going to have to be brave again. Do you think you can do that?"

She nodded.

"Good." Ellie took her eyes off the door, looking down at the girl. "Look at me, sweetheart."

She wiped tears away and looked up, meeting Ellie's gaze.

"We've got to get out of here. That means taking a chance that the creature is either gone or dead. Understand?"

Kathy again nodded.

Ellie nodded back. "Okay. I want you to stay behind me. If that thing attacks us, I want you to run for the exit. Don't worry about me. Don't look back. Just run."

Now the girl shook her head in disagreement. "No, Ellie..."

"Shhh...I want you to promise me, Kathy. You run as fast as you can for the exit. I have a friend outside waiting for me. His name is Jim. He's a good guy. You'll be safe with him."

"What about you, Ellie?"

She flashed Kathy a smile. "Don't you worry about me, sweetheart. I'll be right behind you." She paused. "Now, are you ready?"

The girl nodded.

Ellie released her embrace. As she positioned herself towards the front of the confessional, she prayed to God that the thing was dead. She was taking a big risk with Kathy's life. Her life was one thing. But the girl's life was something else.

"Remember, stay behind me until we're in the clear. Then run for the exit and don't look back."

Renewed shock and fear crawled across Kathy's face. "Ellie, you're bleeding."

Blood dripped from Ellie's gun hand. "It's okay, sweetheart. I'm fine. Remember, stay behind me. Then run as fast as you can."

"But, Ellie—"

Ellie flung open the door. She lunged through the doorway, out into the narrow aisle that ran along the end of the pews from sanctuary to narthex. Kathy obediently followed, staying close.

A loud shriek welcomed them. The wounded ugly quickly advanced.

Ellie reached around her back, grabbed the girl, and pushed her away, up the aisle toward the exit. "Run, Kathy!"

The creature suddenly turned its attention toward the girl, scrambling over the back of a pew to try to reach her.

Kathy screamed.

"Run! Don't look back!"

Kathy turned and ran.

The ugly made it over the back of the pew and into the next row just as Ellie opened fire, hitting the thing in the back. The report reverberated through the church, and the recoil almost knocked the spent and weakening witch off her feet. She cried out from the pain in her blood-soaked neck and shoulder. Still not dead, the ugly turned and advanced on her. She braced herself, took better aim, and shot. Her own cry equaled the creature's wail. But in the end, she remained standing, and the ugly lay dead, sprawled across the back of the pew, blood gushing from the gaping wound.

Kathy ran back. "Ellie!" She flew into her newfound friend, hugging her legs.

Ellie hunkered down and hugged the girl back. "I thought I told you to run and not look back."

"I couldn't leave you."

She released her embrace and looked Kathy in her tear-drenched eyes. "Thanks, sweetheart." She smiled. "I know now I can always count on you to have my back."

Kathy grinned. But her grin faded. "Ellie, you're really bleeding. Bad."

Ellie grimaced. "Yeah, and the injection of adrenaline's wearing off too."

The girl's face took on a quizzical look. "Huh?"

Ellie forced a smile. "Nothing." She stood, grimacing as she did so. "Let's get out of here. What do you say?"

Kathy nodded but still looked worried.

Ellie took the girl's hand and quickly led her toward the exit, eager to see Jim and in a hurry to complete her mission.

Before it was too late.

Chapter 22

Ellie and Kathy met Jim at the front doors of the church. He held his shotgun like a club over one shoulder, and an ugly with a smashed in face lay dead behind him on the sidewalk.

"Ellie, I was just coming for you." Jim gave her a hard look. "You don't look so good."

She gave a hard look right back. "You don't either, James Steady."

Jim looked at Kathy and cocked his head. "Where'd she come from? Immaculate conception?"

Ellie held the girl close. "Something like that. Now let's get out of here. I'll make proper introductions once we're safe inside the car."

All three turned away from the church and ran to the police cruiser. Ellie opened the back door. "Sweetheart, you get in the back, behind the cage. You'll be safer there."

Kathy hesitated.

Ellie scanned their surroundings. All seemed quiet now, but it surely wouldn't remain that way very long. She was sure that uglies would soon be swooping down on them.

"Hurry, sweetheart."

Kathy reluctantly climbed inside, sitting where suspects and perps usually rode, a steel grate separating her from the others.

Ellie slammed the door and climbed into the front passenger seat, Jim next to her, back behind the wheel. With everyone secure within the car, adrenaline drained from her. The shot of epinephrine was wearing off. Blood soaked her bandage. She slumped back in her seat and fought to keep her eyes open. "Jimmy, this is Kathy," she mumbled, "a very brave little girl. Kathy, this is my friend Jim I was telling you about."

Jim looked over his shoulder at the girl. "Glad to meet you, Kathy. We can use the help of a brave little girl."

Kathy leaned forward and peered through the steel grate. To Ellie, she whispered, "You didn't say he's a policeman."

Ellie opened her eyes and smiled. "That's because he's not a very good one."

Jim cranked the engine to life and grinned. "Maybe not. But I'm still a better cop than you are a witch, El."

She laughed then grimaced. "Don't make me laugh. It hurts."

Kathy gasped. "Are you really a witch?"

Ellie nodded. "From a long line of witches."

"Are you going to cast a spell on those monsters?"

Now Jim nodded. "That's the plan, Kathy." He put the car in gear and stomped on the accelerator. "That's the plan."

The cruiser rocketed backwards, out onto the street, emergency lights flashing but siren silent. Tires squealed as it abruptly stopped. Tires spun and squealed again as the car rocketed forward, taking off down the street, back the way it had come, toward the city limits. It maneuvered through town as fast and as best as it could. Flickering streetlights and intermittent fires mixed with the cruiser's emergency lights and headlights, casting a sickly and hellish glow across the cityscape. The ongoing war in the surrounding streets raged on but looked to be slowly dying along with the townspeople. Hunting rifles and shotguns still occasionally boomed in the distance. Screams echoed too. But mostly the streets were filled with the aftermath of battle—crashed and burning cars, demolished buildings, debris, garbage, fires, and dead bodies littering the pavement; a few uglies scavenged those bodies and were on the prowl for more victims.

All three stared out their windows in horror at the carnage and destruction. And in fear of the enemy feeding on the dead and the dying and stalking any living, hidden prey.

"Everyone's dead," Kathy whispered.

Ellie couldn't bring herself to believe that. "No, sweetheart. They can't be. People are hiding, taking refuge wherever they can."

"Even if everyone is dead..." Jim began.

Ellie shot him daggers.

"...and I'm not saying they are." He winced at the slip as he glanced back at the horrified girl. "But still, we need to send these things back where they belong as fast as possible. Before they do finish here and move on to the next unsuspecting town."

As if to punctuate his words, an ugly let loose a murderous shriek and crashed onto the roof of the cruiser.

Kathy screamed in response.

"One of those damn things latched on." Ellie stared at the ceiling.

Jim glanced up then returned his attention to the road ahead. "Hang on." He gunned the engine.

The police cruiser picked up speed, swerving around abandoned cars, running over debris and the dead, and crashing into loitering uglies, hoping to discharge the unwanted passenger on the roof. But the thing held on, screeching, clawing at the roof. Trying to dig its way inside.

Kathy's scream morphed into one continuous wail.

Ellie aimed her pistol at the roof but didn't fire.

Jim increased the cruiser's speed, driving with wild abandon through the streets of Solemn. "Shoot the damn gun, El."

"At what?"

"The whole damn roof if you have to. Just shoot. You might hit the damn thing by accident."

Before Ellie could fire, the ugly swung down from the roof and thumped against the outside of Kathy's window. Still latched onto the car, its hideous face leered at the girl through the glass. It growled with ravenous hunger.

Kathy's wail rose several octaves.

Jim glanced over his shoulder, while Ellie turned in her seat, pistol still at the ready but silent.

"There's your target, El. Shoot it."

She tried to take aim. "I can't get a clear shot through the grating." She was being tossed around in her seat too. "Might help if you held the car on a straight course."

Kathy's wail now rose to tea-kettle pitch.

"Hell with that. Let's do the opposite. Hold on."

He jerked the steering wheel back and forth, sending the car into a fishtail, trying to shake free of the thing. But the ugly held on, wings beating against the side of the car.

Ellie craned her neck to keep tabs on the ugly. "It's not working. It's still back there."

"Son-of-a-bitching, ugly ass fuck!"

Ellie kept her attention on the ugly but was aghast at Jim's outburst. "James Steady...language...little girl."

Kathy's wail was quickly approaching the point where only dogs could hear it.

"If we live through this, and she actually heard me over that shrill, I'll apologize and pay penance later. Meanwhile, hold the fuck on. I'm trying something new."

Jim jerked the wheel to the left and jammed on the brakes, sending them into a 360-degree, gut-wrenching, tire-squealing skid. When they came to an abrupt stop, the thing was effectively bucked off. It shrieked as it flew uncontrollably through the air and crashed into abandoned cars. Without much delay, the cruiser spun its tires, straightened out, screeched forward, and continued its getaway.

Kathy's wail died. Instead, she cried and laughed at the same time.

All three glanced out the rear window in time to see the ugly struggling to free itself from the rubble, obviously injured but not dead.

"Whoo-hoo!" Jim grinned. "Boy howdy, we taught that fucker a lesson or two."

Ellie glanced back and winked at Kathy. "Language, James Steady."

He looked chagrined. "My apologies, Kathy."

Kathy continued to cry and laugh but laughter slowly overcame the tears.

"For penance, three Hail Marys and three Our Fathers, young man," Ellie joked.

Jim grinned. "Hail Mary, full of grace..."

With one headlight blind and the other blinking, the battered police cruiser zoomed out of town, past the city limits. The emergency lights flashed, but the siren remained silent as it sped toward the cemetery and the last, missing ingredient to the spell they hoped would save them all.

Chapter 23

"We're here," Jim declared.

He turned the police cruiser abruptly to the left and sped through the already open gate and under the sign that read *Solemn Cemetery*. Slowing down, he drove past the main office building and the parking lot. Instead, he followed the one-lane, gravel road into the heart of the cemetery, not stopping until they reached the older grave sites. He shut off the engine and turned to Ellie.

"El, we're here. From what I understand, this is the oldest section, just like you wanted."

Ellie fought to remain conscious, drifting in and out, aware but unaware at the same time.

Behind her, Kathy—like a disgruntled prisoner—pressed her face up against the steel grate and laced her fingers through the openings.

Jim gently nudged Ellie. "El, we're here," he repeated.

She moaned, opened her eyes, and gazed up at him. At first, he looked blurry, out of focus, but her vision soon cleared. She reached out a trembling hand and touched his scratched, bruised, and bloodied face. "You okay?" she whispered.

"You're worried about me? What about you?"

She managed a smile and moaned softly. "I'm okay."

"Sure you are." He inspected the blood-soaked bandage and her bloodstained arm and hand. "I better change that bandage."

She moaned. "Do it fast, Jimmy. We're running out of time."

He retrieved the first aid kit from under the seat. Gently, he took off the old bandage and began cleaning and dressing the wound the best he could.

Kathy pressed her face even harder against the grate for a better look. The sight of Ellie's horrible wound screwed her face up into a gruesome-looking mask. "Is she going to be okay?"

"I'm going to be fine, sweetheart."

Jim finished. He winked and smiled at the girl. "Don't you worry. She's one tough witch." He turned back to Ellie, the smile gone, his face a mask of worry. "El, you stay put this time. Let me get the dirt."

"No—"

"Honestly, El, you're not strong enough.

She pushed herself up straight, determined to show him she still had the strength. But the shot of epinephrine had worn off. She groaned and slumped back in dejection.

"Told you so."

She sighed. "Give me another shot."

"Can't. Don't have another EpiPen." He paused. "Let me do it."

"Let him do it, Ellie," Kathy pleaded. "Please."

"El, you need to save your strength for the ceremony. Only you can perform that. Anyone can collect the dirt." Jim grinned. "Even a second-rate cop." He turned on the cruiser's spotlight and lit up the surrounding graveyard. Scanning the area, the harsh light revealed nothing unusual hiding within the deep shadows, in the shrubbery, behind trees, or amongst the gravestones. He turned back to Ellie. "There's no sign of those things anywhere. It'll only take me a minute."

She again sighed, reluctant to let Jim do this alone. But he was right, dammit. She needed to reserve what little strength she had for the ceremony. "I hate it when you're right."

"I know."

"Be careful. Take the iron box with you. Fill it about a third full."

Jim stretched across her. He reached down to the floor, grabbing the iron box resting at her feet, and straightened back up. "You hang on, El. We're almost finished." He turned to Kathy. "And you stay put too, young lady."

With a half-hearted smile, Kathy nodded.

He leaned close to Ellie. "Don't worry," he whispered, "her door won't open from the inside. She's like a prisoner back there...safe and not going anywhere. So you can rest, close your eyes even. I'll be back before you know I'm gone. You'll never even miss me."

She grinned, eyes only half open. "Too late. Miss you already."

He kissed her on the cheek, then he scanned the cemetery with the spotlight one more time for insurance. The bright light still revealed nothing but grave markers, trees, shrubs, flowers, and shadows at the outer edges. Satisfied, he opened his door. Ellie's hand on his arm stopped him.

"Be careful."

"Careful's my middle name."

Iron box in hand, he climbed from the car, quietly closing the door behind him. But after only three steps toward a nearby grave, he stopped cold.

Chitter! Chitter!

Stiffening, he wheeled toward the sound.

An ugly perched on the roof of the car spread its bat-like wings and shrieked.

With the iron box clutched in his left hand, he reached for his pistol with his right, fumbling with the empty holster.

The creature hissed and bared razor-sharp teeth.

"Shit. This isn't good."

With another hideous shriek, the ugly launched itself at him. Both man and beast hit the ground hard.

"Ellie!" Kathy pressed her face against her window. "Ellie! Ellie!" She fought with her door, trying to force it open. Not able to, she pounded her fists against the window in frustration. "Ellie!"

"What is it?" Ellie jerked upright, brought back to life by the girl's screams. Eyes wide, she scanned her surroundings. "What's wrong?"

"Jim. It's killing Jim."

Ellie brought the spotlight around, shining it across the cemetery, stopping it on Jim and the ugly locked in mortal combat. "Jimmy," she cried. Clutching the pistol in her sticky, bloodstained hand, she pushed her door open and scrambled out of the car as if she had just received another shot of adrenaline.

"Ellie," Kathy screamed.

She didn't respond, but Kathy's cry reminded her in the heat of the moment to slam her door shut and not leave the girl unprotected in an open car. Clutching the pistol, she ran toward the battle.

Growling, the ugly pinned Jim to the ground within its wings. It ripped into its prey, tearing away flesh and slurping up the free-flowing blood.

She raised the pistol and fired on the run, screaming all the while.

The shot hit the ugly square in the back. It spasmed. A gaping wound gushed blood. But it refused to go down or release its hold on Jim.

She skidded to a stop a short distance away. This time she took careful aim and fired.

The creature's head blew apart, skull cracking open like an egg. Gory yolk of brains and blood splattered the ground.

She rushed forward. With her foot, she shoved the dead creature away then hunkered down, desperate to know if Jim still lived. The sight of the mangled and bloody thing that was once his handsome face made her gasp. Her love was lost. She turned away, retching and heaving, her insides splattering the ground. What was she going to do without him? She had loved him since high school. He was her first. Hell, he was her only. But maybe he wasn't gone. She hadn't checked for a pulse. Screwing up her courage, she dared to look at him again. She reached out with a trembling hand and felt his wrist for a pulse. There was none. He was truly gone. She hung her head and cried. Sobs choked her as if strong hands clutched her throat in a stranglehold. How could she go on?

"Ellie," Kathy cried.

That brought her out of her grief. She choked back her last sob, wiped away tears. Glancing over her shoulder, she caught a glimpse of Kathy in the back seat of the cruiser, face pressed against the window, palms slapping the glass, a petrified look on her face.

That's how. She wiped more tears away. Kathy needed her. Everyone counted on her. She had a job to do, a ceremony to perform. There would be time for grief later, a lifetime.

She looked back down at Jim one last time. "I love you, James Steady."

With that, she stood. "Time to end this." Scooping up the iron box, she stumbled back to the car to calm down Kathy. Hunkering down, she talked to the girl through the window. "You stay put, sweetheart. You're safe in there." She mustered a small, half-hearted smile. "I'll be right back."

Kathy looked panicked. "No, don't leave me." She slapped the glass with both hands. "Don't leave me."

Ellie put the palm of her hand against the window. "I will be back. I promise."

She stood, not waiting for a reaction or an answer. Carrying the iron box in one hand and the pistol in the other, she cautiously shuffled to the nearest gravesite. There, she dropped to her knees and placed the iron box at her side. She gave her immediate surroundings a quick scan before reluctantly putting the pistol on the ground next her. Using both hands, she clawed with determination at the sod, dumping into the iron box clumps of hallowed ground.

"Time to end this."

Chapter 24

The large, ageless tree stood sentinel over the clearing. The gaping wound still marred the thick, twisted trunk. Through the darkness, the police cruiser raced through the woods and into the clearing, crashing into the backend of the banged-up Ford Mustang. The cruiser's engine hissed, steam rising out from under its hood before conking out.

From behind the wheel, Ellie groaned. She'd been through a war and looked it. Consciousness played hide-and-seek with her. Groaning again, she stiffly moved to check on Kathy, who was now sitting next to her in the front passenger seat.

"You okay, sweetheart?"

The girl nodded.

"There's something to be said for seat belts, huh?"

Kathy absently nodded again as she looked out her window in wide-eyed wonderment. "Where are we, Ellie?"

"This is where we do the ceremony." Ellie pointed. "See that tree?"

"Uh-huh."

"Within that gaping hole is where the uglies were imprisoned many years ago by my great-grandmother."

"She was a witch too?"

Ellie smiled, thin and weak. "Yes, my grandmother and my mother too." Blood soaked through the bandage on her neck. It ran freely down her arm. "All the females in my family."

"Can I be a witch too?"

Ellie cocked her head. Concentration was draining from her much like her blood. "I don't know, sweetheart. I think you have to be born a witch."

"Oh." Kathy stared out her window.

"That doesn't mean you can't help." Ellie took a deep breath, calling on all of the inner willpower she could muster. Somehow, she had to find the strength and courage to go on. "I need you to have my back again, like in the church. Can you do that?"

Kathy turned her attention to Ellie. She nodded.

"Good. I can't do this without you."

"I've got your back, Ellie...*always*."

Ellie smiled. "I guess I knew that before I even asked. Are you ready?"

The girl nodded.

"You must do exactly as I say, understand?"

"I understand."

"You *are* a brave little girl, Kathy."

Kathy managed a smile.

"Let's go."

Ellie opened her door, spilling out, barely able to keep her feet. Kathy hopped out with the energy of youth. Together, they retrieved everything they needed from the car and carried it all past the decaying corpse that still lay there, to the base of the tree. Kathy stared at the dead guy as they maneuvered around him but otherwise didn't react or say a thing.

Exhausted, barely holding on to consciousness, Ellie dropped to her knees. Loss of blood and expending the energy to kill that last ugly had taken its toll. But it was almost over, she told herself. Then she could rest. For now, she needed to be strong. Kathy and everyone else depended on her being strong.

"Kathy, take the salt and pour a ring around us. Hurry."

The girl did as she was told, carefully pouring a protective ring around them.

"No breaks, sweetheart," Ellie warned. "Make sure there are no breaks or gaps in the ring. It's the only thing that'll be between us and those things when they come."

The girl stopped pouring and gulped hard. "They're coming here?"

Ellie nodded. "I'm going to call them here." Dizziness tried to thwart her plans, and she swayed on her knees, but in the end, she managed to right herself and remain conscious and coherent. "Now finish. Hurry."

When Kathy finished, she knelt within the ring.

Ellie knelt there too. She had the iron box resting on the ground in front of her. She opened it. "The dirt from sacred ground is already inside. Hand me the remaining salt."

Kathy did.

Ellie poured the remaining salt into the box and began to chant:

"*Aboon dabashmaya, nethkadash shamak. Tetha malkoothak. Newe tzevyanak aykan dabashmaya.*"

Overhead, lightning flashed in the gray, predawn sky. Thunder boomed.

Kathy gasped, eyes as wide as saucers.

Ellie took the glass vial from her jeans pocket. She poured the holy water into the iron box and slammed the lid shut.

"*Af bara hav lan lakma dsoonkanan. Yamana washbook lan kavine aykana daf.*"

A strong wind swirled into the clearing. Lightning now flashed overhead like a strobe light, and rapid-fire thunder bombs exploded all around. A multitude of shrieks rose above it all.

Ellie raised both trembling arms to the heavens. Blood dripped from the fingertips of one hand. But she held onto life a bit longer and at the top of her lungs, screeched, "*Hanan shabookan lhayavine oolow talahn lanesyana. El fatsan men beesha.*"

Wind whipped and tore at them and the surrounding trees. Lightning continued to flash. Thunder boomed. A swarm of uglies covered the sky like fast-moving storm clouds.

With great effort, Ellie kept her arms extended to the heavens.

"*Hanan shabookan lhayavine oolow talahn lanesyana. Ela fatsan men beesha.*"

With that incantation, the creatures dive-bombed the clearing.

"Ellie," Kathy screamed. She grabbed Ellie's waist and held on for dear life.

But the uglies didn't attack. Instead, hundreds of them streaked past, back through the cavernous hole in the tree from hence they came. When the last horrid creature entered the hollow tree, Ellie picked up the iron box and hurled it after them with all the remaining strength she could muster.

One last flash of lightning lit up the clearing. One last boom of deafening thunder echoed. Then all fell silent and still. The cloud cover dissipated and dawn lit up the sky. The tree had miraculously healed itself, a scar appearing in the trunk where just seconds ago was a gaping wound. Embedded in that scar was the iron box.

"Ellie," Kathy cried, "you did it."

The world spun out of control, and Ellie collapsed within the ring of salt.

Chapter 25

Twenty years later, Solemn was again the quiet, Indiana town where families prospered and grew. As before, bungalows populated the streets, with well-kept lawns and large oak and maple trees. Fallen leaves swirled about the streets and lawns. Children ran and played, laughing and squealing. Parents raked leaves and puttered in their yards. A light traffic traveled the streets.

Gran's house still was in disrepair, in need of a fresh coat of paint. Countless wind chimes tinkled and rang in the breeze. Gargoyles stood guard over a patchwork of herbs, spices, vegetables, and squash.

Inside the house, sunlight streamed into an old and careworn bedroom. A collection of family pictures also brightened the room. They hung on the walls and cluttered the nearby bureau. Some dated back to Gran, Ellie's mother, and Ellie growing up through the years. There was a picture of Ellie and Jim at their high school prom and a picture of Jim the day he graduated from the police academy. Others were more recent: Ellie and Kathy, Ellie pregnant with Jim's baby girl. Jamie as a baby. Jamie growing up with Kathy and Ellie.

Jamie's graduation from high school, and Kathy in her deputy-sheriff's uniform the day she graduated from the academy.

Ellie lay in bed, dying, riddled with cancer. Jamie sat at her mother's bedside, keeping vigil. Sobs choked her throat. Tears rolled down her cheeks. Kathy stood next to the bureau, dressed in her uniform, a stoic look upon her face, watching over her adopted mother and sister.

Ellie moaned and stirred. "Jaime," she whispered, "there's not much time."

Storm clouds gathered outside the window, blocking the sunlight and darkening the room.

"Go to the tree," she continued. "Perform the ceremony."

Jamie wiped away free-flowing tears. "I want to stay here with you, Mama."

Ellie gazed up at her daughter. "Jamie, dear, you must be strong. Go to the tree now. Before it's too late."

Jamie leaned over and kissed her mother on the cheek. "I love you, Mama."

"I love you too, dear." Ellie found the strength to raise a hand and place it on her daughter's arm. "Now go. Make your father and I proud."

Jamie reluctantly rose. She looked down at her mother one last time before turning away. On her way out the door, she gave Kathy a pleading glance. Then she rushed through the house, the front door slamming behind her as she left.

"Kathy?"

Kathy stepped away from the bureau to her adopted mother's bedside. "I'm here, Ellie."

Ellie struggled with consciousness. "She'll need you, sweetheart. Now more than ever."

Kathy nodded. She reached down and squeezed Ellie's hand. "Don't worry about anything. I've got her back."

Ellie smiled weakly. "I guess I knew it before I even asked."

Kathy released Ellie's hand. She went to the closet and retrieved a shotgun and a box of shells before returning to the bedside.

"I love you, sweetheart," Ellie mumbled.

Kathy smiled. "Love you too."

"Now go…make Jim proud."

Kathy turned away. She rushed from the room, footsteps echoing as she hurried through the house. The front door slammed behind her as she left.

Ellie closed her eyes. She tried to hang on, to buy Jamie and Kathy more time. She loved them both deeply and prayed for their success. In the middle of her prayer, she took a deep, hitched breath.

It was her last.

Chapter 26

With emergency lights flashing, the police cruiser sped out of town. Kathy drove. Jamie sat, quiet and pensive, in the passenger seat. Overhead, the sky darkened with foreboding storm clouds. Far off lightning flashed. Distant thunder rumbled. Down the two-lane country road, they raced against the inevitable, finally reaching the clearing in the woods and braking to an abrupt stop not far from the ageless tree.

They both bolted from the car.

Lightning streaked across the sky, heading straight for the tree.

"No," Jamie cried.

Thunder boomed. And Hell again was released upon the world.

Fred Wiehe

LUPINE DREAM

The bite of the beast
The waxing of the moon
Lupine dreams take over the night
The full moon rises
Turning man into beast
A frightening and horrible sight

But now the moon wanes
The nightmares disappear
A new dawn sheds its light
The bite wound heals
The crescent moon fades
The beast again is a man
A man who continues to fight

The Reckoning

In the woods that surrounded the old horse stables, down a path few ever used, people swore they saw faces. Faces carved as if from stone, peeking out from within the rocks, the trees, even the ground itself. Blinking. Watchful. Most discounted it as a trick of the eye, of light and shadow. Those who didn't found it haunting and disconcerting.

To a very few, it was a source of great comfort.

A bright sun began its descent. Dust hung in the air, kicked up by the horses in surrounding paddocks. The smell of horse manure permeated the air. Flies buzzed the horses and people alike. A group of six, young girls had just completed riding lessons and were heading across the stables to the parking area. Another girl who cleaned stalls at the stables in exchange for lessons crossed their path.

"Hey, you little weirdo." Josie pushed Becky out of her way. "Watch where you're going."

Becky stumbled and fell, landing on her bottom, the manure rake she had been carrying now in the dirt next to her.

Josie's friends crowded around, laughing and pointing.

The horses in the surrounding paddocks snorted and stomped at the commotion.

Becky fought back tears but to no avail. Quickly, she wiped the tears away and sniffed the snot back up her nose.

"You little cry baby." Josie kicked dirt in the girl's face.

Becky closed her eyes and cried out. "Leave me alone." Frantically, she wiped dirt from her eyes.

The crowd of girls laughed all the harder. They too began to kick dirt toward the girl at their feet.

"Poor, little Becky," Josie said. "You want to just be left alone?" She hunkered down next to her quarry and long-time target of ridicule. "That's not what you really want, is it? You really want to be one of us. Admit it."

"I just want to be left alone," Becky insisted. She choked back her tears. The next words that came out of her mouth were ones she had wanted to say for a long time but was too afraid. "Why would I want to be one of you? I would kill myself if I were one of you."

Josie got a wild look in her eyes and grinned a demon's grin. Grabbing a handful of small stones, she stood. "Maybe we can help you with that." She chucked a stone, hitting Becky in the head.

The girl screamed.

All the other girls laughed. They too reached down, picked up some small stones, and tossed them at their easy target.

"You'll never be one of us," they chanted. "Never…never…never…"

"Stop that!" Mr. Weir waded into the crowd of young girls, some of the stones hitting him in the legs as he intervened. "That's enough." He reached down, helping Becky to her feet. He checked her over and to his relief there was minimal damage, just a few cuts. Thankfully, the stones had been very small and light. "Are you okay?" He brushed the girl's hair from her face.

Becky sniffed back snot and wiped her eyes, leaving smudges of dirt on her face. She nodded but said nothing. Instead, she stared at the ground as if she thought the entire incident was somehow her fault.

Mr. Weir turned to the group of girls. "You should be ashamed of yourselves." He looked in each girl's face, searching for some sign that one or all felt some shame, some regret, some compassion. He saw none. He could tell their parents, but he wondered if that would solve anything. These mean girls were probably the way they were because of their home life, parents giving them a sense of false entitlement. No. He had a better idea. He stood and looked out over the horizon. The sun had almost set behind the big barn, and a burgeoning gloom began to conquer the sky. It was the perfect time of day for what he had in mind.

"Everyone sit down," he said.

"In the dirt?" Josie protested.

He looked down at her and then at all the girls. "In the dirt."

Reluctantly, grumbling, the girls lowered their bottoms onto the dirt path.

"Form a circle."

They did so, with Mr. Weir and Becky at the center.

"You sit too, Becky." He patted her on the back. "In the circle."

Becky looked unsure.

"Make room for her," he commanded.

The circle of girls made a break, leaving enough room for Becky to sit next to Josie. With some trepidation, she took her spot.

"I'm not going to lecture you on the right or wrong of what just happened or the consequences of your actions," he began. "Instead, I'm going to tell you a story."

Josie rolled her eyes and sighed. Except for Becky, the other girls let out nervous giggles.

"A true story," he continued. "And it happened right here many years ago, back when it was just a boarding stable, rustic and rundown. Back before there were riding lessons and a clubhouse with refreshments. Back before I bought this place."

All the girls fell silent.

"There was a group of women who boarded their horses here. They remind me of you girls except they were adults and should have known better, should have behaved better. I believe there were six of them, as well, just like you girls. And just like Becky, there was one woman, Stephanie, who boarded here that became their scapegoat, the person that was chosen to suffer, who became the target of their anger and bore the blame of all that wasn't right in their petty, worthless lives. And to make matters worse, the reason for the harassment was because Stephie's husband had been badly injured from being bucked off one of their horses after that owner—Pat, I believe her name was—asked him to ride it."

He looked off in the distance as if lost in thought for a moment. Shaking himself free, he continued, "He suffered serious injuries…a concussion with resulting amnesia, multiple broken ribs, a collapsed lung, broken wrist…" He shook his head. "He was actually lucky to have lived through it or that he hadn't become a quadriplegic like that Superman guy, Christopher Reeves."

Looking for a reaction, he studied the faces in the circle. They all looked nonplused. They probably didn't even know who Christopher Reeves was.

Sighing, he continued, "Anyway, right after the accident, this Pat admitted it was all her fault because the horse had already thrown two other people, both of whom had miraculously escaped with only minimal injuries, so she knew the horse was dangerous and still had asked Stephie's husband to ride it. She also promised to pay his hospital bills.

Later of course, she denied all of this, refused to pay the resulting $80,000 medical bills, and started spreading rumors that he had demanded to ride the horse and that it was his own fault he was injured. Since Stephie and her husband had no health insurance, their only recourse was to file a lawsuit. It was because of that suit that everyone hated them. It was because of that lawsuit, that for a prolonged period this poor woman took everything these angry women could dish out."

He studied the girls' faces again. Every one of them except Becky looked bored and unsympathetic.

"Until one night," he continued, "much like this one, she decided to stand up for herself. On that fateful night, she had come to the stables to take care of her horse, waiting until dark in the hope of being alone, in the hope of not having to put up with anymore ridicule, anymore bullying. But that wasn't to be:

Stephie walked her horse Pinto along the dirt path through the woods, both she and the horse enjoying the night air and the solitude. Out of the shadows, two riders on horseback came around a bend toward them.

With a snort, one of the horses reared and spun, the rider almost losing her seat but managing to stay aboard. Stephie's own horse snorted, as well, and tried to break away. But she held onto the lead rope and brought Pinto under control.

The rider also managed to get her horse under control. After doing so, she jumped from the saddle and charged. "What the fuck are you doing hiding in the shadows?" Wanda screamed.

Stephie was taken aback, not knowing what to say or do. The charging woman stopped just short of bumping her, Wanda's twisted and ugly face looming with menace.

"I could've been thrown and killed."

Spittle flew from Wanda's mouth, spraying Stephie in the face.

"It would've been all your fault too, you stupid bitch...out here skulking around in the dark like some weirdo."

Stephie took a step back but squared her shoulders and raised her chin in defiance, tired of being bullied. "It's not my fault you're a bad rider and can't keep control of your own horse."

At that, Wanda's jaw dropped. Her friend Dora trotted her horse forward close enough to bump Stephie and knocked her off her feet.

On her way to the ground, she lost her hold on Pinto's lead rope. The horse spooked from the sudden advancement of the other horse and its rider. He wheeled around and galloped off, one hoof clipping Stephie in the head. She cried out and then lay in the dirt on her back—the two women, the horse, and the night sky spinning and out of focus above her.

Dora backed her horse off, but it still stomped and circled nearby, kicking up dirt and rocks.

"Ahh…poor little Stephie." Wanda, like the horse, kicked dirt and rocks at her target of ridicule.

Groaning, Stephie forced herself to sit up, knowing that if she lay there she would be at their mercy. Then, she tried to climb to her feet.

"Not so fast." Wanda took the flat of her foot and pushed her rival back onto the ground.

Dora dismounted. "Yeah, not so fast. You need to be taught a lesson."

Both women picked up some rocks. Wanda threw one first, hitting her target directly in her left temple.

Stephie screamed, "Stop!" Bruised and in pain, she frantically tried to get to her feet. "Stop!"

Dora threw one of hers, the rock hitting her prey in the shoulder.

"Always trying to police everyone, telling us what to do." Wanda threw another rock. "Well, not this time, bitch."

"Yeah, you're not getting your way this time." Dora threw another rock.

Stephie's screams reached a fevered pitch as she desperately tried to cover up with her arms to fend off the attack.

The commotion brought the rest of the gang running up the trail. Pat, Lori, and Selena all braked suddenly at the spectacle. But rather than trying to stop it, Pat joined in. "Yee-haw!" she yelled, picking up rocks and chucking them with glee at her long-time nemesis. Lori quickly joined in. Selena picked up rocks too but hesitated to throw them, fear etched across her face.

"What are you waiting for?" Lori chucked another rock.

"She's dangerous," Selena mumbled. She looked at the rocks in her hands. "I'm afraid."

"Throw your rocks," Pat demanded.

Still hesitant, Selena threw a rock, hitting her target in the back of the head. Then she threw another and another, now caught up with the others in the frenzy of the moment.

Stephie lay motionless as rocks now flew from all directions.

The owner of the stable followed close behind. "What are you doing?" Kendall pushed through the women and held her hands up. "Stop, you'll kill her."

That was enough to break the fever of violence. All the women stood there in the night, breathing hard, grins on their faces, shaking with adrenaline and hatred.

Kendall hunkered next to the battered and bruised woman, checking for a pulse. "I can't tell if she's alive or not."

"If she is, she soon won't be," Pat hissed.

The stable owner stood, turning to face the other women. "What's that supposed to mean?"

Pat's grin widened. "It means...now's our chance to get rid of her once and for all, maybe even put an end to the lawsuit against me."

"What?" Kendall shook her head. "I can't be a party to this. It's murder."

"Don't be a wuss." Pat got up in the other woman's face. "You're either with us or you're against us." All the women gathered behind her as a show of unity.

Kendall gulped and nodded.

"Good." Pat turned to the others. "We'll bury her right here...alive or dead doesn't matter...Mother Nature will take care of the rest."

"Bury her with what?" Wanda asked.

"Yeah," Dora chimed in, "we don't have any shovels."

"No tools at all," Lori added.

"We can use our hands," Selena offered.

"That's the spirit," Pat said. "Everyone in agreement?"

Everyone, including Kendall, nodded.

Using nothing but their hands, they dug a shallow grave, dumped Stephie into it, and covered her with dirt and leaves.

Afterward, all of them stood around the grave, breathing hard, dirt caked in their fingernails.

"If anyone asks," Pat said, "she hasn't been here, and we haven't seen her."

Wanda added, "Let's round up her horse and put it back. No one will ever know she was here tonight."

In complete agreement, the women returned Pinto to his paddock, put their own horses away, and left for the night.

Unbeknownst to anyone, Stephie wasn't yet dead. She stirred in her shallow grave, unable to see or hear, struggling to breathe. In a panic, she clawed at the loose dirt covering her, fingers digging frantically until they reached the surface and punched through, creating an air hole. She spat dirt from her mouth and gasped on the rush of sweet air that filled her lungs. Weak and woozy, she lay their half buried in the ground, resting her tired, bloodied body, waiting for the night air to rejuvenate her. After some time, she pushed up out of her grave and sat up. She wiped away the dirt caked around her eyes and spat more dirt from her mouth. Blood dribbled down the sides of her face from head wounds. Her bones and muscles throbbed and ached. Groaning and with a grunt, she struggled to her feet but only managed to remain standing for a few precious seconds before she again collapsed. Her head felt as though it had been hit multiple times by a sledgehammer, and stars floated in her vision. Walking was out of the question. She would have to crawl. For what seemed to her like days, she maneuvered herself on hands and knees until even that became impossible, and she was left to push herself along on her stomach, slithering like a half-dead snake through the dirt and grass. Finally, by dawn, she found herself in front of Pinto's paddock. It was there she completely collapsed, the ground spinning with increasing speed. It was there consciousness abandoned her.

When she woke, she was in bed, something beeping in her ear. Darkness surrounded her. She couldn't see anything except for dots of light from what she knew had to be machines that monitored her vitals. She was in a hospital. She knew the sights, sounds, and smells all too well from her husband's stay. She tried to lift her head to have a look around and confirm her suspicion but couldn't. A grunt escaped her lips. A hand squeezed hers.

"Stephie?"

She squeezed the hand back and tried to speak to her husband but nothing came out except a moan.

"It's okay. Don't try to speak. You're okay. You've been sleeping for two days. The doctor said you

have a concussion. You have two broken ribs too and some cuts and bruises." He paused. "Just couldn't let me get all the attention, could you?"

She attempted a smile and squeezed her husband's hand in response.

He leaned forward, kissed her on the mouth, and whispered, "Make them pay, Stephie. Make them pay dearly."

With those words worming their way into her subconscious, she closed her eyes and slept.

Meanwhile, the six bullies met at the stables, the night warm and calm, the horses quiet and lazy.

"How did that bitch survive?" Pat asked no one in particular. "Did the police talk to everyone?" To this question, she expected answers.

All the women nodded.

"They wanted to know the last time I saw her," Wanda said. "And if I was here that night."

Dora nodded. "They asked me the same things."

"Me too," Selena chimed in.

Pat sucked in a deep breath. "Lori?"

She nodded.

Pat turned to Kendall. "What about you?"

The stable owner looked at the ground. "They asked me those same questions." She looked up. "They also wanted to know about all of you. They asked me if everyone here got along. They asked me if she had any enemies."

The breeze picked up, stirring the branches of surrounding trees.

Pat stepped close to Kendall. "And what did you say? Did you tell them we're good Christians?"

"I told them I didn't know. I told them I'm not a den mother, that I'm a businesswoman and only care whether people pay their board."

The breeze was now a stiff wind. It shook the treetops and whipped everyone's hair.

Pat grinned. "Good. But you should have told them I'm a good Christian woman too."

The temperature plummeted with the increased wind. Everyone shivered.

"What the fuck." Wanda hugged herself against the sudden cold.

"Feels like a storm coming in." Dora slipped a sweatshirt on that she had tied around her waist.

"This time of year?" Lori put on a jacket she had been carrying.

"It's her," Selena exclaimed. "Oh my god, it's that bitch. I don't know how. But it's her."

Pat turned toward her little minion. "What are you babbling about?"

An icy rain began to fall. Caught in the wind, the rain seemed to be coming from all directions at once, slamming into their faces and backs at the same time.

"You said it yourself, she's a weirdo," Selena continued her rant. *"Somehow, she's making this happen. She's doing this. I told you she's dangerous."*

Pat scoffed. "Controlling the weather? You're a drama queen, Selena. No one can control mother nature."

With that, the temperature plummeted even more, and the pounding rain turned to sleet. The wind swirled about them in an evil embrace.

"Let's get out of here," Pat yelled.

All six of the women began to run for the cover of a nearby barn. But visibility had turned nearly nonexistent, and the howling wind seemed to direct them where it wanted them to go. Soon they were running blindly through the woods, on the same path on which they had stoned Stephie. Then the sleet turned to hailstones as big as marbles. The lumps of ice pummeled the women as they frantically ran and looked for cover.

Lori was the first to go down. She fell to her hands and knees, the hailstones beating her into submission. Bloody cuts opened on her face and head as she collapsed in the dirt. The ground beneath her began to rumble and shake. The earth's movement rolled her onto her back. The icy lumps grew to the size of golf balls, slamming into her face and chest. The storm muffled her cries of horror and desperation as the ground opened and began to swallow her whole. She sunk into the dirt path, her grave closing behind her until nothing of her was left except her bloodied face, looking like a stone peeking up out of the earth.

Wanda and Dora ran from the path into a clump of trees, hoping the overhead branches would protect them. But the hailstones had become a barrage of icy baseballs that slammed through the canopy. Their only hope was to put their backs to the trees, giving the hailstones as little room as possible to hit them. They both screamed when the trees at their backs split open, and the wind began to push them inside the trunks. But the storm cut off their screams and soon the trunks closed around them until all that could be seen were their faces, the horror of the moment engraved into their features.

Selena and Kendall huddled together against a large boulder, barely conscious from the blitzkrieg of ice and wind, their faces bloody, their bodies beaten and broken. They couldn't even put up a struggle when the large rock at their backs cracked open and pulled them inside, imprisoning all but their grisly faces.

A swirl of torrid wind captured Pat in its clutches, imprisoning her within the eye of its storm. She struggled to free herself from the mini tornado but to no avail. Weak, beaten, and bloody, she fell to her knees. Clutched at her throat. Unable to breathe. The swirling wind had sucked all the oxygen out of the air, creating a vacuum, suffocating her. Eyes bulging, gasping for air, she collapsed to the ground. But before she could expire, the earth opened, swallowing her alive into a makeshift grave and taking possession of her body and soul. All that was left of her was a face frozen in terror—a rock sticking out of the ground.

When the last of the bullies was dispatched, the storm passed as if it had never existed. The trees now stood straight and lifeless, the air calm. The temperature rose to normal levels. The hailstones ended their assault and melted away.

The horses meandered lazily about their paddocks or calmly stood in their stalls as if their lives had never been disturbed, as if nothing out of the ordinary had ever taken place. The night was again quiet and peaceful.

Mr. Weir finished his story. He looked around at the girls sitting in a circle around him. Now, their faces wore masks of shock and fear.

Josie gulped. "I-I'm sorry, Becky."

All the other girls chimed in, "Me too."

"I'm sorry too," Becky whispered.

Josie looked up at Mr. Weir. "I'll never pick on anyone ever again."

He nodded approval. "What about the rest of you?"

"Never again."

"Never."

"Me neither."

"Nope."

"Never."

"Good." He looked toward the parking area. "Your rides are here. See you all tomorrow."

All seven girls jumped to their feet and ran for the parking area, yelling goodbye to each other as they climbed into their respective cars.

When they were gone, he took a deep breath, moaning a bit as he did so, his ribs having never really healed properly since the accident. Dusk was quickly giving way to night, so he turned and walked up the dirt path through the woods in search of his wife. He found her where he knew he would, standing in the spot where she had almost died.

"I knew you'd be here." He approached from behind, putting his arm around her and pulling her close.

Stephie smiled up at him. "I find this spot comforting. It makes me feel that all's right with the world."

He kissed her on top of the head. "It's getting late."

She nodded.

They turned to leave.

Over his shoulder, Mr. Weir called, "Good night, ladies."

From within the trees, the ground, and a large boulder, eyes blinked in response as if begging in Morse code for release and for mercy.

But there would be no release. There would be no mercy.

TRANSFORMED

Fear grips the heart
Panic squeezes the lungs
Terror lives in the soul
Sanity's on the run

Pain takes over the mind
Evil deeds look like fun
Actions are out of control
Sanity's on the run

Violence is a need
Killing one by one
Humanity is stole
Sanity's on the run

Fred Wiehe

My Only Daddy

I heard voices coming from my son's bedroom. He was in there alone, though. No one else was in the house. Who could he be talking to? Himself?

No. I thought I heard another voice, muffled and low.

I crept down the hallway toward his door. The key was firmly planted in the keyhole as usual, even though I seldom locked the door. In fact, the door was open a crack. I could see light from inside his room. I could hear his voice clearly, but I couldn't make out his words. I swore I heard an indistinguishable whispering too. It almost didn't sound like a voice at all but instead like wipers whisking across a car windshield.

Stopping outside his bedroom door, I cocked my head and listened.

"He's my only daddy," Billy answered the whispering.

There was no response, no whisper. Had I imagined it before?

I opened the door the rest of the way. My son stood in the middle of the room, looking up at the ceiling. Sunlight streamed in through the window. It surrounded the boy, giving him an otherworldly glow.

I took a step into the room. A hint of jasmine was in the air, reminding me of my wife's perfume. It couldn't be, though.

"Billy?" I said, taking another step toward the boy.

He turned to look at me. The sunlight behind him seemed to radiate directly from him rather than from the window.

Were all my senses playing tricks on me?

Because the light in my eyes blinded me, I couldn't make out the look on my son's face. I put a hand up to shield my eyes.

"Billy, who were you talking to?"

He didn't answer. He just stared at me from within the light.

I ventured farther into the bedroom, stopping a few feet away. "Billy?"

The scent of jasmine faded. The room darkened as if clouds had just passed in front of the sun, blocking its rays. I could see him now. He stared at me, a blank expression on his usually smiling face.

"Billy?" I stepped close enough to touch him, hunkering down so we were eye to eye. "Who were you talking to?"

He grinned. "An angel."

"An angel?"

He nodded, still grinning.

I sighed. This wasn't the first time he had mentioned angels since his mother died over a year ago. It was the first time, however, that he claimed to talk with one.

I stared at the boy, trying to smile back, but I doubted I did a very good job. "What did the angel say?"

His grin grew wider. "That she loved me."

"That's good," I said, still trying to force my worried frown into a reassuring smile. "Love is always good." I thought for a moment. "I heard you say something about me, Billy. Something about me being your only daddy. What was that about?"

My son's face darkened like the room. His grin faded. "I don't remember, Daddy." He looked down at his sneakers and fidgeted.

"You don't remember?"

"No." His right sneaker kicked at the rug. Then he looked up. The dark cloud vanished from his face. "Can I play outside?" He grinned.

I smelled a faint wisp of Jasmine again. The room brightened with sunlight a bit too. Nothing like before. Still, brighter, though, like his face.

I nodded. "Sure, you go on outside. But stay in the yard."

He wheeled and ran from the room. His feet pounded down the steps and across the kitchen floor to the backdoor. The door soon slammed behind him.

I stood and went to the window. I could see him run across the backyard and jump on the swing. He began pumping his short legs, getting himself going.

I couldn't wrap my brain around the angel thing. We had never been a religious family even when his mother was alive. We had never told him about angels that I knew about, anyway. Where would an eight-year-old even hear about angels? His school was public and nonreligious. Not there certainly.

I watched Billy swing higher and higher. Unnaturally higher. His short legs weren't even pumping anymore and yet the swing was almost as high as it could go, as if someone or something were pushing him from behind.

I opened the window and yelled, "Billy, slow down. No higher. Did you hear me? No higher!"

He giggled and let out a squeal. "The angel won't hurt me, Daddy."

He now swung so high the chain went slack and the swing thumped down as it came out of its forward swing and started backward again. At the pinnacle of the backward swing, he froze in the air for just a few heartbeats as if someone held him there, then he was flying forward again to new heights.

"Billy!"

I turned on my heels and ran from the room, down the stairs and across the kitchen floor to the backdoor. Grabbing the knob, I jerked on the door, but it wouldn't open. I twisted the knob again and pulled. Still jammed.

From outside, Billy's squeals took on a fevered pitch.

"Open, goddammit, open."

Twisting the knob, I pulled with all my might. The door gave way. It flew open, propelling me backwards from the momentum of my own strength. I stumbled and fell onto my ass.

My son continued to squeal.

I scrambled to my feet and hurried outside. By the time I made it to him, the swing had slowed to a calm rhythm. My heart still raced, but I slowed my approach and tried to appear unruffled. The swing slowed even more as I neared until finally it barely moved.

"Billy, you okay?"

He just sat there in the swing, his little hands still clutching the chains, feet dangling. He shrugged. "Sure. That was fun."

I hunkered down in front of him. "Why didn't you slow down when I told you to? Didn't you hear me?"

"I heard you." He nodded. "But I couldn't stop."

"Why not? How did you go so high?"

"The angel. She pushed me."

I stared at the boy, not knowing what to say.

"Don't worry, Daddy." He looked me straight in the eye. A hard, cold look I'd never seen before. "The angel won't hurt *me*."

I gulped. "Who would the angel hurt, Billy?"

"Not me," he repeated.

Gooseflesh crept up the back of my neck and spread across my scalp. I shivered as I stood, towering over the boy. "Go inside," I demanded.

He hopped out of the swing and ran inside. The door slammed behind him.

I was left standing there, inexplicably shaken, a cold uneasiness in the pit of my stomach.

Later that night, after Billy had gone to bed, I again heard voices from his room. I hadn't spoken to the boy about what had happened earlier in the day, both in his room and out in the backyard. Not during dinner. Not during his bath nor while brushing his teeth. Not while tucking him in for the night. I had decided nothing good would be served by bringing it all up again. Besides, I didn't want to think about it. The entire episode had affected me strangely. I didn't like feeling scared of an invisible *angel* or of my son for that matter. Now, though, I could avoid it no longer. Billy's voice and the wipers whispering across a windshield definitely came from his room, just like this afternoon.

I stalked down the hallway, close to the wall, staying quiet. The boy's door stood open just a crack. Light from his bedside lamp snuck through the crack to the hallway.

Holding my breath, I stood at the door and listened.

"He's my only Daddy," Billy said.

Unintelligible whispering answered.

"I can't kill him," he insisted. "He's my *only* Daddy."

My heart stopped. My knees almost buckled. I grabbed the door knob to steady myself. But I didn't open the door. I didn't go in. Fear held me back.

"He's my only Daddy."

Thoughts in my head swirled in chaos. Had I heard him right? Or was it some trick of sound?

"I can't," he insisted. "I just can't kill him."

At that, I screwed up my courage, pushed open the door, and burst into the room.

Billy scrambled out from underneath the bed. He climbed up under his covers and stared at me, wild eyed.

"Who were you talking to?" I demanded.

Breathlessly, he answered, "No one...Daddy."

"What were you doing under the bed?" I edged closer. "What's under there?"

The boy didn't answer. He just stared at me with that wild-eyed, I've-been-caught-at-something look.

"Tell me who you were talking to."

He remained silent, but his wild-eyed look turned to a cold, hard stare. Was that defiance I saw on his face? Who was this boy? He looked nothing like the son I knew.

"I'll look for myself," I said with some hesitation.

He stared.

Slowly, I lowered myself to my knees. I was reluctant to take my eyes off the boy, but there was no choice. Sitting back on my haunches, I bent over, turned my head sideways, and peered under the bed.

From under the bed, *Billy* stared back at me. "Run," he whispered.

The door to the bedroom slammed shut before I could even wonder how my son could be in two places at once, before I could even react to the warning. Only a frantic heartbeat later, something struck from above. It pounced on my back. Knocked the wind out of me. Pinned me to the floor. A strange black mist surrounded me. The stench of jasmine overpowered my lungs. I couldn't breathe. Strong hands grabbed my ankles. No way those hands belonged to an eight-year old. They pulled on my legs, dragging me toward the darkness underneath the bed.

I struggled to break free. Kicked my feet. Clutched at the floorboards to stop myself from being dragged into the unknown.

Somehow, I broke free. Scrambled to my hands and knees. Still surrounded by the mist, still choking on jasmine and not able to breathe, I crawled to the door. Grabbed and twisted the knob. Managed to swing the door open and fall into the hallway. Lying on my back, I kicked it closed.

Something from within the bedroom hit the other side. I planted my feet against the door and held firm—it opening but a crack before slamming shut again. Before another strike, I rolled over, pushed myself to my feet, and lunged at the door. With one smooth motion, I found the key and locked it. A sharp bang came from the other side, but the door held.

Turning, I sat on the floor and leaned back. I tried to catch my breath, slow my heart, get control of my thoughts.

Another sharp bang from the other side. The door vibrated from impact against my back.

No way was this my son. I didn't know what happened to Billy, but this wasn't him. That thing in there was both on top of and underneath the bed at the same time. It was supernaturally strong and tried to kill me. It couldn't be Billy. No way was it an angel either. It had to be a demon, straight out of Hell.

Something again hit the door. An inhuman yowl followed. The sound of it sent lightning bolts of cold shivers throughout my entire being and deep into my soul.

Suddenly, I knew what had to be done. Scrambling to my feet, I hurried down the hallway, down the stairs, across to the kitchen and out the backdoor to the garage. There, I found two cans of gasoline. Back inside the kitchen, I found matches in a drawer next to the stove.

The bangs and yowls continued from inside the bedroom as I returned to the upstairs hallway and began dousing the place with gasoline. I poured an entire two-gallon can in the hallway and down the stairs. I emptied the other can throughout the living room and kitchen. Finished, I stepped outside, struck a match, and tossed it inside. Afterward, I went out the gate to the street and watched as the fire quickly engulfed the house and the demon within it.

***

"You know the rest," Carson said, taking a deep, hitched breath.

Detective Hodges turned off the recorder. Clearing his throat, he said, "You tell quite a *story*. I'll get it typed up for you to sign." He turned and headed toward the door.

Carson's hands were cuffed and attached to the table by a metal ring. He looked up from them. "It had to be stopped."

Hodges opened the door to leave but hesitated. He turned back around, staring hard and cold at his prisoner.

"The demon had to be killed," Carson insisted. "Before it killed me. Before it killed others."

Hatred in the detective's eyes burned. His voice had a rough edge when he spoke. "A year ago, we couldn't prove you killed your wife...your *angel*, you called her."

Carson looked away. "I didn't kill her."

"Now you say your son was a demon and had to be killed." Hodges shook his head in apparent disgust. "You burned your son alive, you son of a bitch. We sure as hell got you dead to rights this time."

Carson looked back up, meeting the detective's gaze with a hard look of his own. "He *was* a demon."

"An insanity plea won't save you. I'll see to that." The detective left, slamming the door behind him.

Carson studied his shackled hands.

He couldn't have been wrong, could he? Not again.

THE IN BETWEEN

Evil lurks in the Netherworld
waiting…watching …
for a chance to escape
to the in between
longing to go
where once again
havoc on the world
it can make

The In Between
Part 2

Cody Butler was dead.

At least his body was dead.

But he was alive; what he knew himself always to have been was alive anyway; he felt the same, thought the same.

He stood on a grassy knoll. Overhead, a blue sky devoid of clouds wrapped itself around the world. A bright sun beamed down. A faint breeze rustled the leafy branches of the surrounding oaks and sycamores. Blue birds in those trees chirped and whistled happy tunes.

He couldn't actually feel the warmth of the sun nor the cool breeze. Still, this was no day for a funeral. He had always imagined funerals taking place on rain-soaked days, maybe with thunder booming in the distance and lightning flashing across the sky. This wasn't that kind of day at all.

Nevertheless, a funeral was taking place below. And it was *his*.

How could that be?

He gazed down on the proceedings. Even though he stood quite a distance away, he could see everyone and everything clearly, as if he had telescopic vision like Superman. Through the crowd of mourners, he could see that the casket perched above the gravesite had his picture set on it. Father Morse stood at its side. His mom, dad, and little brother stood nearby, all three crying with uncontrollable grief.

Shaz—*Cheeze* to almost everyone but his parents—Rupert stood at the graveside too. Cheeze looked the same as ever: a fourteen-year-old stocky boy, with dark skin and curly, light brown hair. His face looked slack and darkness circled his eyes. Honestly, he looked as though he had just lost his…well…his best friend.

Also in the crowd of mourners was Ryn Shade. The fifteen-year-old leaned against her father for support, his arm encircling her in a protective embrace. There were no tears in her big green eyes, but her gaze looked distant, vacant. Her lips, usually full and kissable-looking, were but a thin, hard line. Even so, she looked as beautiful as ever. Her wavy, red hair shone brighter than the sun and fluttered about her shoulders in the soft breeze. The sleeveless, short-cut black dress she wore looked stark against her pale, freckled skin.

His heart hammered his inner chest. The palms of his hands were sweaty, his throat dry. How could this girl still stir such emotions within him if he was dead? It proved that he couldn't be, didn't it?

But dammit, he wasn't alive either.

Oops.

His mom always told him not to curse. He guessed it didn't matter anymore, though. He guessed he could curse all he wanted now…do anything he wanted now.

Big whoop, though. Doin' anything you want don't mean much if you're dead.

But was he really dead? Or was he alive?

He didn't know. He couldn't explain it. He still loved Ryn. Cheeze was still his best friend. He missed his parents and his little brother. He felt the same about everyone and everything. He bet he still looked the same too—a slim fifteen-year old with shaggy, dirty-blond hair and brown eyes.

So how could he be dead?

Still not totally convinced one way or the other, he listened intently. His hearing too seemed blessed with superpowers.

"Today is a day not to mourn Cody's sudden and untimely death," Father Morse said, "but to celebrate his life." The priest paused, choking back his own sobs. "We will remember Cody as track star and honor student at Clement High School, as a faithful altar boy and church member at Saints Peter and Paul, as a loving son to James and Billie, as a doting big brother to Willy, and as a best friend to Shaz, Ryn, and to all his classmates."

Cody turned away. Suddenly he was no longer willing to watch or listen to the proceedings below. Instead, he looked out over the cemetery, past the grassy hills dotted with wildflowers and trees, past the rushing stream and crashing waterfall, past the freeway that led into Red City—the small California town where he lived—all the way to the two-story Victorian house that was his home. His gaze went inside, right through the walls and into the living room, up the stairs and down the hallway, all the way into his bedroom.

Then, as if magically transported, he himself was suddenly there, surrounded by walls covered with posters of TV shows like

Ghost Hunters, *Paranormal State*, *Psychic Kids*, and *True Hauntings*. With the posters was a crucifix his mom had hung on the wall over his bed. He stood now next to that messy bed and amongst the clutter of discarded dirty clothes, books and magazines on the paranormal, electronic gadgets he and his friends had collected in their ghost hunting quest, and his Ouija board, which was still set up on the floor from using it just a few nights ago.

Nothing had changed. Everything was just as he had left it.

With a sudden flash of clarity, he guessed he was neither dead nor alive really. He guessed he was somewhere…somewhere…in between.

He contemplated his circumstances as he stared down at his Ouija board. He, Ryn, and Cheeze were obsessed with the occult and ghosts. They considered themselves ghost hunters like the people in the TV shows on the posters that adorned the walls of his bedroom. At least, they wanted to be ghost hunters like those people. To make money, he had worked a paper route, while Cheeze worked part-time in his parents' store, and Ryn bought and sold electronics on Ebay. They had then pooled their earnings together to buy some of the necessary tools to be legitimate ghost hunters: an electromagnetic field detector, a duel IR thermometer/ambient air thermometer, two infrared motion detectors, a digital voice recorder, three 29 LED tricolor flashlights with holsters, four—because they had to be bought in pairs—Cobra 2-way radios, and a Geiger counter. Besides these high-tech tools, they also relied on the Ouija board, tarot cards, and an old book Ryn had found on how to conduct a séance and disperse ghosts and demons.

He choked back a sob, for he was no longer a ghost hunter. He was now the ghost.

But how? How had he died?

He still couldn't remember. He hadn't been sick. He had no memory of an accident. It made no sense. What was the last thing he remembered?

He concentrated…thinking…trying to remember.

Downstairs, the front door opened. Voices echoed throughout the house—his mom's, his dad's, his brother's. Then he heard Cheeze and Ryn's voices too. Soon more voices mingled with the others, and he couldn't differentiate one from the other anymore.

The wake had started. *His* wake.

He could no longer focus on remembering how or why he had died. He could only obsess on being dead.

Standing at the top of the staircase, he stared down onto the small entryway and the open front door. To his left, mostly out of his line of vision, was the living room. Relatives and friends streamed through the door, some of them carrying containers of food. Everyone either lingered in the doorway or mingled in the living room. Everyone except Cheeze and Ryn. Slowly, they made their way up the stairs toward him. At the top of the stairs, they walked right through him.

Ryn froze.

Cheeze stopped next to her.

Shivering, Ryn turned to to her friend. "Did you feel that?"

Cheeze shook his head.

She turned around, staring back at the top of the stairs, right through where Cody stood. Shivering again, she rubbed at her bare arms.

"What was it?" he asked.

She shook her head in disbelief. "Cold. A cold spot. Like walking through a ghost."

Now he shivered too. "Do you think he's here?"

She got a funny look on her face. "Only one way to find out."

They both turned on their heels and hurried down the hallway to Cody's room.

Cody didn't remember following them but found himself already in his room, looking down at them as they sat on the floor in front of the Ouija board.

Ryn immediately put her fingers on the oracle.

Cheeze hesitated. "Do you really think we should? Remember what happened last time with Cody."

Cody's ears perked up. He didn't remember and wanted to know.

"Nothing happened," she insisted. However, she did take her hands off the oracle.

"That's not how I remember it," he insisted. "Cody swore he saw a gray shadow of some kind over by the closet door."

"It was his imagination." She shook her head. "It had to be."

"Then he said he felt fingers on his neck," Cheeze continued, undaunted. "And he couldn't catch his breath."

"I remember." Ryn looked hard at him. "But nothing really happened."

His eyebrows rose. "Oh?"

Her look hardened even more. "I was just being silly. Nothing really happened, and I'd rather forget about it."

"Okay." He looked away. "But what about Cody?"

"He was okay when we left him," she insisted.

"He died two nights later, and nobody knows what killed him. He was asleep and just stopped breathing."

Now Cody started to remember. Listening to his friends jogged his memory. The three of them had conducted a séance with the board, calling on any spirit or spirits that might be lurking about. The oracle moved to *yes* when they asked if anyone was there. They got very excited and started asking questions. What they got back in answers, though, seemed like gibberish at the time. None of it made sense. They were about to give up when he saw the shadow by the closet door. Actually, it looked as though it had come out of the closet and stood in front of the door. It wasn't exactly a silhouette. It wasn't that well-formed. Still, he could've sworn it was a man standing there. Then it disappeared from sight. That's when he felt the hands on his neck, and he couldn't breathe. Worse, he couldn't move. He wanted to stand up and get away from whomever or whatever had hold of him but couldn't. He believed at the time that the only thing that saved him was his friends releasing the oracle and breaking the spell. Seconds later, though, Ryn cried out and then fainted. She was only out a short time, but when she came to she seemed weirded out.

"I have a bad feeling," Cheeze continued, "that we opened a doorway and something very bad came through it." He paused. "*Something* that killed Cody."

Cody cocked his head and thought hard. He still couldn't remember anything about the night he...*died*.

Ryn's eyebrows knitted together. Her mouth became a hard line, like it had back at the funeral. "You're being a baby. We have to know if Cody's here or not." Her voice lowered. "I have to know." After a moment, she added, "I have to know if he...knows how he died."

Cheeze looked uncertain. His hands still rested in his lap as if afraid to even come close to the oracle. "What if *it* comes back?" He shook his head. "If we open that doorway again, we might not be able to close it."

She put her fingers on the oracle. Her gaze bore into her friend. "Okay, let's say you're right. We opened a door and something came through. Something *evil*." She paused as if to let her words worm their way into his brain. "But what if *it* never went away?" she continued. "What if it's still here? Have you thought of that?"

Now Cheeze had the funny look on his face. "No," he muttered.

"Well, think about it."

He sighed and suddenly looked resigned. "You've made up your mind, haven't you?"

Cody stared at Ryn. He knew that look of determination she now had on her face. He had seen it a thousand times. There was no changing her mind once she got that look. Besides, what if she was right?

"Maybe we can send *it* or whatever back where it came from," she urged.

Cheeze nodded. With obvious reluctance, he placed his fingers on the oracle.

Ryn looked about the bedroom. "Is anyone here?" She waited for an answer. None came. "Cody, are *you* here?"

Cody eyed the oracle. He wasn't sure what to do. He wanted to answer. He desperately wanted them to know he was with them. But how? Could he just reach down and move the oracle? He looked at his hands and wondered. Or did he have to use his mind to move it, like the Force in *Star Wars*. This was all new to him.

Before he could decide how to proceed, the oracle moved to *Yes*.

What had just happened? Had he moved the oracle without even realizing it?

Ryn gasped. "He's here."

Cheeze looked around the room, that funny look still on his face.

Cody too examined the room. He saw nothing out of the ordinary, but something was wrong, a disturbance, again like in the Force in *Star Wars*. He had a sinking feeling in the pit of his stomach that he hadn't unintentionally moved the oracle. That meant someone or something else had.

"Ask another question," Cheeze urged.

Ryn nodded. "Cody, can you tell us how you..." She paused and seemed to choke on the next word. "...*died?*"

The oracle moved, spelling out, *Can't breathe*.

"Crap," Cheeze muttered. "Isn't this freaking you out?"

"Shhh," Ryn admonished. "Cody, why can't you breathe? What's stopping you?"

The oracle moved again. The answer was the same, *Can't breathe.*

Cody didn't understand. He had done nothing to influence the Ouija board. Was someone else impersonating him? Answering for him? He looked about the room but still saw nothing. No gray shadow by the closet door like last time. Nothing out of the ordinary. What had he seen that night? Had he been hallucinating?

"Cody, what's stopping you from breathing?"

The two waited but there was no answer.

That's when Cody noticed the gray shadow. It stood behind his friends. It was almost as if it had somehow stepped out of one or both of them.

"Cody, are you still here?" Ryn asked, her breath now visible, as if the temperature had dropped drastically.

Cheeze shivered, breathing hard, frosty plumes floating from his mouth like dispossessed spirits.

Cody watched the shadow with growing apprehension. What it had in mind he wasn't sure, but he had to do something to warn his friends of its existence. But what?

The Ouija board. He had to move the oracle, get a message to them.

The shadow hovered menacingly over his friends.

A quick message, to the point.

He moved to the Ouija board. He wasn't even sure he could physically move the Oracle, but he reached for it anyway. To his surprise, the Oracle responded to his touch, and he quickly spelled out, *Run*.

Neither of them ran.

Cheeze gaped down at the board.

Ryn remained sitting in front of the board too, looking strangely perplexed.

Frustrated, he reached down and flipped the Ouija board into the air, sending the board and Oracle flying. That got his two friends moving. They both jumped up and backed away. They still, however, didn't run. They just stood there, huddling against the cold.

"Are you mad at us?" Ryn yelled.

"I think that's obvious," Cheeze said, trying to look everywhere at once.

The shadow now stood before them as if readying itself to strike.

Neither of them seemed to notice. They just stood there like lambs to the slaughter.

Desperate measures, Cody thought. Quickly, he moved between his friends and the shadow, blocking its path. That's when he saw the shadow's eyes. They were black, cold, sinister, and strangely familiar.

Was this the thing that had killed him? Had it come in the night, attacked him while he slept, smothering the life out of him? He still couldn't remember.

"Who are you?" he asked. "What do you want?"

The eyes glared, staring through him, as if he didn't exist. Behind him, Ryn cried out. He turned in time to see the girl hit the floor in a crumpled heap.

"Ryn," Cheeze yelped. He squatted next to his fallen friend, unsure of what to do. "Ryn."

Cody turned back to the shadow, but it had disappeared. Where had it gone? Was it responsible for Ryn fainting?

Slowly, Ryn came around, moaning as she did so.

"Are you okay?" Cheeze asked.

She lightly shook her head and rubbed the back of her neck as she sat up. "What happened?"

"I guess you fainted."

Her eyes narrowed. "Don't be a dweeb. I don't faint."

"That's what you said last time too."

She just looked annoyed. "Help me up."

Cody felt helpless, unable to do anything but watch. Cheeze was right. Ryn had fainted at the last séance too. Before that, he couldn't remember her ever fainting.

Cheeze looked around. "Do you think he's still here?"

Ryn still rubbed the back of her neck, as if something had hit her and it was that something that had rendered her unconscious. "Don't know."

"Why do you think he's mad at us?"

She shook her head. "Don't know."

"Do you think he blames us for him dying?"

She looked even more annoyed. "Don't know."

"Are you okay?"

"No," she said, a hard edge to her voice. "I'm going home."

Abruptly, she left, Cheeze hot on her heels. Cody could hear their footsteps on the stairs as they descended and rejoined the wake.

Did the shadow—whatever or whoever it was—want Ryn? Did it mean her harm? He had a bad feeling it did. If the shadow is what killed him then maybe she was next. He had to figure out a way to stop it. For now, though, he needed to keep a close eye on his friend.

That night, Cody appeared in Ryn's bedroom, prepared to give her privacy, but determined to also stand guard over her while she slept. He was still unsure how he would protect her, but somehow he would protect her. To his surprise, though, she was still awake, restlessly pacing the floor. It wasn't until 3am that she stopped pacing. Still, she didn't get ready for bed. Instead, she tiptoed from her room and snuck out of the house.

Where was she going? What was she up to at this hour?

He followed. Before long, he figured out exactly where she was going. She was headed to Cheeze's house. But why?

She used a key to get inside. She probably still had it from when she fed Cheeze's cat while he and his family were on vacation last summer. In fact, he remembered giving her a key to his house too when his family went on vacation. Not to feed their cat. They didn't have one. But to water his mother's plants.

Did she ever give it back? He tried to remember as he followed her inside and up the stairs to Cheeze's bedroom. Once inside, she very quietly and calmly stood beside her friend's bed. He watched, still unsure what she could be up to. Then she turned her head and looked right at him as if she could see him, as if she knew he was there.

And she grinned.

He shivered. The look in her eyes gave him the creeps. There was no way she could see him and know he was there, yet she seemed to be taunting him for some inexplicable reason. Turning away, she climbed on top of Cheeze, straddling his midsection. Amazingly, the guy didn't awaken. He barely stirred. She took out what looked like a large piece of plastic, the kind used to wrap leftovers....*Saran Wrap*. Carefully, she wrapped Cheeze's face and head in the plastic as if he were an unfinished piece of food to be eaten later, tightly holding it there so he couldn't breathe.

Cody wasn't truly alive, so he couldn't actually breathe, but it felt as if his breath were caught in his throat anyway. He couldn't believe his eyes. Why would she do this? More importantly, how could he stop her?

Ryn looked over her shoulder, right at him.

He gawked, unable to respond to the danger, frozen in time. She knew he was there. Somehow, she could see him or sense him. Then he remembered the night he had died. The last thing he had seen was her face. At the time of death, he thought her face was nothing more than in his mind's eye, wishful thinking that he could see her one last time. Now, he realized she had actually been there, suffocating him as she was doing to Cheeze now.

Cheeze didn't resist, didn't fight for his life. He just lay there as if he'd been drugged, letting her steal his breath, his life.

Cody's heart sank. Was it the same for him? Had she killed him so easily, so effortlessly?

Why would she? He loved her. He knew Cheeze loved her too. What had gotten into her?

Into her? Into her!

The shadow? Was she possessed?

That had to be it. He had known and loved Ryn his entire life. She would never—

Yet she was. She was killing Cheeze.

He had to stop her, but how could he when he was stuck in between life and death? Then he remembered he had successfully moved the oracle and had flipped over the Ouija board. If he could do that then maybe he could physically stop her too.

No more time to debate. He rushed Ryn, grabbed her by her shoulders, pulled her from on top of Cheeze, and threw her to the floor. He hated himself for it. Couldn't stand seeing her lying there in a heap. But he had to do it. He had no choice. He tried to remind himself that it wasn't really Ryn he was fighting. It was the shadow demon that possessed her. But it still felt wrong. It was, after all, her body he was hurting. He wanted more than anything to go to her, to help her, but instead he turned away to help Cheeze, to make sure his other friend still lived.

Cheeze, however, was already sitting up, peeling the plastic wrap away from his face. Miraculously, he wasn't gasping for air. In fact, he didn't seem the least bit affected by the attempt to kill him. He climbed out of bed, plastic wrap still in hand, and walked straight through Cody to Ryn. The girl was still sprawled on the floor but stirring back to consciousness.

After Cheeze walked through him, Cody turned toward his friends. Confusion feasted on his mind. He didn't understand anything. What was happening? Waiting, he watched.

Moaning, Ryn sat up. She looked up at her friend standing over her, a disoriented look to her eyes. Soon, though, disorientation gave way to fear.

Cheeze held up the plastic wrap. "So you figured it out." He laughed. "And here I thought you were just a stupid bitch."

Cody stepped forward. He couldn't believe his ears. He had figured it all wrong. How could he have been so stupid? Ryn wasn't trying to kill Cheeze. She was trying to rid him of the shadow demon. Everything else—what he thought was a cold look in her eyes, him thinking she could see him, that she knew he was there—was all his own wild imagination. She was actually trying to save Cheeze.

Panic in her eyes, Ryn struggled to get to her feet but couldn't.

"Too bad you weren't successful," Cheeze said. "Too bad for you." He pounced on her, wrapping the plastic around her face.

She tried to scream, but the plastic wrap squelched it. She kicked and punched at Cheeze but couldn't fend him off.

"No," Cody cried. He rushed Cheeze, ready to do whatever it took to save Ryn.

Before he could do anything, however, the shadow appeared, blocking his way. Those cold, deadly eyes bore into him, stopping him in his tracks. It loomed over him, growing to monstrous size. He couldn't move, frozen in time, a spectator to murder. It was as if the shadow possessed the power to hold him hostage without even touching him.

"Ryn," he cried. He had to find a way to save her. But he needed to find a way to do it without hurting or killing his possessed friend. But how?

Cheeze continued to smother Ryn with the plastic. The fight was going out of her. Her punches looked as if they no longer had much impact, and her legs no longer kicked but instead only spasmodically twitched.

Cody closed his eyes, no longer able to watch. He had to hurry or the girl he loved would soon join him in the in between...or maybe worse. But how was he going to get past the shadow? That's when he remembered the incantation that Ryn had taught him. She had found it strangely enough in a book titled *The Book of Shadows*. How had it gone?

"Demon that threatens me...in this place," he mumbled, struggling to recall the exact words. "Banish it into nothingness...and remove its powers...until the last trace." With each word, his memory of the incantation returned, and his confidence grew. "Let this evil thing flee through time and space."

That was it. He remembered it all. Yet the shadow remained. He needed to repeat it, this time with more confidence, more authority.

"Demon that threatens me in this place. Banish it into nothingness and remove its powers until the last trace. Let this evil thing flee through time and space."

The shadow began to dissipate. Those cold, deadly eyes dimmed as it retreated back into whatever dimension from which it had come. To be sure, he had to repeat the incantation a third time. Everything in threes, Ryn had told him.

"Demon that threatens me in this place," he screamed. "Banish it into nothingness and remove its powers until the last trace. Let this evil thing flee through time and space."

The shadow disappeared completely.

Cody could move again. He rushed Cheeze, plowing into his friend and knocking them both to the floor. By the time the two sat up, Ryn was pulling the plastic from around her face and gasping for air.

"What...what happened?" Cheeze stammered, looking around the room in confusion.

Ryn sat up. She balled the plastic up and threw it at Cheeze. "You tried to kill me, that's what."

"What?"

She gasped and coughed. Color started to return to her pale, freckled face. "In fairness, I tried to kill you too."

"What?" The poor guy looked beside himself. "What the fuck are you talking about?"

Cody had never heard Cheeze use that word before. But then the guy had never been possessed before.

"Well...I wasn't really trying to kill you." Ryn coughed. Took a deep breath. "I was trying to bring you as close to death as possible without killing you, hoping to dispel the demon that was in you."

Her friend gaped. "What?"

She started to cry. "That's what I was trying to do with Cody too." Tears rolled down her cheeks. Sobs choked her throat. "But I failed. I waited too long. Something came over me. I couldn't stop. I couldn't control myself." She looked down at her lap, tears flowing like a waterfall. "And he died. I killed him."

Cody stared in disbelief at the girl he loved. He had been right. He last remembered seeing her face because she was the one who had smothered him.

"Jesus, Ryn," Cheeze hissed. "And you tried the same thing on me?"

She wiped away tears and nodded. "It was the only way."

They sat there on the floor, staring at each other for a long time, Cody studying them both.

"What do we do now?" Cheeze finally asked.

Ryn sniffed back some snot and wiped the rest of the tears away. "I don't know."

"Do you think the demon's gone for good?"

"I don't know."

"I wish Cody was here."

Ryn took a deep breath. "Me too," she muttered.

Cody stood. There was no time to feel sorry for himself and his circumstances. He was dead. There was nothing he could do about that. Ryn had inadvertently killed him. He should hate her. But he didn't. He loved her. And he wanted to save her...Cheeze too. He didn't believe the demon had been dispelled for good. At best his incantation had momentarily kept it at bay, slowed it down. He was sure it would be back. They needed to be ready. He needed to help them. Somehow, he needed to communicate with them. Maybe the three of them working together could send the demon back through the door to wherever it had come from and slam that door shut for good.

He noticed the full-length mirror on the closet door and got an idea. Just thinking about the mirror put him in front of it. He breathed on the reflected glass, fogging it, and then wrote, *Cody's here.* Unfortunately, neither of his friends saw it, and within seconds, the fogged words disappeared. He needed to get their attention first, so he opened the door and slammed it shut with a bang.

Ryn gasped, jumping to her feet.

"What the shit!" Cheeze too climbed to his feet.

Both faced the closet door.

"Who's there?" Ryn asked.

Cody breathed on the mirror. On the fogged glass, he wrote, *Cody.*

Ryn drew in a breath and held it.

"Mother...fuck." Cheeze seemed to have opened the floodgates to that word and couldn't stop.

"Cody," Ryn cried, "I'm so sorry...I'm so sorry... I didn't mean to..."

Cody fogged the mirror. *I forgive you. I love you.*

The girl shut her eyes and bowed her head. Cheeze put an arm around her.

Cody fogged the mirror. *Got an idea.*

Cheeze's eyes grew big. "Ryn, look."

She opened her eyes and looked up.

"I wonder what he's got in mind?"

Cody breathed and wrote. *Ouija board.*

Ryn looked at Cheeze, eyes wide. "We need to get to Cody's house."

They both rushed through the door, down the stairs, and out into the night. Using the key Cody had given her back when she took care of his mother's plants, Ryn unlocked the door. She and Cheeze crept into the house and up the stairs to Cody's room.

Cody was already there, waiting for them.

Ryn set up the Ouija board. Both she and Cheeze sat on the floor around it but kept their hands away from the oracle.

"What do you think Cody wants us to do?" Cheeze whispered.

"Don't know."

On the mirror over his dresser, Cody wrote, *Call the demon*.

They eyed each other.

"I hope he knows what he's doing." Cheeze said.

"He does. I trust him."

They both placed their hands on the oracle.

"We call on the demon who had taken possession of us," Ryn began, "to return to this place and time where it all began."

They waited. Listened.

Cody fogged the mirror and wrote, *Three times*.

Ryn gave a hard, thin smile, and Cody knew it was because he remembered her instruction.

"We call on the demon who had taken possession of us to return to this place and time where it all began."

Cheeze shivered.

"We call on the demon who had taken possession of us to return to this place and time where it all began."

The temperature in the room grew frigid. Frosty plumes of their breath hovered in the air. A wind swirled about the room with great abandon.

Cody tensed. The demon was coming. He readied himself for the onslaught.

The closet door banged open. Through it came the shadow, cold eyes looking like large, black marbles.

At the sight of the thing, Ryn screamed. Cheeze froze in time and space, mouth agape.

The shadow rushed across the room toward the two at the Ouija board.

Cody breathed on the mirror one last time and wrote a parting message. This time, the fog and the message remained, as if it too was frozen in time and space. Then he turned away and rushed the shadow, meeting it head on before it could get to his friends. He and the demon hit like two locomotives. They bounced about the room, his arms wrapped around the evil thing. He refused to look into those black marbles, desperately not wanting to make eye contact.

Holding on tight, struggling to keep the demon under control, he chanted, "I am light. I am one too strong to fight. Return to dark where shadows dwell. Be vanquished with this banishing spell."

Locked in mortal combat, they continued to bounce around the room like a massive pinball.

He could feel the shadow weaken, even if only slightly. *Three times*, he told himself, *three times*.

"I am light. I am one too strong to fight. Return to dark where shadows dwell. Be vanquished with this banishing spell."

He dared to look into the demon's eyes. The black marbles were now but a pale gray. Emboldened, he used all of his strength to maneuver the shadow toward the open closet.

"I am light. I am one too strong to fight. Return to dark where shadows dwell. Be vanquished with this banishing spell."

With that, he forced the shadow back across the closet's threshold that served as the portal into an unknown dimension, sacrificing his eternal soul for the survival of his friends.

The door slammed shut behind them. The air immediately warmed. The swirling wind died.

Cheeze and Ryn still sat in front of the Ouija board, their breath, however, no longer visible.

"Is it over?" Cheeze muttered. "Is the demon gone for good."

Ryn gasped as her gaze drifted to the mirror. On the fogged glass, Cody had written, *Goodbye!*

"They both are," she whispered.

Cody's message slowly disappeared.

"For good."

Holiday Madness

Halloween lurks
Within shadows in my head
Christmastime gremlins hide
Underneath my bed
Trolls crouch at my threshold
Wolf Men come to call
Ghosts haunt my thoughts
And walk my dusty halls
Uglies prowl the night
Hunting for helpless prey
Puppet People don't exist
At least that's what I hope
At least that's what I pray
Vampires step into sunlight
They burst into fire
It's at night that they hunt
It's my blood they desire
But none of these monsters compare
To the stresses and the sadness
Those crazy feelings I get
And strange voices that I hear
That I call holiday madness

Fred Wiehe

Shoot Me

The revolver was in my face before I could even think. Before I could even react. Panic held my mind hostage, thoughts a jumble of useless and senseless images, memories, regrets.

I looked beyond the barrel, staring at the face behind the gun. He seemed eerily familiar yet I was sure I didn't know him.

Who was he? What did he want?

I wanted to ask but couldn't find my voice. My throat constricted, strangling me.

Why didn't *he* speak? Why did he just stare at me with cold, dead eyes?

The silence between us was only broken by the slow and steady thud of my heart, the blood pounding in my ears, and the gasping breath escaping from my open mouth.

He grinned. Not friendly. A grin you'd expect from the devil as he welcomed you to Hell.

"Do you want to die?" he hissed.

What an absurd question.

I swallowed the dry lump in my throat. Tried to work up some saliva.

What would make this stranger show up, gun in hand, and ask such a crazed thing? Was he insane?

Of course I didn't want to die.

I worked my mouth to answer, tried to form the words to plead for my life, but only a pitiful croak escaped.

He leered at me. "Do *you* want to die?"

The barrel of his gun found my temple. Cool metal against my warm skin.

I shut my eyes tight and waited for the inevitable. When it didn't come, I opened my eyes. The man with the gun still leered at me—a patient man, awaiting my response.

I again worked my mouth to answer. This time my voice responded with a dry and strangled, one-word response, "No."

The man looked doubtful. "Why not? What do you have to live for?"

I opened my mouth but to my shock I couldn't readily speak. My mind scrambled for an answer.

What did I have to live for?

Chronic, daily pain resulting from a traumatic, near-death accident? A mountain of hospital and credit card bills? A job I hated? A dream career never fulfilled?

That was it?

I looked up into those cold, dead eyes. The evil grin still played on his face. "Do *you* want to die?"

A tremor shook me. My stomach roiled, and I blinked hot tears from my eyes.

That was it. That's all I had to live for.

Voice shaking and cracking, I whispered, "Shoot me."

Those cold, dead eyes bore through me. I couldn't stand it any longer. I shut my eyes tight, my hot tears drying on my cheeks.

"Shoot me," I demanded, voice stronger, more sure.

Nothing happened. I could still feel the barrel against my temple, but nothing happened.

"Shoot me, you coward."

I opened my eyes. The face staring back at me was a reflection of my own. It was my own hand that pressed the gun to my temple. I could hardly believe it, but mirrors didn't lie.

I again closed my eyes, unable to look at myself any longer. My gun hand trembled, finger poised on the trigger.

"Shoot me."

EVIL

Evil lurks in shadows
It lingers in hallways
Hides in corners
Awaits at the threshold
Pounds at the door

The key is all it needs
Once the door opens
It's ready to pounce
Eager to run amok
Fervent to kill

And only the key
That set evil loose
Upon the world
Can lock it away again
Ending the terror

The Alchemists

"Perfection," Rsnic said. "Only then does the soul and spirit become one." The alchemist glared at his two brethren. "That is what we strive to attain."

The three alchemists stood in their laboratory, a place for experimentation rather than conjecture or speculation. All three wore long, white robes as a sign of following the light, or mother. They were surrounded by alchemical apparatus hanging on some of the walls and lying about on various tabletops and shelves. A large wooden bookcase lined one wall, filled with archaic scientific journals and dusty books.

Smode tugged at his long beard as if to pull it out by the roots. "But must we destroy entire cultures, entire species, to attain it?"

"When tainted with imperfections, yes." Rsnic answered.

"It was we who created them," Smode argued. "Their imperfections are ours. They mirror us." He paced in circles around the oval oven made of brick that stood at the center of their laboratory. It was the link between work and study, practice and theory. A cast iron stand straddled the opening at the top of the oven, and on it sat a glass bowl filled with a boiling blue concoction—an experiment in the process of transmutation that was made from varying proportions of gold, silver, copper, and tin, as well as other less significant metals. The concoction was then treated chemically with mercury and sulphur.

"Stop pacing, man," Canum interrupted. "It's driving me mad." He went to the oven, opened the cast iron door on the side, and stoked the fire. Smoke and ash flew from the opening, along with a few live sparks that landed in his beard. He slapped at them in a frantic attempt to extinguish what could become a disaster.

Rsnic stroked and patted his own beard, as if the sparks had somehow transmuted to his. "That is why we must start anew. We must descend to the darkness of the grave before rising to eternal clarity. The old world must end before a new one rises from the ashes."

Having successfully put out the sparks, Canum nodded in agreement. "Nothing can be created without preceding destruction. You know this."

"Yes, yes," Smode mumbled. "Without sin there is no salvation. Without darkness there is no light. Without death there is no resurrection." He stopped pacing and gave his fellow alchemists an imploring look. "How many times must we destroy whole worlds?"

The other two alchemists gave each other a quizzical look.

"I don't understand you, Smode," Rsnic said. "You already know the answer."

"As many times as it takes to find the quintessence," Canum added, "the agent needed to transmute metals on a molecular level, the agent capable of curing all disease and prolonging life beyond natural limits. The agent needed to attain perfection, to bring us closer to supreme status."

"Only then can we be one with mother and ascend to divine light." Rsnic nodded. "Only then can we ourselves become immortal...become gods."

Smode fidgeted from foot to foot. "But we had created this continent by transmuting elements from five other worlds which we separately created and again separately destroyed over time, building one on top of the other. It is the culmination of a millennia of work and sacrifice." He pulled on his beard. "It's as close to perfection as we've ever been able to attain."

Rsnic frowned. "But it's *not* perfection. We cannot stop until perfection is achieved, until the quintessence is found, until we've achieved immortality." He shook his head. "Really, I truly do not understand you."

Smode looked at his feet. "Do you understand that thousands upon thousands of people will die."

"They are inconsequential." Canum shrugged.

"No more of this," Rsnic declared. "It is time for the descent into darkness, so a new world of perfection can rise into mother's light."

The two gathered around the blue concoction boiling in the glass bowl.

Reluctantly, Smode joined them.

Within the bowl, reflected in the blue liquid, they could see the world below that they had created a millennia ago. Hundreds of thousands of people went about their daily lives, working in the fields and harvesting crops, shopping in the markets, caring after children, playing games, riding horses into battle, governing great cities, writing literature and poetry and plays, creating wonderful art. Species upon species of animals, insects, and plant life also inhabited the world below known as Amidicia.

Seeing it all only served to reinforce Smode's conviction and desire to save the world he helped create. For the first time in his life, tears clouded his vision. His chest ached, and his heart skipped. He didn't understand these foreign feelings, but he knew he couldn't help destroy this world and the people who inhabited it.

"What's that?" Canum asked, pointing into the blue liquid.

Strange ships none of them recognized had anchored themselves just off shore. Hundreds upon hundreds of small boats full of warriors carrying swords, spears, and bows were rowing ashore.

"They don't belong here," Canum cried.

"They're just an anomaly," Smode offered.

Rsnic scowled. "They are further proof of imperfection."

"We did not create these people," Canum agreed. "They are not part of this world. Who are they? How did they get here?"

"The imperfection of the world created them and brought them here." Rsnic ran to a bookshelf, grabbed a dusty book, and rushed back. "We must not dally. We must end this imperfect world now, before more mutations develop, before it's too late."

Smode studied the scene below. The warriors arriving on the shores of Amidicia were certainly not one of their creations; he couldn't argue with that. The world seemed to take a sudden turn, becoming independent of their control and creating its own life. "Maybe this is what perfection looks like," he mumbled.

Rsnic opened the book. "Nonsense."

"Think about it," he argued. "This world has apparently evolved, transmuted if you will, into its own god. It has created life without our help. It has risen to consciousness, attained a sublime state of perfection, became godlike in its own right."

"You are on the verge of hypocrisy," Rsnic warned.

"You have lost your sanity," Canum agreed.

Rsnic began reading from the book, uttering the words of the alchemical dragon who eats its own tale and represents the circle of life. "Raising myself from death, I kill death—which kills me. I raise up again the bodies that I have created. Living in death, I destroy myself—whereof you rejoice. You cannot rejoice without me and my life."

The world below began to tremble at its foundation. Storm clouds gathered. Lightning ripped open the sky. Thunder boomed. Buildings began to crumble. Tidal waves destroyed the anchored ships and buried the advancing army under a watery grave.

"If I carry the poison in my head, in my tail which I bite with rage lies the remedy," Rsnic continued. "Whoever thinks to amuse himself at my expense, I shall kill with my gimlet eye."

"No." Smode could not allow the destruction of what he considered complete perfection to continue. He had to stop it.

Below, mountains collapsed and oceans rose. Screaming people and wailing animals ran for their lives. But there was no escape.

Canum laughed at the destruction and the death.

Rsnic read on. "Whoever bites me must bite himself first; otherwise, if I bite him, death shall bite him first, in the head; for he must bite me—biting being the medicine of biting."

Smode reached across the oven to knock the book from his counterpart's hands. If this is what it meant to follow mother, follow the light, he wanted no part of it any longer. "No," he cried, "enough." In his attempt, he knocked the glass bowl from its stand, sending it crashing to the floor.

With that, the alchemists' sanctuary began to shake. Books fell from shelves. Alchemical apparatus flew about the room, no longer tools of learning but rather weapons of death. The alchemists scattered and ducked to protect themselves.

"What have you done?" Canum cried from underneath a table he had crawled under.

"You fool." Rsnic hugged a support column as if it were the love of his life.

Smode flattened himself to the floor. "What's happened?"

The quake intensified, rocking the laboratory at its foundation. Walls cracked open like eggshells. The floor wobbled and rolled. Chunks of ceiling rained down—a heavy storm of debris.

"You've interrupted the transmutation." Rsnic slid down the column to his knees, hugging it still. "All is lost."

This isn't what Smode wanted. He wanted only to save the world below but instead he had apparently doomed all to destruction, including himself and his brethren.

With that thought, the laboratory completely collapsed, burying the alchemists in mounds of rubble.

Below, having only achieved partial deviation, Amidicia crashed down onto a strange and foreign land, fusing with it and creating a new mutant world. In creating this mutation, both worlds suffered indescribable destruction and uncountable casualties. Great buildings crumbled and burned; the smoke-filled air smelled of death. The people and animals who survived the ordeal were suddenly and unexpectedly thrown together, running and screaming for their lives. The primitive people of Amidicia were thrust into a reality of concrete ground, mammoth buildings, strange and noisy flying machines, and fast-moving, roaring metal animals. In turn, the unsuspecting people of this new land quickly became fast food for the countless species of wild and dangerous animals indigenous to Amidicia but never before seen by them. These wild animals ran rampant, feasting on the fleeing hordes.

In response to this threat, a great army formed behind a red, white, and blue banner of broad stripes and bright stars. This army was composed of flying machines with giant rotating and thumping blades, metal animals that churned forward and knocked over trees and crushed running, screaming Amidicians. The advancing foot soldiers carried weapons of mass destruction that spit deadly, buzzing metal capable of mowing down their enemies. The people of Amidicia fought back with spears, swords, and arrows, but these weapons were no match for the advanced weaponry of the new land. Only fortitude of heart and soul, only the heartiness of body and mind, could possibly save them.

In the laboratory above, Smode rose from the rubble like a Phoenix reborn. He now wore black robes in the tradition of the followers of father and the dark—polar opposite of mother and the light. His heart bled at the sight of the destruction and chaos. He was not prepared for such a wave of sorrow, despair, and fear, emotions he had never experienced as a follower of mother and the light. And in his heart, he knew neither world was prepared for the destructive impact the alchemists had caused.

He also knew neither world would ever be the same.

**To be continued
in
The Alchemists: Dark vs. Light
A Novel by Fred Wiehe
COMING SOON!**

S⊕ngs ⊕f the Night

Standing alone
Surrounded by trees
Under a sky cold and gray
Sounds of the night
The screech of an owl, a wolf's frightening howl
Leave you chilled to the bone and afraid

Rustling of leaves
Snapping of twigs
Movement of shadow and light
It's not just the breeze
Or sound of the owl
As it stirs in the tree and takes flight
It's something behind
Moving steady and slow
That gives you a chill
And a fright

You stand alone
Quiet and intent
Wondering what it could be

Fred Wiehe

You strain to hear
Afraid to move
Afraid to even breathe

It's closer now
Quickening its pace
Maneuvering through the trees
It lets out a howl
A horrible cry
Just as you turn to flee

You're moving fast
It's right behind
Ready to bring you down
You dare not stop
You dare not look
You dare not turn around
Sharp claws rip across your leg
You falter and slow down
You scream as claws strike again
Then you hit the ground

CREEPER

A sky devoid of stars or moon pressed down on San Francisco. A steady drizzle dampened the already chilled night air. Both the street lights and the headlights of cars cast eerie glows across the cityscape. Cars sped along the streets, spraying oil-slicked gutter water into the air. People with and without umbrellas hurried about their business, eager to get out of the foul weather. No one paid much attention to the wailing sirens in the distance. But most did notice the wild-looking man with the blood-smeared face and hands that shrieked like a hurt animal and ran with wild abandon amongst them. Brandishing a bloody knife, the stranger struck out like a viper, cutting and shoving those in his way, the wounded people falling and crying out in shock, pain, and fear as they hit the rain-slicked pavement.

Detective Nick Street followed the wild man. God, how he hated Halloween; every year, all the crazies came out—this Halloween was no different—and the perp he now chased was by far the craziest he'd ever seen. Heart pounding, almost out of breath, the detective ran around or hurdled over fallen, wounded civilians that were left in the perp's wake. His shoes slapped through puddles and pounded on wet pavement as he picked up speed and narrowed the gap. His .38 Chief's Special remained holstered for now, for there were too many civilians in the line of fire. But he would pull it when the time came; he wasn't about to let this perp get away.

No matter what.

Not after what he and his partner Stephanie Staple had seen back at the crime scene—where she remained at least long enough to hurry back to their car and call in for backup before following. Even as Nick gave chase—with Stephanie surely not far behind—he couldn't wipe the horrible carnage of the crime scene from his mind's eye. After fifteen years as a police officer and supposedly hardened to the core, he had never seen or smelled anything quite like it:

The female victim's throat had been ripped open as if by a rabid animal, blood spurting into the air and mixing with the rain like some kind of macabre cocktail. The woman had also been sliced open breast to pubis. Her organs—drenched in body fluids, blood, and rain—spilled out of her as she convulsed and shuddered on the wet pavement. Worse, the perp Nick now chased had been bent over his victim on hands and knees, reminding him of a dog at its food bowl. The man growled too as he ravaged the poor woman's insides.

Nick had jumped from the car and yelled at the perp to stop. The guy immediately jumped up and started running, body organs still hanging from his bloody mouth.

At the sight, Stephanie had stopped to hurl her bean burrito she'd eaten for dinner. Then, after wiping slick remnants from her mouth, she yelled, "I'm calling for backup."

Nick wanted to barf his Carne Asada burrito too as he took off after the perp but more from the caustic odor of the slaughter bombarding him rather than the sight of it. Somehow, he had forced the vile discharge back down his throat and began pursuit.

Now, blocks away from the scene and with the perp just ahead, the horrible stench still hid within his nostrils. His stomach still churned. His Mexican dinner still threatened to charge up his throat. But he held it down and picked up speed just as the perp turned a sharp corner between two tall buildings. He followed but stopped short just around the corner.

Breathing hard, heart racing, he pulled his revolver. Rotten garbage accosted him. He wiped rain from his face and pushed rain-slicked, blond hair from his eyes, straining to see. The narrow alleyway that stretched out before him was dimly lit due to lights coming through several windows from both buildings. Mostly, however, the lighted windows were too high up, and even those had shades drawn. As a result, he couldn't see much and had no idea if the alley was a dead end or not. He knew the perp had stopped running, though, because the slap of his footsteps had fallen silent. In fact, the alley was dead quiet except for the patter of rain and a low growl emanating from somewhere within the surrounding dark. It was no animal that growled, though; he was sure of that.

The perp was somewhere close.

But where?

He pulled a small flashlight from the inside breast pocket of his jacket. He aimed the light with one hand and his revolver with the other as he inched his way through the rain and the dark, down the alley.

The wild man crouched low to the ground at the alley's end, half hidden by wooden crates and garbage cans. The knife he held out, threatening attack. The low growl heard earlier rumbled in the perp's throat.

"Don't move, fuck-wad," Nick warned, inching closer. He shone the narrow flashlight beam onto the perp's face. At the sight, he couldn't stifle a gasp.

The perp sneered, baring bloody teeth that were caked with human flesh and tissue. The knife's blade too revealed remnants of the victim. But it wasn't the carnage or the growl that had caused the gasp. It was the perp's eyes; they were orbs, as black as obsidian, reflecting both light and evil.

Nick repeated the warning. "Don't move."

At that, the perp replaced his growl with incoherent mumblings, whisperings that almost sounded like hissing snakes.

Nick strained to hear, to understand.

"No…yes," the perp hissed. He glanced furtively about as he spoke. "Can't do it. Want to. Need to. No. Can't. Won't. Can. Deserves it. Yes. No. Shut up." He grabbed his head with his free hand and pulled at his wild hair as if trying to rip it out. The other hand still brandished the knife.

Nick kept both the light and gun trained on the target. *He's arguing with himself*, he thought.

"Fucker deserves what he gets," the perp continued, still pulling at his hair with one hand and waving the knife about with the other. "Shut up. No. Tired. Can't. Won't. Yes. Will. Must. No. Shut up."

Nick knew he needed to take control of the situation; the guy was definitely insane. "Put the knife down," he commanded. "No one else needs to get hurt."

The perp let go of his hair. He chuckled—wicked, devilish. "No one else hurt." He chuckled again. "Shit." He gave furtive sidelong glances to his side as if someone crouched next to him. "No one else hurt," he repeated to his invisible friend as if relaying a joke. "Shit. No one else hurt."

"Put the damn knife down," Nick shouted this time.

His mind shouted, *Where's Stephanie?*

"I will shoot," he warned.

"Deserves it. Told you. Must. Yes. Will. Deserves it. Definitely. Fucker deserves all it gets."

One side of the argument suddenly seemed to be winning…and not the good side.

He needed to act quickly. Nick shouted, "Put the—"

The perp's guttural growl cut the warning short. He lunged, the blade of the knife swiping the air as he attacked.

Nick pulled the trigger without hesitation. The report resounded through the alley. His ears rang. Gun smoke burned his nostrils.

The perp hit the pavement, collapsing face down into a rain puddle that quickly turned red with blood. He didn't move or utter another sound.

Still aiming both his flashlight and revolver, Nick inched forward. He kicked the knife away and nudged the perp with the toe of his shoe. Getting no reaction, he used his foot to flip the perp onto his back. He shone the light onto the man's face; the once black orbs were now dim and lifeless. He turned off the flashlight, pocketed it, and just to be sure knelt down to check for a pulse. None.

He stood. Held breath rushed out of him. He felt soaked and exhausted. His athletic body and taught muscles relaxed. His gun hand hung at his side, the revolver's muzzle warm against his wet pants leg.

Not for the first time he thought, *Where in the hell is Stephanie?*

He stared at the crazy, dead man lying at his feet.

Blood seeped from the guy's chest wound, and a steady stream of water and blood trickled along the alley.

He was glad the monster lying at his feet was dead. At the same time, he was sorry he had had to be the one to do the killing; he got no satisfaction out of ending a life, no matter how evil that life had been.

He was about to holster his revolver when he saw it...or at least thought he saw it. Reflexively, he took a step back but strained to see. Something that looked like black oil oozed from the dead man's mouth, nose, eyes, and ears.

At least that's what he thought he saw in the dim light of the alleyway at night. But he couldn't be sure, and it made no sense.

He reached for his flashlight and switched it on. The preternatural oil shimmered in the light as it escaped from every orifice of the now empty shell that once had been a breathing human being.

"What the—?" He couldn't believe his eyes.

Every drop of the black, shimmering oil had escaped from the dead man and collected into a cohesive puddle next to him. There it pulsed as if it were a breathing, living thing, as if it were trying to consciously decide what to do next. But that was impossible. It couldn't be alive. It couldn't reason or think. It was just a puddle of black goo.

But then what was it, and how had it gotten into the dead man? What caused it to suddenly come out after the guy's death? And what did it have to do with the guy going nuts?

He leaned in for a closer look.

In turn, the pulsing, black oil crept toward him.

That gave him the uneasy feeling that it too wanted a closer look at *him*, and he instinctively backed off.

The alien oil now truly became cohesive, almost solid, chaotically changing from one strange shape to another. In the poor light, the shapes almost looked like faces frozen in terror, with multiple, blinking eyes.

"What are you?" he asked, not expecting an answer.

But as if in response to that question, the thing leapt at his face. There, it molded and clamped on tight. He cried out. But the black thing smothered his screams. His finger reflexively pulled the revolver's trigger, firing off all five remaining rounds into the ground and walls around him. As he stumbled backward, he fell to the wet pavement, dropping both flashlight and revolver.

"Nick!"

He heard Stephanie call his name. He heard her footsteps slap against the wet pavement…getting closer.

"Nick!"

But the thing on his face was already breaking apart into smaller bodies and liquefying again. And even though he swatted and scratched at them, futilely tried to grab them and pull them off, they crept across his face and forced their way into his eyes, ears, nose, and mouth. Again he tried to scream but could only choke on the black goo forcing itself down his throat. Soon, the entire oil spill had hidden itself within him. He coughed and choked, kicked and convulsed, as it began to spread through his insides, creeping into his bloodstream, muscles, and major organs—slowly the two becoming one.

As this metamorphosis took place, his heart rate increased and his breathing quickened into a pant. His vision blurred. Sounds were muffled. The world around him seemed nothing but a shadow. He was barely aware that Stephanie now stood over him, her face indistinct, her voice inaudible, her words incoherent.

Then everything went dark.

***

The rain had stopped. Nick woke to an oxygen mask on his face and paramedics checking his vitals. Stephanie stood slightly in the background, concern etched on her pretty face, arms crossed stiffly over her ample bosom.

"He's conscious," a paramedic called out from where he hunkered over his patient.

Stephanie moved closer.

Nick abruptly sat up and yanked the oxygen mask off.

"Whoa, take it easy, cowboy," the paramedic warned. "Not so fast."

Nick took a quick scan of the area. It had been cordoned off with yellow tape. Police and CSI worked the crime scene. The medical examiner and his assistants were taking away the corpse.

"Heart rate and pulse are stabilizing," the other paramedic said, "oxygen levels are normal."

"How do you feel?" the first paramedic asked.

Nick blinked. He felt nothing. Except cold, both outside and inside. "Fine," he responded.

"Do you remember what happened, Nick?" Stephanie asked.

He rubbed at his eyes and shivered. They felt like ice cubes in his sockets. He looked up at his partner. Somehow, she looked different. "Yeah, I cornered the perp," he said without emotion. "The guy attacked me with a knife. I shot him but then slipped on the wet pavement, stumbled backwards, and fell." He rubbed the back of his head. "I'm guessing I hit my head on the pavement."

"Sounds about right," the paramedic said. "You've got a lump back there the size of a golf ball."

"That doesn't explain the irregular heartbeat, elevated blood pressure, and rapid breathing when we found him," the other paramedic said.

"Is everything normal now?" Stephanie asked.

"Looks like it," the paramedic answered. "Still, I suggest he see a doctor, just to be sure. Even though he doesn't seem to have any short-term memory loss, he still lost consciousness and suffered at least a mild concussion. That alone could bring on headaches, blurred vision, confusion, maybe even dementia, which is a decline in cognition and emotion or behavior. My recommendation is that he be under a doctor's care; that's what I'm going to write in my report…a report that will go to *his* captain as well as mine."

"You're talking about me like I'm not here," Nick complained.

"Sorry, Detective." The paramedic held up his index finger. "Follow my finger without moving your head," he said and began moving his finger from side to side, up and down.

Nick's gaze followed the movement without problem.

The paramedic took out a penlight, checking pupil dilation. He turned off the light, rubbed at his own eyes, and then turned the light back on and checked his patient's eyes again.

"What is it?" Stephanie asked. "What's wrong?"

The paramedic turned the light off and sat back on his haunches. His face looked slack, stare blank. "Nothing…I guess." He paused. "Everything looks…normal…I think."

"Am I free to go?" Nick asked as if he were a suspect being held for questioning.

The paramedic snapped out of whatever had taken over him and seemed himself again. He looked at the other paramedic, who shrugged. "Yeah, detective," he mumbled, "we release you from our care." He turned to the other detective. "But make sure he sees that doctor."

Stephanie nodded.

"Help me up."

The two paramedics helped Nick to his feet.

After the paramedics packed up and left, Stephanie discreetly took his hand in hers. "Are you sure you're okay?"

They had been partners for five years and unbeknownst to anyone in the department lovers for the past three. But for the first time, her touch stirred no emotional response. The adoring look in her deep brown eyes elicited no passion.

He pulled his hand away.

In fact, he felt nothing, as if his heart—like his eyes—was a block of ice. And even his partner's beauty and warm, loving touch couldn't melt it.

"I'm sure," he said, shivering.

A combination of hurt and concern shadowed her face. "I think we should get you home. I'm sure the captain won't mind if you wait until tomorrow to write your report."

He nodded. "I agree."

She forced a flirtatious smile. "Good, I'll take you home and tuck you in."

He shivered again. He stared hard at her, trying to remember what it was like to love her, trying to recall the passion and heat they had always generated in bed. But only a dead, cold calm lived where that love and passion used to reside. "Steph," he said, "I think I just want to be alone tonight."

She stiffened, as if his frigid demeanor had somehow jumped to her. Her brow furrowed and her mouth tightened to the point that her usually pouty lips almost disappeared completely.

"You understand, don't you?" he asked, feigning both exhaustion and a sense of cluelessness to her feelings.

She looked at her feet then back to him. "Sure," she said, "you had a close call tonight. I get it. Go home, rest, clear your head." She moved closer and leaned in to give him a discreet peck on the cheek.

He stepped back as if repelled by her advance. "Not here." He gave her a hard stare.

She jerked away, as if slapped in the face.

"Too many people around," he warned, his voice as hard as his stare and devoid of all compassion.

She took a deep breath. "You're right, how stupid of me." She paused, scrutinizing him as if he were a lab experiment gone wrong.

He said nothing more. His cold stare and stiff posture said it all.

"I'll see you tomorrow, detective." She turned on her heel, striding away.

After she'd gone, he realized his hands were fists at his sides, held so tight that his fingernails had dug into his palms, making them bleed. He also realized that he not only hadn't wanted to kiss her but that he had wanted to punch her in the face instead.

Rubbing the knot on the back of his head, he thought, *What the hell's going on? Maybe I do have dementia.*

With those burning thoughts, he hurried from the crime scene without acknowledging or talking to anyone.

But he didn't go home. Instead—without even contemplating his motivations or considering the consequences of his actions—he drove to Stephanie's house, arriving just seconds behind her. In fact—acting on instinct alone—he switched off his headlights, slowed to a crawl, and watched from a distance as she got out of her car.

She slammed the door, strode up the driveway, fumbled with keys as she unlocked the door, and slammed that door as well behind her. Lights went on inside the house.

He drove the car closer and parked just a few houses away. From there, he watched and waited.

Cold tremors wracked his body. Sweat beaded his brow. His still damp clothes clung to him. He clutched the steering wheel as if it were a lifeline to his humanity. But it couldn't save him. Dark thoughts lurked in every corner of his mind. An alien noise hissed in his ears like so much maddening white noise.

The thing inside him had now crept its way into every nook, cranny, and crevice of his being—all the way to his soul. He was no longer Nick Street. He had his memories. He knew Stephanie, who she had been in his life, what she had meant to him, that he had once loved her. But the concept of compassion and love eluded him and no longer meant anything. Stephanie no longer meant anything. He had no feelings for her or anyone. He was someone or something else now. His heart, soul, and humanity were lost.

His grip on the steering wheel now became a stranglehold, knuckles white from exertion. He caught a glimpse of his now completely black eyes in the rearview mirror. Violent and bloody images played in his head like a bad snuff film. The alien white noise tuned in, took voice, insistent in its vicious intentions, its sadistic instructions.

He squinted through the night at Stephanie's house. He glared as she passed in front of a lighted window in her bedroom.

"Do it," he said, his voice a hissing viper. "Kill the bitch. She deserves it."

He shook his head.

"No," he screamed. "Can't. Won't. Mustn't."

"Will," he hissed. "Must. Deserves it. Do it."

"Shut up! No!"

"Yes. Can't stop. Need. Must. Kill the bitch."

"Shut up!"

"Kill the bitch! Now! Do it!"

He took a deep breath and released his hold on the steering wheel. "Do it," he mumbled. "Kill the bitch."

The argument over, he opened the car door and climbed out. He strode with renewed determination and purpose to her front door. A guttural growl erupted from his belly and into his throat as he kicked the door inward. Splinters of wood from the broken door and doorjamb exploded across the living room like shrapnel.

Startled, Stephanie rushed from her bedroom, revolver in hand. She aimed to kill, but her finger hesitated on the trigger at the sight of her partner being the perpetrator. "Nick?"

He didn't hesitate. He met her head on, swatting at her gun with one hand, knocking it away. His other hand was around her throat as the revolver hit the floor with a loud thud. He shoved his girlfriend back, slamming her into a wall.

He heard a sound like something breaking inside her. Her hands clutched at his wrist, fingernails digging into flesh and drawing blood. But the fight was quickly going out of her. And with her pinned against the wall, he tightened his grip on her throat and watched with glee as her eyes rolled back in her head. He listened with satisfaction to the death rattle in her chest and throat.

"Kill the bitch," he yelled, spittle flying from his mouth and washing over her corpse-like face.

"Nick," she choked out as her hand released its grip on his wrist and fell away.

The near-death sound of her voice threw a switch in his blackened soul.

"No," he screamed.

A flicker of light, humanity, memory, or compassion battled against the alien creeping around inside him. And for that one split second he was in control; he released his stranglehold and flung Stephanie across the room.

She crashed into a table and lamp, sending them toppling with her to the floor. There, she lay. Broken. Not moving. Breath labored.

He swirled about the room—a madman turned tornado. He knocked over furniture, lamps, and knick knacks. Everything about him crashed to the floor.

"Kill her," he hissed in his fit of rage.

"No! Shut up!"

Somehow he fought off the alien urges to mutilate and kill. Instead, he channeled his rage toward inanimate objects, tearing framed photos off the wall and smashing them on the floor.

"Do it," his argument continued. "Kill the bitch. Tear her open and eat her insides."

"No! Shut up! I won't!"

"Will," he hissed. "Must. Need."

"No! Won't! Can't!"

"Must," he bellowed. "Kill the bitch."

Argument over, alien again in control, he whirled toward his victim. But she had not been unconscious and motionless during his tirade. She had regained her senses and forced her broken body to hands and knees. She had crawled laboriously across the floor, through the battle's aftermath, and retrieved her revolver. She now knelt, gun aimed at the man she had once loved.

He sneered. "Told you," he hissed. "Deserves it. They always deserve it." He licked dried, cracked lips. "Now kill the bitch!"

"You're not killing anyone, fuck-wad," she croaked.

He yowled like a hurt beast and rushed her.

She didn't hesitate this time. She emptied all six rounds into his chest as he charged, dropping him in his tracks. The thud of his body hitting the hardwood floor and the surrounding wreckage was almost as loud as the report of her gun. Then all went dead quiet.

She remained kneeling. Gun smoke burned her nostrils. She dropped the gun. It hit the floor with a thump. Tears streamed down her cheeks. Sobs choked her throat.

What happened? What turned Nick into a psychotic killer, just like the one he shot?

Oncoming sirens broke the quiet.

Still, she didn't move. Her gaze locked on Nick's body. Her thoughts swirled in confusion. Hysteria knocked on the door to her mind. But she held it at bay, clamping that door shut.

Wiping tears away, she stifled her sobs. She needed to keep her wits. She needed to understand how such a thing could happen. Once she figured everything out, then she could break down. That's how her cop's mind worked.

But then she saw it. Black oil spilled from Nick's eyes, ears, nose, and mouth.

She gasped. She dropped back on her butt.

The black oil or goo pooled on the floor next to Nick's corpse. There, it pulsed and shimmered. Hundreds of eyes blinked open as it began to randomly shape-shift into multiple faces, all frozen in various expressions of torturous horror and pain.

She gasped again as she realized one of those random faces looked like Nick.

When the alien thing began to creep toward her, hysteria took over. Her mouth gaped in a silent scream. Scooting backwards, she didn't stop until her back hit wall.

Outside, sirens blared. Police cars screeched to stops. Cops surrounded the house and prepared for assault.

Inside, her scream finally took voice.

Fred Wiehe

BURNING SOUL

The night is cool
A soft breeze drifts lazily through the open window
Stirring the curtains ever so slightly
But sweat trickles across your brow
It dampens your armpits and soaks into your sheets
You shiver
Your eyes smolder with fever
A strange heat radiates within you
A raging fire
Surging
Out of control
Scorching organs
Blistering tissue
Burning your soul

Rebirth

It comes from the deepest corner
Where dusk thickens into darksome night
Where the witching hour never surrenders
Where dawn never touches
Where vampires hide from burning sunlight
Waiting
Resting
Awakening
Reborn to the night

Fred Wiehe

Predator & Prey

He woke in complete darkness, choking on his own vomit.

Reflexively, his head jerked forward, he hacked it up, spitting most of it out. He gagged and almost threw up again, the overpowering stench permeating the already stifling air. But somehow he held it down.

Still, chunky rivers of hot vomit trickled from his nose and mouth. The rivers ran down his chin and dripped to his bare chest. From there, he could feel them making their way to his abdomen. Then down to his exposed loins.

Panic strangled his thoughts. He was naked. Why?

And his arms were being ripped from their sockets; he stood but not on his own power. Leather straps bit into his wrists, stretched his arms over his head, and kept him upright. Only the tips of his toes touched the floor.

He swung his head from side to side in hope of seeing something…anything. But the darkness engulfed him. There was nothing to see.

And he paid dearly for the sin of movement, for that slight exertion woke tiny demons with hammers in his head. They pounded against the inside of his skull, pulverizing his already fragmented wits to dust.

He screamed. Choked on it. Barely made a sound.

His heart banged in his chest. Terror bubbled in his stomach, spewing forth in an eruption of his insides. More rivulets of hot vomit flowed down his naked body.

He hacked and gagged, breath racing through his war-torn throat. But he managed to croak, "Dear Lord, help me."

A buzz in his ears answered that prayer. The darkness around him now seemed to shimmer like blacktop in the hot sun.

He spat out the last remnants. "Lord, help me."

The buzzing turned to garbled whispers. The shimmering darkness separated into formless shadows.

He raised his head to the heavens. "Lord, hear my prayer," he croaked louder, "save me from this hell."

Although still incomprehensible, the whispers now seemed to taunt him. The formless shadows took almost human shape.

He wasn't alone. Whoever these predators were that kept him prisoner were in here with him, hiding in the darkness, apparently afraid of the light—God's light.

Terror again bubbled in his stomach and rose into his throat. This time he swallowed the burning bile back down, refusing to play the part of frightened prey any longer. Instead, he found his courage and his voice. He cried, "Lord, hear my prayer…have mercy."

A sound—like a door opening—answered that prayer. A bright light stabbed his eyes. He turned his head away and squinched his eyes.

The incomprehensible voices grew louder until finally they coalesced into one intelligible voice—a boy's voice.

"The Lord won't hear your prayers, Father Ray," the boy said.

He turned toward the harsh light, squinting into it, letting his vision adjust. Soon he could open his eyes a bit wider. That's when he realized that he hung in a closet from a hook in the ceiling, like a piece of rotting meat.

Then he focused on the boy before him. The boy stood in the closet doorway, a well-lit yet nondescript room behind.

"Bobby Garcia?" he mumbled in recognition.

It couldn't be. He hadn't seen Bobby Garcia in at least eight years, maybe ten. Yet here the boy stood, looking just the same—still ten years old, dark hair falling across his forehead and into his brown eyes.

As if appearing out of nowhere, a group of boys suddenly crowded the room behind Bobby—Jimmy Mullin, Brad Cooper, Ken Garth, and others he couldn't name but recognized as one-time altar boys. They all looked just as he remembered, although—like Bobby—it had been years since he had seen most of them.

Bobby pushed hair out of his eyes and looked the priest up and down. The boy grinned—wicked, menacing.

"God help me," Father Ray begged when he realized he had an erection...without meaning to...against his will; he couldn't help it... the sight of the boys... "Have mercy."

"No, the Lord won't hear your prayers, won't help you," Bobby assured, the grin still playing across his young face. "And there'll be no mercy. Not from *Him*. Not from us."

The boy revealed a large hunting knife from behind his back. "No mercy," he repeated, pointing the sharp blade at the one-time predator's hard on. "No mercy." He advanced on the priest.

Father Ray screamed.

***

The funeral was over. Almost everyone had left the cemetery. Only a group of young men remained at Father Ray's gravesite.

Bobby Garcia stared down at the casket in the yet-to-be-filled grave. He pushed dark hair from his dry, brown eyes.

Jimmy Mullin stood next to Bobby. The other young men crowded close behind.

"A heart attack was too good for him," Bobby muttered.

Jimmy put a hand on Bobby's shoulder and gave it a gentle squeeze. "If there's any justice in this universe, he'll rot in Hell for eternity."

Bobby nodded.

The other young men—all fallen prey to the priest at one time or another—muttered in agreement. With that, they turned as one and walked away.

***

He woke in complete darkness, choking on his own vomit.

Reflexively, his head jerked forward, he hacked it up, spitting most of it out. He gagged and almost threw up again, the overpowering stench permeating the already-stifling air. But somehow he held it down.

Still, chunky rivers of hot vomit trickled from his nose and mouth. The rivers ran down his chin and dripped to his bare chest. From there, he could feel them making their way to his abdomen. Then down to his exposed loins.

Panic strangled his thoughts. He was naked. Why?

And his arms were being ripped from their sockets …

Fred Wiehe

SUCCUBUS

She stalks the night
A seductive apparition
Feeding her insatiable appetite
On men's lack of inhibitions
Their fantasies she delights
Their desires she fulfills
But payment to be satisfied
Is blood, death, and hell

BIMBAI

Where he comes from no one knows
To some, he is an answer to their prayers
To others, he stalks out of the shadows
He's a figure of death
Born of their nightmares

Fred Wiehe

Resurrected

An
Aleric: Monster Hunter
Novella

Chapter I

A dark figure stalked out of the darkness, a slight limp impeding his progress. He wore a black trench coat, and he had pulled his black fedora down low, hiding half his face. The night hid the rest. He watched two cops chase a Gypsy down the street, all three disappearing around the corner. With the cops gone, he limped closer to the apartment building the Gypsy had come out of and stopped out front. He stood next to the steps, back pressed against the wall. He had no interest in the Gypsy or his home or in why the cops had given chase. However, he was grateful to the Gypsy for getting the cops out of the neighborhood.

His interest lay in the three prostitutes standing on the corner, selling their perverted wares. Such creatures did the Devil's work. They tempted men into sin, thus recruiting them into the service of evil. Such creatures— Satan's minions—didn't deserve to live. The air was too precious for them to breathe. The earth was too beautiful to be marred by their wicked glamour. God instructed him to rid the world of these vile temptresses and their immoral ways; he was the wind and they were the locust. And like locust, the world would be a better place without them. Men would again be safe once prostitutes were completely exterminated.

The scalpel in his coat pocket would be all he needed. At least one of these lurid and loathsome creatures would not see the light of day. And with God's help, he would eventually send them all back to Hell where they belonged.

He took one step toward his destiny, but something underfoot stopped him from going farther. He reached down and picked up the object that he had stepped on, annoyed at it for delaying his mission. He examined it in the dark as best he could. He held in his hand a memory stick. What files it contained, what secrets it revealed would have to wait for later. He pocketed the memory stick. He would plug it into the USB drive of his computer later to discover its mysteries.

First, he must do God's work.

A lone prostitute now stood on the corner, the other two having already snared defenseless flies into their seductive webs. He took the scalpel from his pocket and limped toward her.

"Hello, my dear," he said, voice just a pitch above a whisper. He held the scalpel down at his side, out of sight but ever at the ready.

The whore turned toward him. "Well, aren't you the fucking gentleman." She grinned and sidled up to him until their bodies almost touched.

He took an involuntary step backwards and eyed the sinful specimen with disgust. She looked much older than he had expected, even with the garishly thick makeup and the poor lighting from the dim streetlight. Under an open leather jacket, she flaunted her body in nothing more than a halter top and shorts. The cold San Francisco night caressed her bare body parts, raising gooseflesh across her skin and exciting her nipples to erection under the tight top.

"What's the matter? Don't be embarrassed. Your cock can't be that small." She reached toward him, the nails of her hand painted the color of blood.

Before the dreaded creature could touch him, he brought the scalpel up and slashed it across her throat. The sharp blade sliced her open from ear to ear.

"It's not," he rasped.

Dark blood gushed from the gaping wound. She made a gurgling noise as if in the throes of drowning. A second later, she dropped to the pavement like a sack of rotten potatoes.

Blood splatter covered his face and clothes. But he didn't mind. In fact, he relished the carnage.

Picking up the horrid thing by the leg, he dragged her toward the curb. Just then, a black van screeched around the corner and squealed to an abrupt stop. The side door automatically opened as the driver climbed from the van.

"Help me with her, Icky," the killer commanded.

Silently, the twisted and deformed figure hurried to his master's side, and together they hoisted the body into the backend of the van.

The killer joined the body in the back while the misshapen driver climbed behind the wheel.

With a slamming of doors, the black van sped off into the night.

Chapter 2
Two Nights Later

A storm cloud of depression darkened Aleric's mood and weighed on his shoulders. Pearsa, his first *human* girlfriend in almost two hundred years, had left that day by bus for parts unknown, afraid for her life, afraid that Jeta—his vampire wife—had not truly perished in the fire that burned down Pearsa's fortunetelling parlor. Wasso—the young Gypsy he had saved from Dr. Ratterman and King Tene's evil plot of artificially creating zombies—had moved out and was now staying with Pulika and Mala—the young Gypsy couple he had taken under his wing. So, except for Odin—the raven who shared his apartment—he had the place to himself; he was alone. Alone to dwell on his losses, even Jeta, if she was indeed gone.

He also worried about the loss of Dr. Ratterman's memory stick. He had stupidly dropped it while fighting and killing the Neanderthal Ratterman had turned himself into by taking his own experimental serum. If anyone with scientific knowledge found that memory stick, they would have the means of creating a mass amount of zombies.

He growled like a rabid dog.

And it would be his fault.

But it wasn't just depression and worry that plagued him. He also physically felt like shit. A feverish chill shook him and he groaned at the dull, throbbing pain inside his head. Hobbling to the bathroom with an arthritic gait, he stretched out the tired muscles in his back and neck. The aching joints in his knees and ankles cracked as he went. He blinked back hot tears and rubbed at his burning eyes.

Soon, he stood in front of the toilet, relieving himself of a full bladder. He stared out the bathroom window at a night that looked like he felt—sickly, chilled and congested, with a persistent post nasal drip that dampened the city streets and moistened the windowpane.

The night could very well be sick, but he couldn't; he hadn't had so much as a mild cold in almost two centuries, since starting to share blood on a constant basis with Jeta.

Finished, he shook off the last drop, put himself back inside his pants, and flushed. At the sink, he washed his hands, splashed cold water on his face, and peered at his reflection.

For two centuries, he had looked twenty-nine or thirty, certainly never older than thirty-five, and then only after abstaining from sex and bloodletting with Jeta for an extended period. Partaking of supernatural blood after a fresh kill sustained him during those times but not to the same effect.

Now, seemingly overnight, the centuries pummeled him. He hardly recognized the man staring back at him: Cavernous darkness circled both of his blood-shot eyes, and crow's-feet pulled them into a squinty stare. Deep crevices lined the corners of his mouth. Gray strands ran through the raven-black curls of his long hair. Stubble salt and peppered his face.

He coughed uncontrollably, hacked up a putrid, green glob, and spat it into the sink.

"Damn," he hissed.

Jeta had always been his salvation and damnation. Not for the first time he wondered if he could survive without her. It was her blood in his system that kept him young, gave him the boundless strength, energy, agility, and grace to hunt and kill monsters. It was her blood that provided him with preternatural night vision, animal-like instinct for survival, and crystallization of thought. And even though he wasn't immortal, it was her blood that made him very hard to kill.

His hands began to shake. Sweat beaded his brow. The throbbing in his head turned to pounding. He gripped the sink to steady himself.

He needed it now, supernatural blood to keep him going.

He stared at his reflection. "Fuck you," he told it. "Fuck your addiction."

He owed the curse that Jeta shared with him more than he had ever wanted to admit. Even when he had dreaded her frequent visitations and abhorred their coupling, he knew it to be true.

Now, without her, he had proof. He felt like a heroin addict going cold turkey, and he had aged seemingly overnight. He doubted very much that he could live solely on nightly hunts and the fresh kill of supernatural beasts. Maybe he was a fool to believe he could. Maybe he was a fool to have ever considered a life without Jeta.

But for Pearsa's sake—for the Gypsy girl's survival—he would have to try. In the last couple of days he had come to the undeniable conclusion that he loved the fortuneteller more than life itself. He had also come to the conclusion that her life was more important to him than Jeta. No matter the consequences, whether it meant his demise or not, the dark and twisted relationship between Jeta and himself had to end. It was time to kick the addiction of their rutting and sharing of blood. It was past time to discard the guilt and blame for his one-time bride's abduction and eternal damnation. He had carried that burden in his heart for far too long.

It was time to admit that his bride no longer existed at all except through supernatural glamour. It was time to admit that she was nothing more than a damned soul, a creature of the night. It was time to admit that there was nothing left to love. It was time to make sure she was dead.

Taking one last look in the mirror, he squared his shoulders, steeled himself for the challenge ahead, and left the bathroom in disgust. He hobbled through the dark, back to bed. Plopping onto the edge, he sat opposite the open window. Ragged curtains fluttered inward with the chilly breeze and cold mist.

Could he effectively break the two-century-old spell?

He stared out the window at the neon lights tinting the cityscape. He took a deep breath. "Jeta," he whispered, "come to me."

She did. After entering through the window as a wisp of fog, she materialized at the side of the bed. The city lights outside the window served as a backlight but kept her face hidden in deep shadows.

"I've been waiting for you to call to me, my love," she whispered, moving closer, face still hidden. "It was only a matter of time."

"I thought you had perished," he lied.

She moved close enough to touch. "Never, my love."

From under a pillow, he drew a stake constructed of aspen wood. Swiftly, he brought it up and plunged it hard and deep into the vampire's chest.

Jeta's eyes bulged and flashed red. She gasped and croaked. Blood gurgled in her throat, spilled from her mouth, and gushed from around the stake in her chest. She jerked and convulsed with violent spasms.

"I'm sorry, my love," he whispered, "for us both."

The light in her eyes burned out, and she fell into his arms.

He gently held his lover's still body—for he would forever love her—and he cried for the first time in two centuries.

From his perch, Odin squawked, "Nevermore."

Chapter 3

Aleric lay in bed well after the sun lit the morning sky. After having plunged the wooden stake into his wife's heart, he drank what little blood drained from her. However, she must not have fed in a while, for there was very little, not enough to stave off his deterioration. Without more, he continued to wither into old age and show further signs of withdrawal. He had barely found the strength to discreetly dispose of her body.

Could it be that he was nothing without his vampire bride? Could it be his exploits and legend owed her everything and himself nothing?

He grabbed his midsection and curled into a fetal position. Gritting his teeth, he rode out another abdominal pain. His face and ears flushed with heat, feeling as though they'd spontaneously combust. Chills struck his extremities. At the same time, sweat dribbled from every pore, dampening his shirt and plastering hair to his head. His heart raced. One leg tried to keep up, jerking in place as if trying to run all on its own.

He needed nourishment, supernatural blood to give him back a modicum of youth and strength. Again, he wondered whether survival without Jeta was possible. Her blood in his system had acted as an opiate, instilling euphoria and making him feel indestructible. Now that she was gone, he was alone and left to his own devices for the first time in two centuries. It wasn't just his doubts about having the physical strength. He also had doubts concerning his mental fortitude.

He was reminded of the *swato* about the conceited mosquito and the old candle that burned eternally. According to this Gypsy story, the mosquito thought himself to be unequaled in the whole earth. But the wretched little candle scorched and roasted anyone foolish enough to test their strength against hers. Hearing of her reputation, the mosquito couldn't resist the challenge. He was choked with anger to think that anyone in the world could be stronger than he. So he pulled his cap over his eyes, thrust his hands into his pockets, and set out in the direction of the ruined castle where the candle lived. Once there, he forced his way inside and confronted the candle—cursing, insulting, and mocking her. But no matter what the quarrelsome, little mosquito tried, the candle kept her temper, not even glancing his way. Enraged, knowing no fear, the mosquito stepped back and gave the candle a blow under the chin with his fist. The candle in quick retaliation devoured the mosquito's hand with her flame. The mosquito ran home, crying and hurt. Still, he was not brought back to his senses. As soon as his fist healed and no longer gave him pain, he went off to again find and pick a quarrel with the candle. In fact, nine times more the mosquito did battle with the candle and nine times more he saw himself vanquished and nine times more he ran home, crying and hurt. No matter how many times the candle burned him, the mosquito could not stay away, could not swallow his pride, could not resist the temptation or allure of the candle's eternal flame.

Aleric clutched his abdomen, gritted his teeth.

He was indeed the prideful, little mosquito. So full of himself and his legend. Whereas, Jeta had been the candle. For two centuries, he hadn't been able to resist her allure no matter how many times her eternal flame burned him. And now he was to blame for finally snuffing her out, and as a result, he was also to blame for his own ultimate demise.

A knock at his door brought him out of his misery and self-loathing. Who in the hell could it be this early? He curled up tighter. There was no reason to get up. He wasn't expecting anyone.

Another knock.

Probably just someone trying to sell something.

"Who's there?" Odin squawked.

Fucking bird. If he could find the strength, he'd kill the damn thing.

Another knock followed.

"Aleric, you home?"

A woman's voice.

"Aleric?"

Mala. Pulika's young wife.

Gritting his teeth, he rolled out of bed and staggered to the door.

"Who's there?"

"Shut up," he growled at the raven as he opened the door.

When Mala saw him, she gasped. "You look horrible."

He tried to smile but it was more of a grimace. "*Nais tuke.*"

Mala giggled. "You're welcome."

"Come in," Odin squawked.

"For once I agree with the damn bird." He stepped aside. "Come in."

She did.

He closed the door behind her. "You look well, very pretty."

Mala smiled. She wore a yellow sun dress with matching *diklo*, a sky-blue cardigan, and sky-blue slip-on shoes. "Thank you. Nice of you to notice." She scrutinized Aleric even closer. "Are you okay? Pulika's worried. He said you looked like death the last time he saw you." She paused. "He was wrong. You look worse."

Aleric gritted his teeth against a sudden onslaught of abdominal pain. Otherwise, he hid his suffering well, fighting against doubling over. "Would you like to sit?" He motioned toward the sofa.

Mala shook her head. "I can only stay a minute. I was just in the neighborhood and promised Pulika I would check on you."

"You two worry too much."

She looked at her feet. "We love you. Without you, Pulika would still be working the meat rack in the Tenderloin, allowing pedophile scum to use him for money. You saved him. You saved us."

He eyed the girl. He had forgotten just how young they were. Although married, Mala was only fifteen and Pulika sixteen. "I love both of you, as well. Tell Pulika, I will be fine."

She looked up and smiled. "I'll tell him."

"You never said why you're in the neighborhood."

"Oh, I'm telling fortunes door to door." She pulled out a deck of tarot cards from her sweater pocket.

For the first time, Aleric noticed the clipboard in her hand. "I never knew a clipboard to be used for divination."

She giggled. "Oh, that's just to get people to open the door. I'm hoping they'll think I'm gathering signatures for a petition or something."

He laughed but then turned serious. "*Mandar tsera tai kater.*"

"We will not take more money from you. We must stand on our own."

He shrugged. "There are worse things than taking money from *gadje* for telling their fortunes. It is better than working, I suppose."

She shook her head and smiled. "Besides, Wasso's lawsuit will pay off soon."

He nodded. "Oh yes, the slip and fall in Safeway's produce section."

"They're getting ready to settle now. Soon we'll have no worries."

He nodded with understanding. "How is Wasso? He is still...*human?*"

Mala opened the door to leave. "There's been no relapse...no sign of the zombie virus." She stepped into the hallway. "*Zhan le Devlesa tai sastimasa.*"

"Go with God and in good health," Aleric repeated back to her.

As he watched her descend the stairs, an uneasy feeling in the pit of his stomach came over him. He couldn't be sure if it was a premonition of bad things to come or just another wave of nausea and pain brought on by his continuing deterioration.

He prayed it was the latter.

Chapter 4

With a jar cradled in the crook of one arm, the killer limped across the kitchen to the basement door. After unlocking and removing the padlock, he opened it, the door creaking like a rusted coffin lid. Darkness greeted him on the other side. He flicked the light switch on the wall, illuminating one bare bulb that dimly lit a long, wooden staircase. Slowly, he descended, steps creaking underfoot, into the cold and musty catacombs beneath his home.

He flicked another light switch at the bottom of the stairs, illuminating the first underground room in flickering, dim fluorescent lighting. The stark combination of gray, concrete walls and a gray, concrete floor made this room look like an air-raid bunker leftover from the Cold War. It was almost empty except for a walk-in freezer against the far wall and the makeshift office underneath the staircase where he had set up a desk, chair, lamp, computer, printer, fax, and phone. He also added a space heater by the desk for comfort. As a warning system, he had installed a red light on the wall above the desk that blinked whenever anyone rang the bell at his front door, and live video fed to his computer from a small camera installed above that door.

A doorway in the wall opposite the stairs led to a dark, narrow hallway. Beyond that hallway there was an identical room. Except this room he had decorated in a coroner's décor, complete with a stainless steel dissecting table at its center and a stainless steel medical tray on wheels next to it. On the tray, he had laid out various surgeon needles, scalpels, probes, forceps, refractors, explorers, clamps, extractors, scissors, drills, syringes, and hypodermic needles. He also had a Stryker autopsy saw, mouth gags, and an assortment of narcotics, opiates, and barbiturates. Unlike the first room, he had equipped this one with surgical lamps that provided bright, harsh light. He had also lined the walls and the floor in a heavy, clear plastic to catch blood splatter. Ironically, whenever he stood at the center of this room, surrounded by the plastic, he always felt as though he were back inside the protective embrace of his own mother's womb.

Two more bunker-like rooms stood just off a short hallway from the autopsy room. These windowless rooms had steel doors that locked and unlocked from only the outside. In each corner of the rooms, he had installed a video camera up by the ceiling; these cameras also fed live footage to his computer. Both rooms at the moment were completely empty, but soon he'd have a houseguest or two to again occupy them.

Carrying the jar as if it were a baby, he crossed the first room to the walk-in freezer. When he opened the large, metal door, a blast of arctic air punched him in the face, as if frozen tundra lay within. He crossed the threshold into the icy world to add this new specimen to his growing collection.

Five more wombs, each nestled and frozen in its own jar, waited for their sister to join them.

He grinned with satisfaction as he placed the jar on a shelf with the others.

That's six prostitutes, Satan's minions all, who could no longer tempt men into sin, who could no longer litter God's world with their bastard offspring.

He hugged himself against the cold and scanned the large freezer.

There was room for more, though, plenty of room. And when he filled this freezer, he'd build another, for God's work was never done. The world was overrun with sinners, and it was his job to exterminate them all.

He left his trophies behind, stepping from the freezer and shutting the metal door. Although cold too, the room stretching out before him felt cozy compared to inside the frozen world he had just left. Limping, he crossed the room to his makeshift office and sat at the desk, the warmth of the space heater caressing his legs. The memory stick he had found a few nights back, just before ridding the world of one more sinful bitch, rested on the desk next to the computer, waiting for him to discover its secrets.

Maybe God had left the memory stick for him to find, with heavenly instructions on how to continue the daunting task ahead.

Picking it up, he plugged the memory stick into a USB port and waited for the files to reveal themselves.

He had the strangest feeling that what he was about to learn would transform his mission somehow, that God was about to provide him with a new weapon in which to fight the world's evils and punish its sinners.

But only one main folder existed on the stick, marked *Wilhelm Ratterman, M.D.*

He expected more. And who was this Doctor Ratterman?

Maneuvering the mouse, he clicked on the folder, opening its secrets.

That was more like it; at least a dozen files existed in this one folder. One file was marked *Research Notes*. The other files were all named *Experiment*. The only difference was a number added to each file to represent sequential order.

He clicked on *Research Notes* and sat back in his chair. What he read astonished him:

Dr. Wilhelm Ratterman had endeavored to discover both the secret to immortality and to tap into the hidden strengths that all humans have in time of extreme stress and great danger. It had been his hope to solve the mystery to everlasting life and to find the secret behind courage; why some people fear nothing, while others fear everything.

To help in his experiments, he had used Gypsies as guinea pigs, giving them what they thought were flu shots.

The killer smiled to himself.

Dr. Ratterman truly was brilliant. The flu vaccine shortage had given the doctor the perfect setup. He had been able to innocently inject unsuspecting people—mostly Gypsies provided by a man named Carranza Tene—with his formula, under the pretense and generosity of a free flu shot. At that time, most people had been happy to just get their shot, what with the vaccine shortage, and hadn't questioned from where it had come. Because most of his subjects had been Gypsies, no one of any consequence had missed them when the experiments went awry. According to Ratterman, only other Gypsies noticed when one of their own went missing, and usually they assumed their friend or loved one moved on to greener pastures; such was their nomadic lifestyle. And even if other Gypsies had suspected foul play, the doctor still hadn't worried. He had been assured by Tene that no Gypsy would ever go to the police—they just didn't do such things. Besides, apparently King Tene had all of these other Gypsies scared into submission; not one of them had caused any trouble.

But perfect setup or not, Ratterman's first attempts at discovery had all ended in dismal failures. The first test subjects had all died within a few hours—the exact opposite of immortality. A new formula and a second group had proved no better. Then, like a bolt of lightning from the heavens, inspiration had struck the doctor. He had come upon the idea of isolating the zombie virus and artificially producing it, for zombies possessed many of the attributes he wished to unearth, being supernaturally strong, unafraid, extremely aggressive and vicious, and basically immortal unless killed or starved.

Of course, in his attempt at courage and immortality, the doctor hadn't wanted to become a member of the undead, slowly transforming himself into a walking, decaying corpse. No, he had hoped to discover the exact dosage needed in the formula to produce the effect he wanted without degrading his own cell structure.

With each new batch he had come closer to success. Zombie transformation and molecular cell damage in each progressing test group had slowed considerably.

Normally, according to the doctor's research, symptoms of a zombie infection appeared quickly, usually within an hour. After developing flu-like symptoms—fever, chills, headache—the victim fell into a zombie coma that lasted for six hours until waking in a catatonic state. Once fully transformed, a zombie degraded rapidly too, entering stage three within a few days.

However, his test subjects had both transformed and degraded evermore slowly with each newly refined formula. In his last entry, the doctor had felt positive that sooner or later he would hit on the exact dosage.

The killer read the last of Ratterman's notes, wondering what had happened to the good doctor. Had the poor soul injected himself with an unsuccessful batch of his own serum? Was the doctor now a walking, decaying corpse? Or was he dead?

It didn't really matter. Ratterman was of no consequence except for the fact that God had seen fit to reveal the doctor's strange experiments.

Yes, he firmly believed that God had left this memory stick for him to find. It was definitely a sign, providing him with a new strategy in which to fight sin. No longer would merely ridding the earth of the plague known as prostitution be enough. No longer would merely death be ample justice or punishment for these vile servants of Satan. He now had the capability to exact a more fitting and devastating punishment upon these loathsome creatures. And in the process he'd also deal severely with the sinful men who succumbed to such temptations. Imagine their surprise when these sinners find not pleasures of the flesh with these wanton women but instead pestilence and ultimately death.

At the thought, he let loose with a wicked chuckle.

Just then the red light over his desk began to blink. Someone was at his front door. Switching the computer monitor to live video feed, he stared at the pretty, young woman who had rung his doorbell. She wore a blue sweater over a yellow sundress with a matching scarf covering her pitch-black hair. In her dainty grasp, she held a clipboard.

Grinning, he slowly stood and limped toward the makeshift autopsy room. There, he fixed a syringe with a hypodermic needle, filling it with the quick-acting barbiturate, Pentothal.

Maybe this unexpected caller wasn't a professional prostitute, but he believed most women by nature were whores and sinners. Besides, she'd make a great test subject and had come to him at a time when he needed her most, like a gift from Heaven.

Back out in the first bunker, he slowly ascended the stairs, fully prepared to accept this new houseguest into his home.

Chapter 5

Carranza Tene's brother sat on the edge of the motel's bed, swaddled in darkness. Boldo Tene listened to the shower run in the bathroom and wondered why he wasn't in there, soaping the taut and luscious body of his young mistress. He should've been. Instead, he languished with self-pity, thoughts as dark as the room, dwelling on his brother's nemesis and murderer—Aleric Toma Bimbai.

Even though Bimbai hadn't actually pulled the trigger, the bastard was as responsible for Carranza's death as if he had; he was sure the bullet that killed his brother was meant for the monster hunter, and since there was no way to know who had fired the fatal shot, he would exact his revenge on him.

The problem was he had no viable plan. All past attempts on Bimbai's life had failed miserably. Gypsy henchmen, hired assassins, Ratterman's monster, and even the vampire Kinski had all met the same dismal fate when confronting the two-hundred-year-old Gypsy.

Death.

He stood, pulling the terrycloth robe tight around his otherwise naked, hairy body. He tied the cloth belt about his pot belly to keep the robe closed, and paced around the small, dark room.

Maybe the stories were true. Maybe Bimbai was immortal. According to the legends, the monster hunter had died once before, centuries ago, and had come back. Some say that he lost his soul on the treacherous journey from the blackness of death back into the light of life. Some say that even though he again walked among the living, the light of life no longer shone within him. Instead, he walked somewhere between life and death, between blackness and light, through a landscape of never-ending shadows, dark and foreboding.

He shivered at the thought. If true, he'd never get his revenge.

No, there had to be a way. Nobody's immortal. Although difficult, even vampires could be killed. And so could Bimbai.

But then he remembered the first time he and his brother had confronted the man and the legend. It was the time of the Gypsy riot, more than ten years ago, when *Roma* from all over had massed together on ten acres of rented meadowland high in the foothills of the Sierra Mountains, organizing in rebellion against paying the tributes Carranza demanded as their self-appointed king and forcing him and his brother to rush there with their soldiers to squelch the revolt.

Bimbai was there, leading the rebellion, looking barely twenty-eight rather than like a two-hundred-year-old legend. But he had a cold, predatory look in his eyes, and the gun rig strapped around his shoulders sported two holsters with twin pearl-handled revolvers.

Still, the Tenes hadn't believed the stories about this Gypsy being descended from King Tshukurka. They hadn't believed that the young man standing before them had died, had come back to life, and could never die again. They had considered the stories hogwash until Carranza shot Bimbai high in the chest, and they both witnessed the charging Gypsy still coming at them like immortal fucking Christ.

He stopped pacing as he remembered staring in awe and fear at the barely bleeding gunshot wound Carranza's gun had inflicted, a wound that should've been fatal but seemed no more bothersome to Bimbai than if he were shot with a paintball.

Into the darkness, and not for the first time since that fateful meeting, he recited a curse for a malignant disease to waste the monster hunter. *"Te malavel les I menkiva,"* he whispered.

More than ten years later, he and his brother had still been rebuilding their power base, putting down mini revolts, and waiting for the curse on Bimbai to work.

"Te malavel les I menkiva."

Bimbai had made Carranza eat crow that day ten years ago. But the monster hunter should've killed the king. That was a fatal mistake because the tribes fractured again after the legend relinquished all rights to the throne and returned to his hunting, allowing the Tenes to again put the screws to all those who had risen up against them, demanding and collecting money as tribute, just like before. And soon they were almost as strong as before the riot, maybe stronger.

But now Carranza was dead, and he was left to carry on, alone. Now *he* was the self-proclaimed King of the Gypsies.

And Bimbai still lived.

"Te malavel les I menkiva."

"You want him dead," someone whispered from behind.

His breath choked in his throat as if those words were actually hands throttling him. He whirled toward the voice. "Who the fuck is it?" he croaked. Reaching for the nearby lamp, he fumbled with the switch.

A man stepped from the shadows, into the dim light.

The Gypsy stiffened. He clutched his robe and pulled it tight, as if it were protective chain mail rather than terrycloth. "How the fuck did you get in here? What the hell do you want?" He looked closer. "Goddammit, I know you, don't I?"

The man sneered. "You want him dead," he repeated—a statement, not a question.

He stared hard at the man's face. "Yeah, I fucking know you," he insisted. "Your name is Jones. You're the Nazi sonofabitch Carranza hired a while back to kill Bimbai. You fucking set my brother up, double-crossed him."

Jones stepped closer. "You and your brother wanted him dead then. *You* want him dead now." His voice hissed like a poisonous viper. "He denounced your brother as king and called him a pretender, a bastard fake, and instigated the uprising. For that alone you'd have anyone else's legs broken. But for your brother's murder, the bastard surely has to die."

Boldo gaped at his uninvited guest. A shiver shot up his spine with the impact of an atomic bomb, mushroom cloud of gooseflesh spreading across his scalp. "How do you know of my brother's death? Are you some kind of goddamn mind reader?"

"No, not a mind reader. I'm the one who fired the gun that killed him."

The Gypsy scowled. "You fucking sonofabitch." He squared his shoulders, ready to take on his brother's murderer.

"I wouldn't if I were you." Jones flashed fangs.

Boldo stumbled backward, clutching at his terrycloth chain mail. "*Strigoi*," he murmured.

"Things have changed a bit since we last met," Jones confirmed. He laughed.

The Gypsy pulled the curtain cord, his inner clock sure it was morning. The curtains separated. But what pressed against the window was not morning sun but an almost underwater murkiness. Salvation would not come in the form of daylight.

Snarling, the vampire moved in—a predator cornering its prey.

Boldo pressed his back against the cold windowpane. "Stay…the fuck—" His dry, constricting throat choked off the words. His heartbeat thumped in his ears. Pressure built within his head, gut, and chest, fear threatening to erupt from every pore and orifice.

"It's not you I want dead, Gypsy," Jones hissed. "If I did, you'd be dead and drained already." He stepped back, relinquishing ground to his prey as a sign of trust. "Like you, it's Bimbai I want dead."

Boldo eyed the vampire with suspicion. He maneuvered closer to the door and possible escape, finding his voice as he moved. "Then kill him," he said. "Why fucking bother me?"

Jones opened his arms as if anticipating a hug. "I want payment for my efforts."

For sake of money, the Gypsy screwed up his courage. "Why the fuck should I pay you for something you're sure as hell going to do anyway? Besides, *you* murdered my brother, not Bimbai; you admitted it."

Jones took ground back, stepping closer to the retreating Gypsy. "Bimbai was my target, not your brother. The king is dead because of the monster hunter." He shrugged. "And if you don't pay? I'll kill you and your lovely, young mistress first." He bared fangs. "Now, will payment be made in money or in blood?"

Boldo pressed his back against the door. He choked off the leak between his legs, a short squirt of wet fear escaping down his leg. Blinking back hot tears, he choked, "Both…I'll fucking give you both."

Jones halted his advance. He gave the Gypsy a quizzical stare. "An interesting offer," he mused. "How do you suppose to do both?"

Boldo gulped. "How much goddamn money did you fucking want to kill Bimbai?"

"A hundred grand," Jones said without hesitation.

The Gypsy nodded. "Give me a fucking break on the price—say, fifty thousand—and I'll supply you with fresh kills, fresh blood."

Jones' eyebrows rose at the prospect.

Boldo knew he'd seized the vampire's interest. "You can start with her," he said, nodding toward the closed bathroom door. "She's fucking yours. I give her to you."

"Is she Gypsy?"

Boldo nodded.

Jones grinned, showing a hint of fangs. "I've always wanted to fuck a Gypsy."

"Now's your chance."

"I didn't say it had to be a female bitch." He looked the Gypsy up and down with a measured stare. "Just a Gypsy bitch."

With eyes bulging, Boldo stepped back. Another squirt of wet fear escaped down his leg.

The vampire laughed. "Relax, fat man. You're not my type."

Boldo breathed a bit easier but kept his distance and his robe pulled tight.

"You know," Jones said, "I could just take her anyway and still demand the hundred grand."

The Gypsy screwed up new courage. "But if you take the goddamn deal, she'll be just the fucking beginning," he promised, his voice a low, conspiratorial hush.

Even deathly fear of this horrid creature couldn't keep his mind from its evil calculations. The chances of Jones actually killing Bimbai were slim; the vampire Kinski couldn't do it, and many others hadn't been able to either. This fledgling vampire surviving the monster hunter's revengeful wrath for an unprovoked attack was even slimmer. And once Bimbai disposed of Jones then no new victims would be needed. And, more importantly, no money either. Then again, there was a slight chance the vampire could succeed. The prospect of Bimbai's cold body on a slab in the morgue would be well worth a few innocent deaths and a relatively small payment of money. He had everything to gain—his own life and possibly Bimbai's demise—and not much to lose; he could always get another mistress and there was a ready supply of Gypsies he could offer to the vampire. The more he thought about it, the better he liked the idea.

"I can keep you in goddamn fresh blood for some fucking time," he continued. He dared to edge closer, his confidence returning. "You strike me as being relatively new to your fucking…*situation*."

Jones snorted. "You have no idea."

Boldo nodded. "It could get goddamn difficult finding the fucking blood you need to survive," he confided. "Kill too fucking many and you'll have every sonofabitch that hunts monsters for bounty on your ass. You fucking know. You were one."

The vampire considered the Gypsy's words.

"And then there's the fucking ASA to consider," Boldo added. "You don't want those cocksuckers on your fucking ass."

Jones frowned at that prospect. He'd worked as an independent asset for them in the past. They were almost as relentless and ruthless as he.

"I can supply you with all the goddamn Gypsies you fucking want, women and men," Boldo continued, seeing he had the vampire caught in his deceptive web. "The shit-fucking police won't miss them. The goddamn ASA neither. No one will be on your fucking ass about them. You'll be goddamn invisible. Never hungry. I'll take fucking care of everything."

Jones nodded in agreement. "I accept your offer," he said, "but fifty thousand isn't enough. Make it eighty."

Boldo took a great breath. Negotiating with a vampire was tricky business. And this vampire was already a killer before being turned. "Sixty-five thousand," he said as firmly as he could muster, "not a fucking dollar more."

The vampire grinned. "Seventy," he said, "and you've got a...*fucking*...deal."

The Gypsy nodded in agreement.

"I want the money by tonight...cash," Jones insisted.

Boldo nodded again. He took a step toward the closet.

"Where are you going?" Jones spat the question out like maggot-riddled meat.

The Gypsy sprung another leak between his legs and immediately stopped. "My c-c-clothes," he stammered. "Let me get the fuck out of here and let you get on with your...*business*."

Jones bared fangs. "You can get the fuck out of here like that."

Boldo hesitated. He didn't want to leave the motel room in just his urine-spotted robe. But he dared not challenge the vampire.

Jones advanced on him. "Get the fuck out."

The Gypsy hurried to the door, fumbled with the lock and the security chain. He ran into the parking lot in full retreat. Robe flying open. Bladder bursting.

Chapter 6

Jones closed the motel-room door. Locked it. Slipped the security chain in place. After undressing, he padded to the bathroom door with the stealth of a predator. Even through the closed door, he could sniff the girl's scent. Hear the steady thump of her carotid artery and the rush of her blood.

His own heart beat with the furious speed of a caged rat on its exercise wheel. He went rock hard between his legs at the thought of the naked Gypsy girl in the shower. Poised at the door, he ran his tongue across teeth and fangs in anticipation of the feast, the violence.

Being a vampire had its perks; he'd always prided himself at being coldhearted, unforgiving, and murderous, but he'd never known this kind of darkness, power, and bloodlust. Already, he barely remembered life as a mere human. He was now perched at the top of the food chain and relished that newfound strength and dominance.

Bursting through the door, his body mutated as he attacked, stuck halfway between human and wild animal. He shredded the shower curtain with extended claws, yanked it free of the rod, and pounced.

The unsuspecting girl spun toward the attack, her beautiful Gypsy face a frozen mask of horror. Raising her fists in self-defense, she screamed.

But the vampire's fangs clamped onto the girl's throat and cut the cry short. Hot blood surged into his mouth. Taking his prey off her feet, he slammed her into the wall and thrust himself between her legs. Biting down harder, he consumed as much of her gushing blood as he dared, not wanting to drain her completely, at least not yet. The girl punched his shoulders with meek fists and gurgled like a drowning victim in his ear. Hot, steamy water continued to pound him, putting up a better fight than the girl, as he feasted on blood and sex.

Chapter 7

Boot Deufer clomped like a cloven-hoofed demon, cowboy boots echoing as he strode along the long, deserted corridor. He walked with hands deep in the pockets of his blue jeans, head bopping in time to the Rolling Stones' *Sympathy for the Devil* playing on his iPhone, shaggy-red hair falling into steely-blue eyes. Under his black, corduroy sport jacket, he carried twin .357 Colt Pythons, both slumbering in a double-holstered rig. A Glock 20 semi-automatic rested in a single holster attached to his belt behind his back. A Smith & Wesson .45 Chiefs Special hid in the top of his right cowboy boot, waiting patiently to blow someone away. His right hand fingered the switchblade he carried in the pocket of his jeans, caressing it like a loving suitor.

At the end of the hall, he came to a lone door, the *ASA* emblem and the title *Deputy Director* emblazoned on its front. The Agency of Supernatural Affairs was a black ops division of the Department of Justice. Only high level officials knew of its existence. Their main purpose was extermination of zombies and vampires, as well as lesser-known supernatural creatures. By day, they scoured the countryside for likely hiding places of the undead. By night, they patrolled high-crime areas, places the undead would frequent in their quest for victims.

He had worked as an independent *facilitator* for the company many times, contract work their agents had neither the talent nor the stomach to perform; ASA agents had no problem terminating supernatural creatures and beasts, but killing humans—cold-blooded murder—was another matter. He made no such distinction.

Killing was killing.

He didn't knock, didn't break stride. Barging into the office unannounced, he slammed the door and plopped himself down into the leather chair opposite a mahogany desk and the black man sitting behind it.

Deputy Director Fisher started and then fidgeted in his chair at the sudden interruption. Nevertheless, he finished signing the document in front of him before putting down his pen and eyeing the young assassin sitting across the desk.

"Unplug," he commanded.

Boot ignored the directive—head bopping, red hair flopping to his favorite song.

The deputy director sighed. "Please take out the earbuds, Mr. Deufer."

Boot plucked out the earbuds and closed the music app, killing the Stones. With a slight swing of his head, he shook red bangs away from his eyes, chuckling to himself when his gaze fell on Fisher, and he saw the deputy director tremble.

He had that effect on people and used it to his advantage.

Fisher cleared his throat and fidgeted more. "I have a contract for you, Mr. Deufer."

Boot clucked his tongue and grinned. "No shit."

Fisher took a deep breath. "Yes…well, this is no ordinary contract, no ordinary target," he continued, keeping to business. "We've already lost at least one facilitator who attempted to fulfill this contract."

The assassin snorted. "I'm no ordinary *facilitator*."

"True. Still, you deserve to know exactly who and what you're going up against."

A casual wave of a freckled hand responded as a sign to be briefed on the intended target.

"His name is Aleric Toma Bimbai," Fisher said.

Boot stiffened. He leaned forward with interest. "Gypsy," he spat the word out as if not able to stand the foul taste of it.

"Not just any Gypsy. He's a bounty hunter, a very dangerous man, who's gotten in the way of this agency one too many times."

He answered with a hard, cold laugh. "What's the matter, deputy director, doesn't Bimbai play well with others?"

Fisher leaned back in his chair. "To put it in your terms, Mr. Deufer, no he does not. And we're tired of him amusing himself on our playground. Recently, he jeopardized a major operation involving the extermination of zombies massing together at Cannery 51. Because of him—"

"I couldn't give a rat's ass," Boot interrupted.

The deputy director swallowed his words, mouth pursed as if he'd just bitten into a lemon. "You might care about his reputation then," he ventured, "a reputation that goes far beyond the ordinary. There are stories…legends, really…that swirl about him like a thunderstorm." He paused and then mumbled, "I don't believe them, of course…immortality and such. After all, he's not a—"

Leaning across the desk, the assassin roared, "I don't give a freaking rat's ass. Just give me his dossier."

Fisher leaned back, took a handkerchief from the breast pocket of his suit coat, and wiped a combination of sweat and spittle from his face. "Very well, Mr. Deufer," he murmured, "don't say I didn't warn you." He opened a desk drawer, pulled out the file on Bimbai, and tossed it onto the desk.

Boot grabbed it. Opening the file, he felt like a kid at Christmas. Killing and money always excited him. But he'd kill a Gypsy for free; the money was just a bonus.

"There's not much here," he mumbled as he shuffled through the documents, "only cases where Bimbai got in your way."

The deputy director nodded solemnly.

"No picture…just a sketchy description…a list of possible addresses…and no background information except for wild rumors and crazy stories."

Fisher cleared his throat. "Like a ghost," he murmured.

Flicking a shock of red hair from his eyes, Boot looked up to make eye contact.

But the deputy director refused—eyes cast down.

"You call this freaking intelligence?" The assassin threw the file at the deputy director, hitting the man pointblank in the chest. Papers scattered across the desk and onto the floor like blood spatter. "Ghost," he scoffed, "Gypsy scum, more like it."

Fisher nodded.

Boot stood, eyeing the man across the desk from him with disdain. "No matter," he said, voice cold and flat. "I'll take care of this little problem for you."

The deputy director fished inside a desk drawer. He pulled out a canvas pouch and handed it across the desk.

Boot snatched it. Without counting the money, he stuck the pouch in the pocket of his sport jacket. He plugged the earbuds back in and switched on the Stones. *Sympathy for the Devil* blasted in his ears. Making a gun with forefinger and thumb, he pretended to shoot the deputy director. Then with a wink, he bopped his way back out into the hall and on to the mission of facilitating Bimbai's demise. Like the Devil, laying souls to waste was what he did best.

Gypsy or not. Legend or not.

Chapter 8

A shroud of dark clouds blanketed the city and held the sun hostage. A chilling wind bit into Aleric's face, tousled his curly, long hair. He put up the collar of his Western duster, plunged his hands deep into its pockets, and pulled it tighter. He fought against the current of people rushing about on the streets of San Francisco. Car horns blared, traffic crawled to a snail's pace, and car exhaust choked the ocean freshness out of the air. Up ahead, a row of cabs waited for fares.

He jumped into the backseat of one. "Hall of Justice," he instructed.

The young cabbie's radio screamed back. "The notorious serial killer known only as Zero Sin has held the city of San Francisco hostage for months, abducting prostitutes and dumping their dead bodies days later on the streets and in back alleys after surgically removing their wombs. This morning, another body was found in an alley off Post Street in the Tenderloin. The unidentified victim's womb was removed, and the killer again left the Bible verse, John 8:7 as his calling card written in the victim's blood on the sidewalk:

Let any one of you who is without sin cast the first stone. And as always the killer added, *The stone is cast.* The bloody message was signed simply, *Zero Sin.*"

"Turn that crap off," he barked.

Reluctantly, the cabbie complied. Quickly, he pulled out into traffic without signaling and without hesitation, horns blaring disapproval.

Aleric, like the cabbie, paid no heed. Instead, with the radio now silenced, he lost himself in thoughts of Pearsa.

His love was running scared, lost within the nomadic life of a Gypsy. The girl didn't carry a cell phone, and there was no way to get word to her of Jeta's demise except through the Gypsy network. The network was reliable but slow, especially compared to the instantaneous communication most people enjoyed today. Because of that, it would be some time before the girl's return.

Of course, even if Pearsa returned today, she couldn't help with his deterioration. Only Jeta could've done that.

The cab pulled to the curb, screeching to a halt outside the Hall of Justice. "Twenty-three, fifty," the cabbie said, turning to face his passenger.

He handed the young man a twenty and a five. "Keep it."

The cabbie turned back to his steering wheel. "BFD…lunch off the dollar menu again."

He ignored the cabbie. Normally, he'd make anyone piss their pants for such a remark, but he hadn't the energy, strength, or inclination now to respond. Instead, he climbed out of the cab, his back in spasms, his joints aching. He stretched and flexed as the cab sped off, leaving behind a dark cloud of exhaust. Choking and coughing, he turned away. Somehow, he had to find the force of will within himself to rise from the ashes of dependency. Determination swelled within him. He refused to just sit back and wither away, so he planned to go down doing what he'd always done best—fighting monsters. That meant a hunt. That was why he came to the Hall of Justice. He needed a wanted poster to give him a clue on where to start. There was always a monster, demon, or beast that needed termination. And in doing battle with these assorted creatures, he'd not only make some money but get a much-needed fix of supernatural blood.

He eyed the massive, church-like building that stood before him and began the ascent of what looked like a million marble steps, past pillars the size of redwoods on both sides and on across the marble entryway to the heavy, oak doors. He reached for a thick, steel ring that served as a door handle but stopped before pulling the door open.

Suddenly and inexplicably, he felt like a field rodent, with the dangerous, watchful stare of a viper tracking his every move. A glance over his shoulder and a quick scan of the street and surrounding buildings told him nothing. But the slick, greasy feeling in the pit of his stomach refused to go away.

He ignored it, leaving it to whoever watched to make the first move.

Entering the building, his combat boots echoed in an entryway that opened up onto a huge lobby with domed ceiling and ornate woodwork. Also in the lobby were armed security guards manning metal detectors and x-ray machines; no one got into the Hall of Justice without a thorough search. With no valid ID, no firearm permit, and armed to the teeth—a Mossberg 590A1 compact, pump-action shotgun with pistol grip hidden within a pocket on the inside of his duster; a classic,

Dirty Harry .44 Magnum in his shoulder holster; a Glock semiautomatic pistol tucked into his belt; a survival boot knife in a quick-release sheath clipped to his right boot; and a smaller knife within a hidden pocket of his pants—he wasn't about to get through security. But then he didn't need to get through.

Rather, he kept to the entryway where they posted bulletins on felons, both human and supernatural. Scanning the board, he searched for both easy pickings and a blood type with the most nourishment.

Not every supernatural creature provided the same amount of sustenance in their blood. Zombie blood—gunk—was useless, providing no nutrition and running the risk of infection. Goblins, gremlins, ghouls, trolls, and such provided varying degrees. Werewolf blood was good. Vampire blood was best. But he didn't quite feel up to doing battle with a werewolf or a vampire.

In fact, he found only one creature amongst the posted bulletins worth going after. He yanked the poster off the wall and studied it.

WANTED: DEAD
FOR RAPE & MURDER

SKOOKUM
$5,000 FOR ITS HEAD
Last seen in the Santa Cruz Mountains

He scowled.

Skookums were creatures of the Otherworld, difficult to catch and with an uncanny ability to disappear into thin air when cornered. These wild men of the woods were known to abduct women and forcibly engage in sexual intercourse for crossbreeding purposes. So, he could believe the rape charge. But never had he heard of one turning cold-blooded killer; he definitely had a hard time swallowing murder charges, and he hated to track one down and kill it under false pretenses.

But he couldn't afford a conscience now. Besides, he wasn't a judge. He was a bounty hunter. He didn't concern himself with guilt or innocence. He only fulfilled warrants, eradicated the world of undesirable supernatural creatures, and collected sizable sums for his efforts.

Still, Skookums were big, hairy beasts that stood anywhere from seven to nine feet tall and weighed up to twelve hundred pounds. They were powerful and could put up quite a struggle.

He scanned the board once more. But nothing else was even a remote possibility. He had no choice.

On the plus side, the benefits from the wild beast's blood would almost equal that of werewolf blood. And the five-thousand-dollar reward wouldn't hurt either.

He crumpled the poster and stuffed it inside the pocket of his duster. Before anyone could protest, he turned on his heels and shuffled to the door.

Outside, he raised his face to the sky. Sunlight had finally punched a small hole through the grey shroud, ending the vampire's day. The dark clouds that had been hovering over his mood dissipated with the sun's return, as well. No longer did he feel as if he were under the watchful gaze of a predator, cornered prey waiting for an attack.

Slowly, he made his way home, in desperate need of a few hours of rest to ready himself for that night's hunt.

Chapter 9

The young girl's screams echoed through the catacombs. She cried and wailed, begged for freedom, promised she wouldn't tell, pleaded for mercy.

All to no avail.

To the killer, her cries were like a symphony—perhaps Mozart's Requiem Mass—and he was the conductor, the maestro. But it wasn't Mozart's highly debated, last composition that played repetitively in his head and found its way to his lips as he worked. Instead, he hummed *The Searchers'* pop classic *Love Potion #9* in honor of selecting Dr. Ratterman's ninth experimental trial of the zombie serum—a love potion of sorts for his houseguest.

He had set up a makeshift laboratory within the first room of his underground bunker, just off the doorway that led to the autopsy room. Specific compounds and assorted ingredients that he needed for Ratterman's formula—including zombie *gunk*—he had procured himself through black-market contacts. He had sent Icky out to buy the more common supplies he didn't already have on hand, such as test tubes, beakers,

Bunsen burners, and rubber tubing. He had moved a large stainless-steel cabinet in from the autopsy room. The top he used as a table to set up his equipment and conduct his experiments. Underneath, there was plenty of storage for excess supplies. Right now, brewing concoctions bubbled in heated beakers and moved through labyrinths of rubber tubing.

He had chosen potion number nine from the files because, according to the doctor's notes, this one had achieved at least partial success, for Ratterman's purposes anyway. The test subjects that had taken this batch still became card-carrying members of the walking dead, of sorts. Their cell structures deteriorated and rotted like other zombies, but they transformed at a much slower rate. Also, the degenerative process with this formula seemed to peak and then stop rather than continue to break down cell structures until body parts began to fall away and nothing much of the zombie was left. In other words, these dead didn't rot away and were still functionally useful—for eternity in theory, unless something was driven into their brain or they were beheaded. Even more importantly, the zombies created with #9 still had brain function. Yes, they eventually lost their identities, their selves, but they continued to reason and behave somewhat normally, at least until the need to feed on human flesh and brains overtook all other thoughts, all rationale.

The killer entered the autopsy room, the plastic protection crackling underfoot and *Love Potion #9* still on his lips. He stared down at the screaming girl strapped to the stainless steel table.

The kind of zombie this girl would become fit his needs perfectly. Transformation would be slow enough and deterioration would be minimal enough that, on a street corner late at night, men soliciting her services wouldn't notice she was dead until it was too late. Yet her bite would be just as venomous and deadly as any other zombie.

The killer prepared a hypodermic needle with the love potion. With this formula leaving the girl's brain function reasonably intact, he felt sure he could control the monster he was creating. She would do his bidding and thus the Lord's bidding, for they were one in the same.

Over the girl's screams, the killer said, "You should be honored. You will be the first of your kind, an undead angel doing the Lord's work."

Apparently not convinced, the girl struggled against her restraints and sent her scream into a high-pitched, ear-piercing squeal.

The killer leaned forward. "Only God and I can hear you." He injected #9 into his patient. "And neither of us is listening."

Now it was just a matter of time before the Lord's undead angel walked the earth in search of sinners.

Meanwhile, he could sit back and enjoy the song of her screams.

Chapter 10

Mala screamed.

Her wrists and ankles were bound, strapped down to a cold, metal table. The asshole standing over her had just stuck her with a hypodermic needle, injecting her with something he called a *potion*. Panic swelled in her heart as a burning sensation bubbled through her bloodstream. She couldn't help but think of Wasso and what he had gone through, being injected with Ratterman's zombie serum. All she could do was pray that something similar hadn't happened to her.

"Aleric!"

Her only hope was her friend. He had helped Wasso, finding the antidote, saving him, and even disposing of the evil doctor who had injected him.

"Aleric!"

But how could Aleric save her? He didn't even know she was in danger. He didn't even know where she was or how to find her.

Her heart felt on fire. Her brain threatened explosion.

Oh, why did she have to go out into the *gadje* world? She should've stayed home where she belonged, with Pulika and Wasso.

She writhed on the table, struggling against the effects of the potion, fighting to remain conscious. But she was losing the battle, losing herself.

Darkness engulfed her.

"Aleric…"

Chapter II

Deep in the forest of the Santa Cruz Mountains, Aleric hunted the Skookum. Night swallowed the countryside. The overhead canopy of thick branches and heavy foliage blocked out any hope of moonlight or starlight. Before Jeta's demise, his night vision had been flawless and clear. Now, he could barely see past the end of his nose. His other senses were no better. His hearing seemed muted. His sense of smell detected nothing out of the ordinary.

Under his breath, he cursed. Much to his dismay, he was turning human. Worse yet, he was turning old and human. He would probably die tonight. The Skookum would surely tear him apart. No matter. Maybe it was time. Maybe two hundred years was a long enough life.

Out of breath, he stopped his trek through the forest and hunkered down in a small clearing to examine the ground. He really was hunting blind. He could see no sign of tracks or any other indication that the Skookum had come this way or was anywhere near the vicinity.

"Cretchuno!"

He knew it was bad luck to take Christ's name in vain but his frustration was mounting. The best he could apparently hope for was that he'd stumble upon the creature or it stumbled upon him.

A twig snapped.

There was no missing it. Not even in his diminished state. Something or someone was nearby, stalking him.

He pulled the survival boot knife from its sheath. Stood. Cocked his head. Listened.

Everything went deathly silent.

He sniffed the air. If he didn't know better, he'd swear he smelled vampire. He cursed again under his breath. He hated not being able to trust his own senses.

The attack came swiftly from above. It hit him in the back, sending him flying forward and somersaulting across the ground. When he came to a stop, he lay face-down in the dirt, his knife lost to the night. A growl rumbled from above. Quickly, he rolled onto his back, kicked his legs forward, and catapulted onto his feet, adrenaline thankfully coursing through his entire being.

The growl rumbled from a dark figure standing before him. Night shrouded the figure's face. The faintest scent of vampire wafted in the air.

"Hello, my old *friend*," the figure growled.

Aleric cocked his head. His senses truly were out of whack. He thought he recognized that voice, and if he was right, it didn't belong to any vampire.

"Jones?"

The figure moved closer, into a sliver of moonlight that had managed to cut through the forest canopy.

"Jones," he hissed confirmation of his adversary.

Not a vampire, but a predator of another sort. Someone must've put a price on his head. Jones never did anything unless money was involved. It was the only explanation as to why his old rival would be stalking him in the middle of the night, in the middle of nowhere.

"Who?" he asked. "Boldo? The ASA?"

Jones only scowled.

Aleric shrugged. It really didn't matter who. "How much?" he asked, mildly interested in what his head was worth.

Jones flashed fangs. "I'd kill *you* for nothing."

Aleric took an involuntary step back. After two hundred years, he thought nothing could surprise him anymore. He was wrong. And at the same time, right; he *had* smelled vampire.

"Your fucking Gypsy whore did this to me." Jones moved even closer.

This time Aleric didn't retreat. "Jeta's dead. I killed her."

"I know. I felt her die." The vampire ran a tongue across his teeth and fangs. "All the more reason to kill you. She was a whore, but she was my master, nonetheless."

Fangs bared, he lunged at Aleric's throat.

Aleric caught him in mid-flight, putting the vampire in a stranglehold. The two hit the ground on impact, Jones on top, Aleric on his back. He continued to choke the vampire, holding the thing's fangs at bay just inches from his face.

A crack of gunfire split the night.

The bullet hit the ground next to Aleric's head, kicking up dirt. A second shot chased the first, this one hitting the vampire square in the back. Jones cried out and spasmed. With the vampire weakened, Aleric pushed the thing from on top of him. Jones tumbled away as he climbed to his feet.

Again, gunfire cracked.

Like a metal mosquito, the bullet buzzed Aleric's ear. He wasn't sure who was the intended target, him or Jones, but at that moment it didn't matter. What mattered was unless the shooter was using silver bullets, the vampire wouldn't stay down long.

The next shot kicked up dirt at his feet.

That got him moving. He wasn't about to miss this golden opportunity to get much needed vampire blood. Jones was down at least temporarily and weakened. Despite the threat of catching a bullet, he needed to strike now.

Groaning, Jones began to climb to his feet.

Aleric bulldozed into the vampire, sending them both crashing back to the ground. They rolled in a frenzy of flailing arms and kicking legs, bullets whizzing all around them. With Jones weakened, it was Aleric who managed to get the upper hand. He bit into the vampire's neck—instead of the other way around—sinking teeth into flesh and drawing first blood. He clamped his mouth down tight, greedily sucking as much of the vampire's blood as he could.

With the monster hunter still attached and feasting, Jones growled and mewled at the same time as he struggled to his feet. They spun in circles, bullets whizzing about but missing their mark.

Out of nowhere, a large, hairy creature crashed through the foliage. It let out a beastly yowl as it grabbed the two adversaries, pulled them apart, and flung them in different directions.

Aleric hit a tree and thumped to the ground. He saw stars, and his world spun out of control. But he could also feel the vampire blood begin to course through his veins, giving him a shot of supernatural adrenaline. By the time he climbed to his feet, his vision had crystallized.

Jones had recovered, as well, but he was limping off into the forest to lick his wounds and surely ready himself to do battle another night.

The Skookum stood in the clearing. It beat its chest King Kong style and yowled. Two bullets slammed into the beast but only served to piss it off. Not sure where the attack was coming from, it struck out at the only adversary it could find.

Aleric.

Like a rampaging bull elephant, it charged.

Aleric sidestepped the attack and managed to slip around onto the beasts' back as it rushed past. He climbed the thing as if it were a redwood. Reaching the top, he hooked an arm around its throat, both choking it and holding on for dear life. Thankfully, the vampire blood was now reviving his entire being, bringing renewed vigor to every muscle, joint, and nerve ending, acting as a fountain of youth. Without it, the Skookum would demolish him. And it still might. But at least now, he had a fighting chance.

The gunfire ceased. Whoever had been taking potshots must have given up. Now it was just him and the Skookum, two adversaries squaring off and doing battle.

The beast spun and bucked, desperately trying to throw its unwanted rider.

He held on, choking the thing. Big, hairy arms reached back at him, grabbed at him. But he stayed on and kept a hold. The problem was he was never going to bring it down this way. It was too big, too strong. He'd lost his knife to the night. That left shooting it. But there was no way he could reach either the shotgun or the Magnum. His only choice was to let go.

He did just that. In free fall, he reached within his duster, pulled the Mossberg free, and pumped a round into the chamber. He managed to get a shot off before he hit the ground and just as the beast spun around to face him. He thumped to the ground, back and head slamming against dirt and duff. Simultaneously, the shotgun's blast slammed into the Skookum's chest, leaving a hole as big as a moon crater. Blood gushed from the wound, and the beast toppled like a fallen redwood. It crashed to the ground right next to him, a crushing deathblow just missing the monster hunter.

Groaning, he sat up and checked himself for broken bones. He struggled to catch his breath, and he was sore as hell, but it didn't feel as if any ribs had been broken. His limbs felt intact. Without further delay, he got to his knees, bent over the beast, and hungrily drank the thing's blood, letting the supernatural elixir finish the job the vampire blood had started, restoring his youth and bringing him back to the land of the living, at least temporarily. He would need this newfound strength, for when finished, he'd need to find his knife and cut off the thing's head to collect his reward.

Only then would he worry about the shooter and whether he was the intended target.

Chapter 12

With the C14 Timberwolf sniper rifle slung over his shoulder, Boot Deufer maneuvered through the woods, slowly making his way back to his SUV that he had left parked on the nearest access road. A mixture of anger and awe swirled through his brain. Anger at himself for missing his goddamn target multiple times. Very uncharacteristic, even considering the heavy blanket of darkness and the distance from which he took the shots. Awe for Bimbai, who was either the luckiest fucker in the world or who was truly the legend described in his dossier. Maybe it was a combination of both.

He stopped. Pushing back a shock of red hair from his eyes, he cocked his head and listened. He could've sworn he'd heard something moving through the brush. Not a human. And certainly not the goddamn Skookum. Nothing that big. Maybe a large dog or a coyote. But now there was nothing. Maybe it was just his imagination. Didn't matter. A dog or a coyote didn't concern him. He could handle either easily. It was humans and monsters that concerned him. He could handle them too. But he'd learned long ago not to let down his guard. It's why he was so good at his job. It's how he stayed alive.

He started off again, climbing a hill to the road where he left his rental car. With no further warning, the attack came from behind. A huge wolf pounced onto his back, bringing him down and dragging him back down the hill. With his face in the dirt, he tried to fend off the growling thing, but the wolf had him pinned to the ground under its weight, large paws pushing on the back of his head, keeping his face buried in the dirt. It didn't bite him, though, or try to harm him in any other way. It just continued to growl, its wet nose pressed against his neck, almost nuzzling him.

An instant later, the wolf transformed into a man, who continued to pin him to the ground with supernatural strength and sniffed his neck and hair as if still an animal.

"Who the fuck *are* you?" Boot croaked.

The man laughed. "Have some sympathy for the Devil," he whispered, as if he could read minds. "Besides, you and I want the same thing…Bimbai…dead."

Boot then realized the man on top of him was the vampire he'd shot in the back. Panic swelled in his chest. He tried to push up, legs kicking at the same time. But his struggle was futile. The vampire—even wounded—was too strong.

"You're going to help me," Jones hissed. "I'm going to be your new master."

"Fuck you."

"No. I'm going to fuck you." Jones pushed his hardened cock into Boot's ass and pressed fangs against his throat. "Right after." Fangs penetrated throat. And he sucked on his victim like a passionate lover.

Boot screamed. But his scream was quickly swallowed by the night as he relinquished his humanity to the world of the undead.

Chapter 13

The killer's experiment had been successful.

Mala sat on the floor of her cell. Except for the yellow *diklo* on her head, she was naked and exposed. Slowly, she was turning into the undead. Still, she was torturously mindful and self-aware, cognizant of her surroundings. She understood nothing would ever be the same, and soon, she would lose the ability to remember her name, her past.

Icky stood outside her door, staring through the barred window at her rotting nakedness, licking his dried and cracked lips as if she were a meal that he craved to devour.

Mala gave a deep growl and bared rotted teeth as warning to the deformed pervert.

But Icky grinned his own rotted grin. "Me likes a good fight." He licked his lips. "All the better." He reached down and rubbed his hard-on through his pants.

She growled and snarled.

"Ooo…me likes." He rubbed himself harder. With his other hand, he slipped the key into the lock and turned it. The lock clicked, but before he could open the cell door, the basement door opened and footsteps thumped on the stairs.

"Icky, it's time to do God's work."

At the sound of his master's voice, he took the key out of the lock and slid it back inside his pocket. He took one more glance at the naked zombie and gave his hard-on one more stroke. "Me be back," he warned her.

Mala growled and snarled.

"Icky." The killer stood at the bottom of the stairs. "God's work waits for no man."

Icky licked his lips and turned away. "Yes, master."

Double sets of footsteps thumped upstairs. The door closed. The lock clicked in place.

Mala stopped growling, stopped snarling, and slumped back against the cold, concrete wall. Tears rolled down her decaying cheeks and sobs choked her undead throat.

She didn't notice that the iron door to her cell stood ever-so-slightly ajar.

Chapter 14

The killer was one with the night in his black fedora and black trench coat. He also wore the surrounding San Francisco fog like a cloak of invisibility, secure in his belief that God provided the cover to protect him as he went about *His* work.

Two whores stood on the corner of Post and Bush Streets in the Tenderloin District. Business was apparently slow due to the dense fog. Few cars drove by. No one walked the streets.

He pulled the syringe of love potion #9 from the deep pocket of his trench coat and limped toward the whores, slipping the plastic cover from the hypodermic needle.

"Good evening, ladies," he said.

The two whores startled, having been taken by surprise being approached in the fog. When they saw him, they relaxed a bit. After all, he looked of money.

"You fucking scared us," one whore said.

He smiled and bowed slightly. "My apologies. I'm in need of a date this evening. There's a gala I must attend and have no one to escort. It would be somewhat embarrassing to show up without a beautiful woman on my arm. I'm willing to pay twice your usual fee."

Both whores eyed him with skepticism. But money was money.

"You're both very beautiful," he lied, "I'm not sure I could choose between you, but alas I can only escort one of you."

The two whores looked at one another.

"You go, Carmina," one said. "With everything you're going through, you deserve a special night and can really use the extra money."

The killer smiled. "I can assure you it will be a special night."

Carmina looked around. "I'm not fucking walking."

"I have a car and a driver waiting down the street, just a short distance." He extended his arm, bent at the elbow.

Carmina snickered. "What do you think, Lizzy?"

Lizzy nodded her approval and mouthed the words, *fucking money*.

Carmina again snickered. Still, she slipped her arm through the killer's. "A *gala*, huh? I've never been to a fucking gala. Am I dressed okay?"

"You look beautiful," he assured, "perfect, in fact." He bowed to the other whore. "Good evening, Madam."

He and Carmina turned around and walked off into the fog.

"You said you'd pay double?"

"Of course."

"That would be two goddamn hundred an hour. You sure that's okay?"

"Perfect."

A black van roared up the street and squealed to a stop next to them. Carmina gasped as he stuck the hypodermic into her neck, injecting her with #9. The side door to the van automatically opened. He threw her into the van. While she lay there, he ripped open her top and quickly carved *Zero Sin* into her skin, just above her breasts. As the door closed again, the van sped off, quickly lost within the dense city fog.

"Perfect."

Grinning, he tossed the spent syringe and needle into the gutter. He didn't worry about leaving fingerprints or DNA behind on it. His black-leather gloves would prevent that from happening.

Turning around, he limped back toward the second sinner. She had her back to him as he approached out of the fog and pulled a scalpel from his pocket.

"Excuse me, Madam."

Lizzie spun around, eyes wide. "Where the hell's Carmina?"

He smiled. "She sends her regards." He held up the scalpel, relishing the sudden look of fear on the whore's face.

Lizzy screamed.

He silenced that scream in one, swift slash of the scalpel across her throat, opening her from ear to ear. Blood gushed forward. She made a strange gurgling sound and dropped to the pavement.

He stood over his victim, fighting against the urge to remove her womb. He didn't have time to wait for Icky to return with the van, so they could take the body back where he could efficiently perform the surgery. His deformed assistant needed to get the other whore back to put her under lock and key before she began to turn. That complicated things. Maybe he could perform the surgery right there on the city street? He looked around. The fog prevented him from seeing too far, but he appeared to be alone. Still, there probably wasn't time to do a proper job. He would have to be satisfied with signing his work.

Hunkering down, he ripped open Lizzie's top, exposed her breasts, and with the scalpel wrote *Zero Sin*.

Chapter 15

Aleric felt resurrected. He arrived back in San Francisco with renewed vigor and boundless energy, walking the city streets, lost within its cold, foggy embrace. The combination of vampire and Skookum blood that now coursed through him would last for days, maybe even weeks. He would deliver the Skookum's head to the authorities in the morning and collect his much-needed money. For now, it rested in his freezer, safely away from where Odin could get at it; the damn raven would eat anything.

As he strolled through the streets, his thoughts turned to Pearsa. There was no telling how long it would take her to come back to him since he didn't know where she'd gone or how far she had traveled. He didn't know much. Except she was gone, and he still felt lost without her.

A woman's scream pierced the night, bringing him out of his self-pity. It lasted but a split second before being cut short, but with his senses once again fine-tuned, he was able to pinpoint from where it came. He rushed down the street toward the cry. Even through the fog, he was able to make out a dark figure up ahead. It was dressed in a trench coat and a fedora and was kneeling down in the street. Without breaking stride, he raced toward it, boot heels echoing in the otherwise quiet night. The figure, hearing his approach, jumped to its feet and ran off. Even noticeably limping, it disappeared quickly into the surrounding darkness and thick fog.

He slowed his pace as he approached where the figure had been kneeling. That's when he saw the body. It was a young girl, he guessed a prostitute from the way she was dressed. Her throat had been sliced open, and she now lay in a pool of her own blood. He hunkered down and checked for a pulse just to be sure. As he thought…dead. But to his surprise, as if the killer were an artist signing his work, the bastard had carved a signature into his victim's exposed breasts.

Zero Sin.

"*Cretchuno*," he whispered.

He stood and scanned the night. No sign of anyone. How could anyone limping move so fast? He looked down at the dead girl again. Since she was beyond help, he decided to find a pay phone to make an anonymous call to the police. Afterward, he spent the rest of the night hunting the limping figure in the trench coat and fedora but to no avail. What he did find, however, was a clue to Zero Sin's identity. A bloody surgeon's scalpel. And in the handle were the carved initials, A.F.

Chapter 16

Pearsa gripped the arm of her seat with one hand—the other arm in a cast and sling—knuckles white, fingernails digging in. The plane bucked and kicked through the turbulent air over the Rockies.

"Just think what you could do with two hands," the tall, blond flight attendant said with a slight lisp and a wink. "You could really hold on for dear life, honey."

Looking up, she gave the male flight attendant a tight-lipped smile. She sat in the middle seat, no one next to her on either side with the plane more than half empty. Her small, carry-on bag took up the seat next to the window. She released her death grip on the seat and instead put a protective hand on her broken arm—a badge of honor left over from her encounter with that vampire bitch, Jeta.

The smiling, young man with the drink cart had a name tag that read, Jimmy. "You could use a drink," he said, giving another wink.

She gave Jimmy a nod. "Vodka, please," she said. Then she mumbled, "And Xanax."

Jimmy tapped her arm. He said, "Honey, the vodka I can do, but you have to supply your own sedatives."

She gave the flight attendant another tight-lipped smile, not thinking she'd said that last request loud enough for him to hear.

"Ice?" Jimmy asked, reaching for a plastic cup.

She nodded.

"Don't worry, honey," Jimmy said as he poured vodka from a tiny bottle, "the captain swears we'll be through this turbulence soon." He handed her the plastic cup.

She took it with a trembling hand and immediately gulped half down.

"Here," the flight attendant said, "take another." He snuck another bottle into her hand and winked. "You look like you're going to need it."

"Thank you, Jimmy." She made a move for her carry-on bag. "How much?"

The flight attendant waved a hand at her and with a toothy grin, he pushed his cart farther down the aisle.

She downed the rest of the vodka in her cup. As she did so, a young woman with jet-black hair and wearing a white gown tiptoed past in bare feet. She headed toward the first-class section at the front of the plane.

"Jeta?" she whispered, almost choking.

She hadn't gotten a good look at the woman's face, but otherwise the woman looked a lot like her rival, and she couldn't help but jump to her greatest fear—somehow, despite word of Jeta's demise through the Gypsy grapevine, the vampire had survived and found her.

The woman maneuvered like a specter around—or was it through—Jimmy and his cart. An instant later, she disappeared through a curtain separating the two classifications of passengers.

Pearsa's hand shook as she struggled with the cap to the tiny vodka bottle, loosening it with her teeth and finally twisting it free with her good hand. Throwing the cap aside, she didn't bother with the glass of ice but instead downed the vodka straight from the bottle. She finished it in two gulps, throat burning, eyes tearing.

Within a vodka-induced haze, she absently reached for the silver *treshul* that hung from a chain about her neck. Aleric had given her the crucifix for protection against vampires, it being both a blessed, religious symbol and made of silver.

Staring at the curtain just a few feet away, she tried to convince herself that the woman she had seen couldn't have been Jeta. The vampire was supposed to be dead. Aleric had gotten word to her, and she trusted her lover at his word.

She continued to finger the *treshul* as she eyed the window. The shade was pulled down, blocking out any light. Was it day or night? In a blind panic, she reached across the empty seat and pushed the shade up. Weak daylight greeted her. She looked around. Other passengers had their shades up and were looking out. Still, not much sunlight penetrated the plane. Maybe the vampire could exist during the day if she remained out of the direct light from a window.

She wished she had gotten a better look, even just a glimpse of the woman's face. The jet-black hair, white gown, and bare feet could've been just an unfortunate coincidence. But what about the way the woman carried herself, almost floating past Jimmy like a ghost.

Probably just vodka-induced imagination, an optical illusion, she told herself.

Still, she felt an undeniable urge to get a closer look.

Screwing up her courage, she unbuckled her seatbelt. She used the back of the seat in front of her to pull herself to her feet. She stepped into the aisle as the plane hit a rough air current. The turbulence threw her sideways into an old man sitting across the aisle. To steady herself, she had to grab onto the man's shoulder.

The old man glowered. Under his breath, he grumbled, "Gypsy."

She released her hold. Ignoring the disparaging remark, she continued on toward the fateful curtain. Heart pounding. Head dizzy with vodka.

But the flight attendant and his cart still stood in her way. She saw no clear way around him.

"Excuse me, Jimmy," she murmured.

Jimmy looked up while pouring a passenger a drink. "You okay?"

"Yes." She forced a Mona-Lisa smile. "But I need to get to the restroom," she said, indicating the one just outside the curtain in front of them.

"That's going to be difficult, honey. There's just no room. There's one at the back of the plane, though."

She glanced over her shoulder. "Oh, yes," she mumbled, clearing her throat. "To be honest, Jimmy. There's a young lady that came up the aisle a few moments ago. I think I recognized her. She went into first class. I just wanted to see if it was really my friend."

The poor guy looked perplexed. He shook his head. "No one came past me, honey."

"Are you sure?"

He looked at the cart blocking the aisle then back at her. "I don't see how she could've."

She bit her lower lip and nodded. "You're probably right."

Jimmy gave her a sympathetic wink and handed her two more tiny bottles of vodka. "Maybe these will help."

She tried to smile in gratitude but could only manage pursed lips. With vodka in hand, she turned on her heel and stumbled down the aisle toward the rear restrooms.

She no longer had to see the young woman for herself. Jimmy had told her what she needed to know. Only something supernatural could've gotten past the flight attendant and his cart unseen and without incident.

She stuffed herself into the confined bathroom, slammed the door shut, and locked it. Staring at her pale reflection, she uncapped one bottle with her teeth. She spat the cap onto the floor and gulped the vodka. Finished, she uncapped the second bottle but didn't immediately drink it. Gathering herself, trying to slow her racing heart and panicked thoughts, she instead sipped this one, hoping to make it last, wondering how long she could remain safely within the locked bathroom with San Francisco still hours away.

The plane bucked. She knocked into the sink, her cast clunking against it.

If she was lucky, maybe the plane would go down before the vampire could get to her.

She took another sip of vodka and fingered the silver crucifix.

But she knew she could never get that lucky.

CHAPTER 17

Icky chained the whore to the wall of her cell. He had left the cell door open because his captive was still unconscious, and there was no worry of her escaping. Once he had the girl secured, the hunchback hunkered down, licking his dry, cracked lips and rotted teeth.

Mala in the next cell growled.

He paid her no mind. His full attention was on the whore before him. Opening the girl's blouse, he pulled it apart, exposing her breasts. The sight of the whore's nipples immediately hardened him. He reached out with a dirty, gnarled hand, hesitated, and then brushed his fingers across one tit and nipple. He groaned, rubbing himself with his other grubby hand.

"Me likes," he mumbled. "Ooo…me likes…"

The growls next door continued.

That just excited him more. Now he squeezed the whore's tit as if it were a melon he needed to test before buying.

Mala banged against her iron door. The master hadn't wanted her shackled. But he wasn't worried. He knew she was secure in her locked cell.

He stopped rubbing himself and now used both hands to disrobe the unconscious whore. Once she was completely naked, he stood before her, pulled down his pants, and began to masturbate in earnest.

"Ooo…me likes…me likes…"

Lost in self-induced lust, he didn't hear or pay attention to the approaching growls from behind. He was too busy ejaculating all over the undead woman lying at his feet. By the time he did hear the approaching growls and turned toward the sound, it was too late.

From a crouch, Mala pounced, clamping her mouth around Icky's exposed penis. She bit down hard and ripped the appendage away from her victim.

Icky screamed. His hands pressed against his bleeding crotch as he fell backwards, on top of the whore he had just ejaculated upon.

Mala spat out the chewed penis and pounced again, this time landing on her jailor's chest and sinking her rotted teeth into his neck.

Icky's piercing screams—like him—died a slow painful death.

Chapter 18

When the killer arrived back at his lair, he found the front door standing open.

"Icky," he muttered.

That idiot. What was he thinking? Anyone could've wandered inside and discovered his secrets.

"Icky," he yelled.

Slamming the door behind him, he limped through the house, discarding his trench coat and fedora as he went.

"Icky!"

A stiff punishment was in order—a beating for sure. He stomped into the kitchen but then stopped in his tracks. The basement door stood open too. Before he had just been angry at Icky for stupidity and forgetfulness, but now he had to wonder whether something was seriously and dangerously wrong.

He stared at the open doorway for some time, unsure of what he should do, unsure of just how much danger all of this presented. What if something had happened to Icky? What if the zombies were roaming free? If they were, the danger might not even be in the basement. Those things could be anywhere in the house.

A shiver shot up his spine. He gulped and peeked over his shoulder to make sure nothing was behind him. Nothing was, but that just meant he was in no immediate danger.

Another thought provoked a new shiver. Maybe they weren't in the house at all. Maybe the open front door didn't mean someone got in but instead meant the zombie whores got out.

Where in God's name was Icky? He needed answers. And he needed help in searching the house.

But he was getting ahead of himself. First, he'd have to look in the basement. Maybe there was no need for concern. Maybe the zombies were still in their cells. Maybe Icky was down there right now playing with his zombie toys. Of course if he was, he'd be punished. But that would still be better than the alternative.

He asked God for protection as he crossed the threshold to the basement and descended the stairs. At first glance, he didn't see anything out of the ordinary. Then he came to the cells that were supposed to imprison the zombie whores. The cells were empty except for a corpse. His hunchback assistant lay in a pool of his own blood within one cell, pants down around his knees, bleeding out from his crotch, face half eaten. Not far from the body lay his dismembered cock.

He sighed and muttered, "We're all works in progress."

Only this time there was no way Icky could learn from his mistake, no way to better himself, no way to atone for his sins. In the end, he had lived and died a loathsome creature.

Just to be sure his assistant didn't come back from the dead, the killer retrieved a pair of surgical scissors. He shoved them through the hunchback's ear, into his brain. With that taken care of, he searched the entire house from top to bottom, but there was no sign of the zombie whores. Thanks to carelessness and perversions, they were loose.

No matter. That was the plan all along anyway. He was less in control of the situation than he planned or wanted, but the results would be the same. Soon the miscreants and perverts of this city would feel God's wrath.

Meanwhile, he began to clean up the mess that was once Icky.

Chapter 19

Aleric returned home to his second-story apartment on Post Street after a night of searching for the limping figure that had fled the murder scene. All he had to show for his trouble was a scalpel with the initials A.F. engraved on the handle. A.F. was Zero Sin. But who in the hell was A.F.?

"Nevermore," Odin said in way of greeting.

Not for the first time, he regretted reading the bird Edgar Allan Poe.

The raven was perched on the coffee table in front of the sofa. The remote control sat on the table in front of the large, black bird. Odin pecked at the remote, channel surfing. The TV flipped from channel to channel at lightning speed. No sound came out of the accompanying speakers, so either the volume was turned down or the sound system was on mute.

He plopped down on the couch and put his feet up on the table next to his roommate, combat boots still on.

The raven finally settled on a news channel. A pretty, blonde anchorwoman filled the screen.

"Good choice." He reached into the pocket of his Duster and pulled out the raven's breakfast. "Here you go." He plopped the dead rat onto the table.

Odin squawked then immediately began to tear into the rodent.

On the TV screen, the blonde anchorwoman was replaced by what appeared to be a dead man. And to his eyes, the dead man looked to be chewed up from a zombie attack to boot. This took him by surprise because he wasn't aware of any current or new infestations, either in the city or any outlying areas.

"Turn it up," he commanded.

Odin paused in his breakfast long enough to hit the volume button in three successive raps.

The blonde anchorwoman came back on. "Early this morning, a policeman in the Tenderloin came across this man, Alejandro Torres, a forty-three-year-old who lives in the Mission."

A picture of the man before being bitten and ripped into appeared in the upper right-hand corner of the screen, so viewers could still see the pretty blonde.

"Mr. Torres was being ravaged by two naked women. The two women ran off when the policeman approached. They have not been found."

He shook his head. How in the hell can two naked women avoid apprehension and go unnoticed? Only in San Francisco.

The TV again showed the dead Mr. Torres. He was indeed ravaged, shirt ripped off, chunks of flesh missing from his face and torso, one hand still clutching a yellow scarf.

The anchorwoman continued, "When asked if this could possibly be the beginning of a zombie outbreak, police spokeswoman Lt. Jane Armory said that she doubted it. She claimed the two women apparently did not move or behave like typical zombies."

He again shook his head. The two women were caught eating their victim, but they didn't behave like zombies? Yeah, right.

The anchorwoman continued, "Lt. Armory also stated that Mr. Torres is under close observation at Mission Hospital. He's expected to recover."

That got his attention. He was sure the victim looked dead. How had he survived?

"But if he takes a turn for the worse and expires then the zombie question will be answered." The blonde smiled her pretty smile as if she were talking about puppies and children rather than death and the undead. "Mr. Torres' reanimation or lack thereof would confirm one way or the other whether there is concern of a new zombie outbreak. Until then, the police will treat this case as a random assault and will work on identifying and apprehending the two suspects."

"*Cretchuno!*" He couldn't believe his ears. It confirmed what he had always believed: Cops were fucking assholes, lacking in both logic and imagination.

"Turn it off. I've heard enough."

Between bites, Odin complied.

Aleric wasn't about to wait on Mr. Torres to expire and turn. First, he planned on visiting the victim in the hospital to terminate the threat. Then, he would hunt for the zombies. After all, how hard could it be to locate two naked zombies roaming the streets of San Francisco?

Soon, he would find out.

He raced for the door. When he opened it, Pulika stood on the other side, poised to knock.

"*Droboy tume Romale*, Pulika." Aleric eyed the skinny boy. Something was wrong. Dark bags circled Pulika's eyes, and his curly, black hair was even more disheveled than usual, sticking up and out in all directions. "What is wrong?"

Pulika tried to catch his racing breath. "Mala, she's…she's missing…didn't come home last night. I-I've been looking for her all night."

Aleric led the boy to his sofa and sat him down next to Odin.

"She…went out yesterday…to tell fortunes…door to door."

Aleric nodded. "She stopped here to see me."

Pulika wiped tears away and choked back sobs. "Where can she be? What's happened to her?" Then he turned angry. "I told her not to trust the *gadje*."

"Aleric will find her," Odin squawked. The raven hopped onto Pulika's lap.

"Trust the bird," Aleric said. "He speaks the truth."

Pulika wiped away more tears and pet Odin. "I trust him." He looked at Aleric with pleading eyes. "I trust you."

Aleric patted the boy on the back. "Go home. I will bring Mala to you when I find her."

Pulika did as he was told.

Aleric raced to the hospital. Worry and fear fed on his mind. He should've listened to his gut. It tried to warn him that Mala was walking into danger the morning she visited. If he hadn't been in such a deteriorated state, he might've listened. Now she was lost, wandering through a city infested with naked zombies and a serial killer.

But as worried as he was for Mala, he first had to get to Mr. Torres. The danger of him turning into the undead was immediate and imminent.

Chapter 20

As Aleric strode down the hallway, he caught sight of a uniformed cop posted outside Mr. Torres' hospital room. For all he knew, there could also be plain clothes detectives nearby or roaming the hallway. He wasn't going to be able to just walk up to the door, go in, and take care of business. He thought about finding the linen closet where the hospital kept extra scrubs, stealing a pair and masquerading as a doctor. But that plan had too many possible flaws and too many opportunities for him to be discovered. Besides, it was also too time consuming. Instead of stealth, he needed a diversion. Something that would get the cop to leave the door unattended for a short time and occupy everyone's attention. He figured he could always go old school and pull the fire alarm.

Before he could do anything, a woman's scream exploded from inside Mr. Torres' room. The cop didn't react right away, hesitating as if unsure of what the scream meant or what to do about it. In that hesitation, Aleric took action, stampeding past the cop and barreling through the closed door.

The thud of the door banging against the inside wall challenged the woman's scream but only for a moment. The bang of the door silenced quickly, whereas the scream rose to almost glass-shattering pitch.

Inside the room, he pulled up short. A zombie that was once Mr. Torres sat in bed. It bit into the nurse, and not for the first time by all appearances, ripping off a large chunk of flesh. Blood spurted everywhere. The nurse's scream slowly died as she went into shock.

"Cretchuno," he swore.

They hadn't even been smart enough to restrain Torres while they waited to see if he would turn or not, costing the poor nurse her life.

He pulled his large knife from the sheath at his boot and attacked, sending the blade of the knife deep into the zombie's skull, piercing its brain and putting it out of its misery. He pulled the knife free. The nurse lay across the zombie's lap, still alive but barely. Loss of blood and shock would soon finish her off. Then she would turn too. He raised his knife to do what he knew he must.

"Freeze!"

With knife poised for a deathblow, he turned his attention toward the source of the command.

The cop stood in the doorway, revolver drawn and aimed. "Don't move or I'll shoot. You're under arrest."

Aleric snarled. "*Hush kacker, gadje!*"

The cop looked confused, hesitant.

In the excitement of the moment, Aleric had forgotten himself and spoke in Romani to this *gadje* pig. "Shut up and listen, *gadje*," he repeated in English. "This poor woman is dying and then she will turn, just like Torres."

Indecision plagued the cop's face. He gulped hard. "I can't let you do it."

"Shoot then." Aleric shrugged. "*Te aves yertime mander tai te yertil tut o Del.*" With that, he plunged the knife into the nurse's skull, piercing her brain, preventing her from turning. He pulled the knife out and cleaned the blade on his pants.

The cop lowered his weapon. "What did that mean?"

Aleric grinned. "I forgive you and may God forgive you as I do."

Sheathing his knife, he strode past the cop and out the door. With sirens blaring in the distance, he hurried out of the hospital. He desperately needed to find the two naked zombies. He was sure Dr. Ratterman—even though dead—was responsible. Or at least his serum was responsible. Even worse, the significance of the yellow scarf in Torres' dead hand suddenly and inexplicably hit him, and he was sure that when he found the two zombies, he would find Mala too.

Chapter 21

Pearsa's plane landed at dusk. Bag in hand, she quickly headed for the exit. But then she saw Jeta and pulled up short. At least she thought it was Jeta who was heading for the same exit. Certainly, it was the same dark-haired beauty from the plane—barefoot and wearing a white dress. She still couldn't make out the woman's face, though. She had to get a closer look to be sure. But did she dare?

She must. She had to know.

Jeta exited through the automatic doors.

Pearsa took a deep breath and hurried after her. Once through the automatic doors, she put on the brakes and scanned her surroundings. Cabs were lined up along the curb, taking on passengers. People rushed to and fro with luggage. But the vampire was nowhere in sight.

She looked up and down the walkway, examining everyone getting in and out of cabs, as well as each passerby.

Still no sign of the vampire. How could she have disappeared so quickly?

By turning into mist or maybe a bat, that's how.

At that, Pearsa's knees almost buckled. Her heart slammed against her ribcage. More and more, she was convinced that Jeta still lived and was stalking her.

"Miss, you okay?"

The question brought her out of her thoughts and fears. She turned around.

A young man with shaggy, red hair, a crooked grin, and steely-blue eyes stared back at her. "You okay, miss?"

The guy's eyes flustered her. They seemed to bore into her, straight through to her soul. "Yes, yes," she stammered, "I'm all right."

The young man nodded. "Need a cab?" He pointed over his shoulder to the yellow cab parked behind him.

She nodded and smiled.

"Here, let me help you. Getting around can't be easy with a broken arm." The cabbie stepped forward and took her bag. He popped the cab's trunk and threw the bag inside. Then he opened the backdoor.

"Thank you." Pearsa climbed into the cab. The door slammed behind her.

The cabbie was behind the wheel in seconds, starting the engine.

Please allow me to introduce myself...

The cabbie grabbed his iPhone and turned off the music playing through the radio. "Sorry, I forgot to turn that off. I normally don't play music when I have a fare."

"That's okay. The Stones, right?"

The cabbie nodded. "Where to?"

She hadn't given where she would stay much thought. With her fortunetelling parlor burned down, the only place left for her to go was Aleric's, so she gave the cabbie the address and then sunk back into the seat and cradled her broken arm, trying to relax.

But that wasn't to be. There would be no peace of mind as long as she worried that Jeta was still out there. The vampire bitch had already tried to kill her twice. The only reason she had returned to San Francisco was because Aleric had sent word that Jeta was dead. Why would he do that if it wasn't the case? He wouldn't. But she was sure she saw Jeta with her own eyes. Lost within this labyrinth of confusion, she paid no attention to where the cabbie was taking her. Soon, the cab pulled up in front of an old warehouse.

The cabbie turned in his seat and looked back at her. "Time to get out." He flashed fangs.

She opened her mouth to scream, but nothing came out. All she could manage were choking sounds. Blood pounded in her ears.

In a flash, the vampire was out his door and opening hers. He grabbed her by the hair and dragged her from the car. All the while, he whistled *Sympathy for the Devil*.

She punched with her one good hand and kicked with both legs as she was dragged to the warehouse, taken inside, and dragged across a massive, empty room into a lit office. The vampire slammed the door and released his hold on her hair. She fell to the floor.

"Boot, stop whistling that fucking tune."

The vampire cabbie stopped.

Breathing hard, panic rising in waves from her gut to her throat, she looked up to see an ugly man with a scar and a buzzed haircut sitting royal-like on a tattered sofa. Next to him was the barefoot Gypsy in white.

"You're not Jeta."

The ugly one flashed fangs. "No, she's not. My mistress is dead. This is my ... *assistant*."

The girl smiled. No fangs; she wasn't yet a full-fledged vampire.

'She's a damn good facsimile, though," the ugly one continued. "Don't you think?"

Pearsa didn't answer. Her attention was instead drawn to the three dead bodies that littered the office floor.

The ugly vampire cackled. "Those were gifts from King Boldo." With the back of his hand, he caressed the face of the barefoot Gypsy sitting next to him. "I'm gaining new appreciation for Gypsy blood."

Boot snorted. "It's the only thing Gypsies are good for."

"Now, Boot, they're good for a fuck too."

"Who the hell are you?" Pearsa pushed her long hair out of her face. "And what the fuck do you want?"

"My name's Jones. Maybe Bimbai told you about me."

"Why would he speak to me of scum like you?"

Boot reached down, grabbed her by the hair, and shook her head. "Show some respect, Gypsy cunt."

Jones cackled. "It's okay, Boot. Let her have her moment. Soon, she'll be licking my cock and begging for more."

She struggled to her feet. Her broken arm dangled at her side in its cast, the sling having been torn away in the struggle. "Don't count on it, you piece of shit." Her bravado hid her terror, both from the vampires and from herself.

Jones stood, facing his prey. "For now I need you alive. You're the cheese to catch the mouse." He ran his tongue along his teeth and fangs. "But don't press your luck, bitch. Alive doesn't mean unharmed." He smiled. "Maybe I'll give you to Boot as a plaything."

She hated herself for what she was about to say, but she had few—if any—options. She didn't want to end up Boot's plaything or end up drained of her blood like the three Gypsies on the floor. "Guarantee my safety, and I'll help you. I'll give you Bimbai on a silver platter." She needed to bide her time, make them think she would help them, and hope her lover could figure it out and save her.

Jones and Boot laughed. The barefoot girl just looked confused.

Jones said, "I can see now what Bimbai sees in you. But why should you help us?"

She shrugged and tried to look coy. "A girl will do anything not to die."

Jones stepped close. "I accept your offer. But I don't trust you. You'll betray me first chance you get." He reached out and grabbed her by the shoulders. "There is a way to guarantee your loyalty, though."

She reached for the silver *treshul* and held it up for the vampire to see.

Jones looked mildly annoyed. "Lavinia, the crucifix."

Before she could even anticipate, the barefoot girl was on her, yanking the crucifix from around her neck. The very next second, the vampire's fangs penetrated her throat. The sharp pain brought a gasp to her lips, tears to her eyes, and panic to her heart.

She had miscalculated. Her plan had backfired.

As she lost more and more blood, the room began to spin, her eyes glazed over, and her head felt empty and light. Panic was soon replaced by complacency, and pain was replaced by pleasure.

She groaned and held on tight until darkness swept her completely away.

Chapter 22

Night settled on the Tenderloin District. The streets turned into wind tunnels, a cold chill blowing along the front of buildings on both sides of the street. Aleric plunged his hands deep inside the pockets of his duster and hunched his shoulders as he stalked the streets, visiting the scene where Torres was attacked, looking for clues. What he found sickened him. Out of the gutter, he picked up Mala's dirty *diklo*, confirming his worse fears.

"Cretchuno!"

He still had to wonder how two naked zombies could avoid notice and capture. But then it was San Francisco, where strangeness occurred daily, and people hardly noticed anymore. What he hoped was that Mala and her zombie friend were still hiding somewhere nearby.

Out of the darkness, someone came towards him. It looked to be a man, walking with a slight limp. The man who killed that prostitute the other night had walked with a limp. A block away, the man turned a corner down another wind-swept street.

Aleric started up again, quickening his pace. Before he could reach the corner and continue his pursuit, he was attacked from behind by growling zombies. They jumped on his back, teeth gnashing at his neck and face. But he was stronger than his attackers and didn't go down. Instead, he spun, taking the things on a merry-go-round ride. Before either could bite him, he succeeded in throwing them clear, sending them crashing onto the pavement and rolling into the gutter.

When the zombies jumped to their feet, he saw that one of them was Mala. He was embarrassed for her nakedness and sickened by her condition. But he had no time to dwell on it.

The two attackers wasted no time, splitting up, one to the right and one to the left, advancing on him from two sides. Mala and her friend were definitely no ordinary zombies. They were too quick and fluid in their movements, and they didn't just blindly attack as if on instinct like most undead. Instead, they coordinated their efforts. They had a plan. They came at him, crouched low, growling and ready to attack, ready to bite.

He sidestepped Mala as she advanced on his left, pulling his knife at the same time and plunging it deep into the skull of the other zombie as it pounced from the right. Black gunk splattered the ground as he pulled out his knife and the thing thumped to the ground. Mala was back on him in a flash, screeching and jumping onto his shoulder and back. He could feel her hot, fetid breath on his neck and face. He had to overpower her, and quickly. Before she could bite, he flipped her over his shoulder to the pavement. In an instant, he had his duster off, throwing it over her head and wrapping her in it like a protective cocoon. Using the blunt end of his knife, he hit her in the head, knocking her unconscious.

With Mala subdued, he examined the dead zombie at his feet, noticing something carved into its skin, just above its breasts. He hunkered down for a closer look. As with the dead prostitute, Zero Sin had signed his work.

It must have been the serial killer who found Ratterman's memory stick and reproduced one of the serums. It was the only explanation.

"*Cretchuno.*"

It was his fault this was happening again. It was he who had lost the memory stick with Ratterman's files on it. Mala would not have gone through this if not for his carelessness.

To save Mala, he needed to find Zero Sin. If the killer had the serum then he must also have the antidote.

The limping man was his only clue.

He stood. After returning the knife to its sheath, he lifted Mala, slung her over his shoulder, and hurried off in pursuit. He turned the corner, hoping the trail had not gone completely cold.

But it had. There was no sign of the guy and no clue as to where he could've gone.

He stood there, the wind whipping around him, unsure of what to do next. A squeak and a bang accompanied the whistle of the wind. He looked toward the source. A sign in front of a large Victorian swung back and forth on hooks, banging against the wooden frame from which it hung. The sign read: Albert Finch, MD Psychiatrist.

Interesting. He took the scalpel he had found from his pants pocket. The initials A.F. were carved into the handle. Coincidence? He didn't believe in coincidences.

He made his way up the stairs to the front door and rang the bell. No answer. He shrugged. That wouldn't stop him. He tried the door. Locked. That wouldn't stop him either. Setting Mala down, he took the scalpel and stuck the blade into the bottom half of the keyhole on the doorknob. He applied pressure in one direction and then another, wiggling the scalpel around in the lock until he heard a click.

He was in.

The door swung open. He picked up Mala and crossed the threshold, pocketing the scalpel and unholstering his .44 Mag. Darkness prevailed inside. At least the street lights outside cast a sickly glow. Inside the house there wasn't even that. Luckily, since drinking vampire and skookum blood, his night vision had improved.

Cautiously, he inched his way into the room, avoiding furniture as he moved, scanning for signs of anyone hiding within the shadows and listening for any movement. He made it across the front room without incident. The next room turned out to be a kitchen. A dim, sliver of light sneaked out from underneath a closed door that stood against the far wall. He quickly scanned the kitchen before moving to the door. An open padlock hung from the door's latch. Either someone forgot to lock it after coming back through or they were at that moment on the other side.

Waiting.

Gently he set Mala down and opened the creaking door, sounding an alarm to anyone who might be on the other side. Damn. But there was nothing he could do. The door was open. The alarm had been sounded. He now stood at the top of a long, wooden staircase, lit only by one bare light bulb. Knowing full well that whoever lurked in the basement knew he was coming, he slowly descended. Stairs creaked underfoot, further warning of his descent. From the last stair, he stepped down into a large, cold and musty room. Overhead, fluorescent lights flickered in and out, emitting a low *ping*. Gray, concrete walls surrounded him. A gray, concrete floor stretched out underfoot.

There was no sign of life.

The room was home to a makeshift laboratory, complete with brewing concoctions bubbling in heated beakers and moving through labyrinths of rubber tubing.

Most likely one of Ratterman's experiments. Before leaving, he would destroy it.

Also in the room was a desk with a computer under the staircase. But far more interesting was the walk-in freezer against the far wall. He made his way to the freezer and opened the large, metal door. There were only glass jars lined up on shelves. What was in them, he didn't know or care. All he cared about was that no one was hiding inside the icy world.

He searched the rest of the basement but found nothing of consequence; just the typical trappings of the average serial killer's den: harsh light, steel table, surgical tools, cells, lots of heavy, clear plastic, and blood. He crossed back into the lab.

The attack came immediately and without warning. Zero Sin had been waiting for him, hiding against the wall, just on the other side of the doorway. The killer attacked from behind, hooking an arm around his throat and shoving a hypodermic needle into his neck, just below his right ear.

Before the deadly serum could be plunged into him, he reached around, grabbing his attacker and freeing himself from immediate danger. He flung the bastard across the room, sending him crashing into the laboratory equipment. Tables flipped. Beakers and test tubes shattered, glass flying everywhere. Spilled concoctions splattered the walls and floor.

Zero Sin lay amongst the debris, disheveled and dazed, moaning and shaking his head.

Aleric holstered his .44. With the hypodermic needle still sticking out of his neck, he advanced, glass crunching under his heavy boots. Before his adversary could even think of recovering, he pulled the needle free and stuck it into the back of Zero Sin's own neck, plunging the serum into his system.

Afterward, he hunkered in front of the shocked and subdued killer and sneered. "I'm not one of your defenseless victim's, *Albert.*"

Zero Sin stared, realization of what just happened crossing the features of his face. "No, no, what have you done?"

"It's time to pay for your sins." Aleric took a fistful of shirt and hauled the asshole to his feet. He dragged his adversary back through the plastic room to one of the cells.

Zero Sin struggled, kicking his feet and flailing punches at Aleric's arm and legs. "You can't do this. I'm an instrument of God. *He* will never forgive you. You will be damned if you do this."

The warnings fell on deaf ears as Aleric threw Zero Sin into the cell and slammed the iron door shut. He looked through the barred window.

The killer scrambled to his knees. "There is an antidote. Give it to me and all will be forgiven. Don't…and you will be damned to hell for all eternity."

"I'm listening," Aleric answered. "Where is it?"

"On the stainless steel tray, next to the surgeon's table. The vial with the white label, marked *Forgiveness*."

Aleric retrieved the vial and a hypodermic needle. He held it up to the window. "Is this it?"

The killer was still on his knees as if in prayer. "Yes, yes…give it to me."

Aleric filled the hypodermic with the antidote. He answered, "Let us do evil, that good may come, whose damnation is just. What then? Are we better than they? No, in no wise; for we have before proved both Jews, Gentiles, and Gypsies that they are all under sin; as it is written, *there is none righteous, no, not one*." He sneered. "Romans, Chapter 3, Verse 8, 9, and 10, you righteous prick."

Defeated, the killer gaped but said no more.

"I have someone else, someone truly righteous, who is much more in need of this. Goodbye, Albert. May God show you mercy I couldn't."

Aleric turned away and quickly ascended the stairs, administering the antidote to a still unconscious Mala. He then returned to the basement. With the lab already destroyed from the fight, he went to the computer. There, he found Ratterman's flash drive. He crushed it under his heavy boot. Afterward, he wrecked the computer beyond hope of recovering any files.

Before leaving, he visited the cells. The zombie that was once Albert Finch rushed the iron door, rotting teeth snapping at the window, desperate to get at him. By the look in the thing's eyes, he knew that Albert was still in there somewhere, painfully conscious and aware of who he had been and what he now had become but unable to stop or control his zombie urges.

Aleric turned away.

Zero Sin's reign of terror on San Francisco was ended, and finally Dr. Wilhelm Ratterman's evil experiments, like the doctor himself, were truly dead. More importantly, Mala was saved.

With his business finished, Aleric left the unholy house.

Maybe he could sleep tonight once Mala was safely home. Maybe.

But he didn't think so.

Chapter 23

Mala was conscious and talking before Aleric left her in Pulika and Wasso's care. Mercifully, she didn't remember anything of being undead. He prayed that would always be the case. With her in good hands and resting comfortably, he returned to his apartment.

Odin immediately squawked at him.

"*Cretchuno*, Odin, be quiet."

He slammed the door. But then he stopped. Something wasn't right. He could sense it.

Odin again squawked a warning.

He looked around. Someone had been there. He sniffed the air. Vampire.

Unsheathing his silver-bladed knife, he cautiously searched the entire apartment. As he thought, only the lingering smell of the damned thing remained; the vampire itself was gone.

"What did it want, Odin? Why was it here?"

The raven squawked and flew to the table in front of the TV. "Nevermore." Odin danced around as if standing on a hot plate.

He followed the bird to the table. "Damn." Reaching down, he picked up the silver *treshul* lying there.

Odin picked up a piece of paper and danced around with it in his beak.

He took the paper from the raven. Only an address was written on it. After reading it, he crushed the paper into a ball within his fist.

The vampire had Pearsa.

Chapter 24

With no thought given to his own safety, Aleric rushed to the address on the piece of paper. It turned out to be an old, empty warehouse in the China Basin. He had no plan and no backup. His attack would be straight on. Whoever the vampire was, he'd destroy it. His only thought was to save Pearsa.

The door was unlocked. He entered a dark, massive room, utterly empty. A lit office stood on the other side of the room. A beacon of light came through a large, front window, calling to him in the surrounding darkness. His boots echoed in the void as he crossed to the office door. He did not hesitate. He threw the door open.

What waited on the other side brought him up short. Bodies of Gypsies lay strewn about on the floor. Four of them. By the tattered sofa against the far wall stood a woman with her back to him. She wore a white dress, was barefoot, and had long, black hair.

He sucked in air. "Jeta…"

But it couldn't be. His wife was dead. He had plunged the stake into her heart himself and drank the last of her blood.

"Jeta," he said her name again, louder.

The woman in white turned.

It wasn't Jeta. It was an imposter, a Gypsy girl posing as his one-time bride.

The door behind him slammed. He wheeled toward the sound.

Jones and a red-haired man stood between him and the door, between him and escape. It didn't matter. He wasn't looking to escape.

"Here to finish the job, what you couldn't finish out in the woods?" He eyed the redhead with Jones. "I see you brought help." He sneered. "You're going to fucking need it."

Jones cackled. The redhead next to him flashed fangs.

He shrugged. "Even two vampires won't give me much trouble."

"You're awfully sure of yourself, Gypsy," the redhead growled.

"Show some respect, Boot." Jones took a step forward. "You're talking to a goddamn legend." He paused. "Do you like my facsimile of Jeta?"

Aleric didn't acknowledge the existence of the girl behind him. "Where's Pearsa?"

Boot stepped up alongside Jones.

Fake Jeta moved in closer from behind.

But he didn't flinch. Let the attack come. "Where'd you get these Gypsies?"

"Your friend King Boldo offered them up as sacrifice for his life." Jones smacked his lips. "Gypsy blood…delicious."

Aleric stiffened. "Boldo Tene is no more king than his brother."

"Nevertheless." Jones spread his arms out, palms up. "He gave up these three for us to feed upon."

Aleric glanced about the room. "I count four."

"Oh, one of them you gave us." Jones grinned.

Boot snickered.

"Pearsa?" Aleric muttered. He looked around again. One of the bodies had an arm in a cast.

Jones cackled.

Aleric went to Pearsa, hunkered down next to her, and felt for a pulse. There was none. What was he to do without her? Enraged, he stood with fists tight at his sides.

Jones shrugged again. "I guess you're too late."

"I'll kill you."

Boot growled. The girl hissed.

"All three of you."

He pulled the silver-bladed knife just as the girl lunged at his back. He turned and grabbed her by the throat. With one hard squeeze, he crushed her windpipe. The sickening crack of it echoed in the small room.

Boot was on him before he could even discard the girl's corpse, so he used it like a club to beat the vampire off, knocking him across the room. Then he threw the corpse at Jones, slowing the vampire's advance just long enough to make a counter move with his knife, slicing forearm.

Jones howled. Smoke rose off the silver-induced wound. He cradled his arm and fell to his knees.

Aleric advanced to finish the job, but Boot intercepted him, knocking him off his feet. Grabbing Boot as he fell, he brought the vampire down on top of him. He held Boot in a bear hug as he planted the blade of his knife through the temple and into the brain. The vampire collapsed, mortally wounded and bleeding out. After slurping up a bit of blood, he shoved the corpse away and jumped to his feet in one smooth motion.

But Jones was already on him, knocking the knife from his hand and shoving him backwards. The momentum took them both through the large window, smashing glass and hurtling them into the room beyond the office. The two rolled as one for several feet before breaking apart and going their separate ways.

Jones came to a stop in a crouch, ready to lunge despite the wounded arm.

Aleric rolled up onto his feet, into a shooter's stance, .44 drawn and aimed.

Jones grinned. "Bullets won't stop me," he growled. Then he leapt.

Aleric fired.

The sound of the shot echoed off the walls of the warehouse. The bullet hit the vampire in mid-leap, sending him crashing facedown onto the concrete floor. Blood pooled underneath him.

Using the toe of his boot, Aleric kicked the vampire over onto his back.

Not yet destroyed, Jones looked up in shock, blood oozing from both the chest wound and his mouth.

"Silver bullets," Aleric growled, holstering his revolver. He retrieved his knife, and returned, standing over his conquered nemesis.

The vampire coughed and gagged on his own blood. "Finish it," he choked.

Aleric knelt down. He poised the knife over the vampire, the tip of the silver blade resting against its chest. *"Te del o beng ande tute. Te xal tu phuv."*

Jones spat out blood. "What the fuck does that mean, Gypsy?"

"The devil shall take you. The earth shall devour you."

Jones spat blood into Aleric's face. "Get on with it, Gypsy scum."

Aleric licked Jones' blood from around his mouth and chin. *"Guav cho muy."* He leaned closer. "That means, fuck your face." He jabbed the point of the knife into the vampire's chest. Slowly and painfully, he cut out the creature's heart.

The ensuing screams were like the high-pitched yowls of a wolf being slaughtered.

He held up the still beating vampire heart. Before it could stop, he ate it raw. He left the corpse where it lay and went to the other vampire, still lying on the office floor, mortally wounded.

He knelt down next to Boot. *"Guav cho muy,"* he said as he carved into the vampire's chest and removed its heart. This one had only the slightest beat, but he ate it anyway.

He stood. The life force of the vampires surged through him like an overdose of steroids. His heart beat so hard he thought it might break through his ribcage. His limbs felt on fire. His senses were heightened, on edge. He hadn't felt this powerful and invincible since sharing blood with Jeta.

Still, no matter how vigorous he felt physically, emotionally he was broken. Pearsa was gone, taken from him forever.

He turned away from the unanimated vampire at his feet, making his way to his love. But she was gone. The other three bodies were still there, but hers had disappeared. How could that be? He had felt for a pulse. There was none. The dead don't just get up and walk away.

Unless…

He turned and hurried out of the office, his footfalls echoing through the warehouse. How could he let it happen again? He failed Pearsa just as he had failed Jeta almost two hundred years ago. He flung the door open and crossed the threshold into the San Francisco night. Throwing his head back, he howled at the moonless sky, his cry of despair reverberating to both Heaven and Hell.

Chapter 25

Movement from the other side of the closed door mercifully shook Aleric from his morose thoughts and burgeoning guilt concerning Pearsa and her plight. He waited in the dark bedroom of the scum Boldo Tene, sitting in a rocking chair, long coat open and hanging to the floor. A compact shotgun lay across his lap. His hand tightened around the pistol grip.

The door creaked in protest as it slowly opened. A slither of light entered the room, amputating one side of the room from the other with the precision of a surgeon's scalpel. A blanket of darkness still covered the far-left corner of the room where he waited like a coiled rattler. However, unlike that snake, he would give no warning before he struck.

"We can be alone here," Boldo promised.

"What about your wife?" the young girl with him asked.

The self-proclaimed king appeared in the doorway. He stood sideways and motioned for his companion to enter. "She's gone, visiting her mother."

The girl hesitated on the other side of the doorway. "I don't know."

Boldo put his back to the room, fully exposed within the backlight from the hall as he tried to coax his young companion into the room. He opened the door wider and flipped the light switch, standing awash in a flood of sudden light.

Aleric remained coiled yet silent.

Upon seeing him there, the girl in the hallway cried out, turned, and ran away down the hall.

"Hey," Boldo yelled, confused by the fleeing girl.

"The girl shows good sense," Aleric said. "Maybe you should too."

"What!" The king wheeled around.

Aleric raised the barrel of the shotgun and aimed it at the squat and heavyset Gypsy standing before him. He had already pumped a round into the chamber. But he didn't shoot. Instead, he waited for his prey's confusion to wane, waited to be recognized and acknowledged.

He didn't have to wait long.

Like a growing storm, a look of confounded horror quickly darkened the king's face. "Bimbai!" he yelled. "Shit! Fuck!"

The shotgun blast boomed like thunder inside the small room. The round slammed into Boldo's kneecap. He screamed like a stuck pig and crashed to the floor, grimacing and grunting as he struggled back up onto his good knee.

Swift and graceful, Aleric drew his knife and threw it with deft expertise from across the room. The silver blade planted itself squarely into his prey's shoulder.

The king yelled. He slumped back onto the floor, back and head banging against the wall behind him.

Aleric rose from the chair and crossed the room with vampire-like quickness. He hunkered down and leaned close. *"Marel tu o Del."*

Boldo gaped, pain and shock twisting his face.

"But I can't wait for God to punish you." Aleric pulled the knife free. "He will have to wait his turn. I'm first." Neatly and precisely, he sliced open the king's throat.

As if playing his own death dirge, Boldo gurgled and gasped as he slowly bled to death from the gaping wound that traveled from one ear to the other.

"That's for Gypsies everywhere," Aleric whispered.

He wiped the silver blade clean on the dead man's clothes. His mission was completed. With Boldo now joining his brother Carranza in death, there were no more Tenes left in the world. All the so-called, self-proclaimed kings were dead, their reign of terror over.

And the one true king, the only living ancestor to King Tshukurka, stood and turned away, losing himself in the San Francisco night.

Chapter 26

Aleric stumbled into his second-story apartment, exhausted. The satisfaction of killing the likes of Boldo didn't last. He knew he should be pleased, but Pearsa weighed on his mind and his heart.

Plopping onto the edge of the bed, he sat opposite the open window. Ragged curtains fluttered before him like soiled apparitions. Outside, the city's neon lights tinted the night sky blood red. Inside, the dark caressed him like a gentle lover. His trusty bottle of Jim Beam rye waited on the end table for him, a true friend. He grabbed it and took a long slug to help him sleep, to help him forget his misfortunes and failures.

Through the open window, Odin abruptly returned home from a night of scavenging. The bird landed on his master's shoulder, a remnant of dead carcass still clutched in his beak, as if having brought the thing back as a trophy.

"Odin, must you bring your midnight snacks home with you," Aleric complained.

The large, black bird stared out the window, ignoring the complaint.

"I'm not impressed," Aleric said. "Like a Gypsy, you steal your food. What dog or coyote did you cheat that chunk of meat out of?"

As if in protest to the allegation, Odin left his master's shoulder. The raven flew to the small table in front of the television and plopped the chunk of flesh down. With his beak, he hit the remote. The TV came on, casting an unearthly glow across the dark room. The bird ripped into his snack to the sound of a late-night horror movie.

"I am Dracula."

"It's really good to see you. I don't know what happened to the driver and my luggage and...well...with all this, I thought I was in the wrong place."

"I bid you welcome."

Wolves howled.

"Listen to them...children of the night. What music they make."

"Odin, turn that crap off and go to bed," Aleric demanded.

"The blood is the life, Mr. Renfield."

The unearthly glow and Dracula's voice both instantly vanished with a click of the remote.

Odin flew to his perch.

Aleric shook his head. After one more slug, he put his friend Jim Beam to bed, as well. He undressed with laborious, drunken movements, clothes and weapons discarded in a pile on the floor. Naked, he sat back down and stared out the window.

"Pearsa," he whispered, "come to me."

She did not disappoint him, appearing as if having traveled on a wisp of otherworldly smoke, an apparition of ethereal, angelic beauty.

But he knew it was not heaven from which she had arrived.

"Nevermore," Odin warned from his perch.

The warning fell on deaf ears. He couldn't resist. "Pearsa," he whispered her name again.

She floated toward him with ghostly grace, slipping the gown she wore off her shoulders and letting it drop to the floor. "Do you love me?" she asked, her voice deepening into an almost inhuman growl.

He gazed into the lovely face he had once loved, and smiled.

She laughed, slid into bed, and pulled him down on top of her. Grabbing his erection, she spread her legs and slipped him inside while he cried out with the pain and the ecstasy of being engulfed by her inner flame. After slicing her own throat with a long, sharp fingernail, she penetrated his with her fangs.

As they rutted, the two shared blood.

From his perch, Odin called, "Nevermore."

Neither man nor vampire heeded the warning.

And Aleric's resurrection was complete.

The Collected Nightmares

THE DEVIL'S PRAYER

Rage is right
Fury is good
Killing is order
Human blood is delicious

Fred Wiehe

STRANGE DAYS

I looked into a mirror.
But saw not my reflection.
Instead, I stared into the eyes of a monster.
And in that instant, I saw the terrible things I had done.

DEAD GIRL

Wyatt had never believed in love at first sight.

Until now.

As soon as he saw her, he knew she was the one. She was perfection—long, brown hair, big, green eyes, milky skin, a splash of freckles across her nose, kissable, full lips. Besides the physical attraction, he felt he instantly knew her, had always known her. He couldn't have, of course, because he had never met her before, that he could remember anyway. And if he had met her, he was sure he would remember. Still, she seemed so familiar, so instantly recognizable. He knew her but he didn't. He couldn't explain it. Somehow, she stirred emotions in him he had never felt before and unearthed fragments of memories in his consciousness that he knew he had never really experienced, could have never really experienced.

He sighed, gaze locked on her. She was indeed perfection. The problem?

She was also dead.

She lay in a crumpled heap on the sidewalk, a pool of blood under her head, a trickle of blood coming from her nose, broken blood vessels in the whites of her eyes, the back of her head caved in.

His breath caught in his throat. His heart both pounded with excitement and ached with grief. He missed her. But how could he miss someone he had never met. And he wanted her so badly. Not in a creepy way. He wasn't a necrophiliac or anything like that; he had no desire to fuck a corpse. It was that he felt connected to her somehow. Another time and another place they could've been married, lived in a small house with children, a happily ever after fairy tale.

Now that would never be.

"Did you know her?"

"Huh? What?" He shook himself free of his fantasy. The real world focused around him. He stood on the corner of Haight and Ashbury streets in San Francisco. The dead girl at his feet was sharp contrast to a neighborhood known for its 1960s counterculture of free love.

Did love or passion have anything to do with this girl's murder? He never understood people who claimed to kill in the name of love.

Red and blue emergency lights splashed across the night, the nearby houses, the pavement still wet from an earlier rain. A crowd watched from behind yellow crime-scene tape that cordoned off the corner. Uniformed cops stood guard.

"Did you know her?"

He glanced at the plain-clothes cop standing next to him, a guy who reminded him of Columbo from the 70s TV show, minus the rumpled raincoat. He wanted to answer Columbo's question with a yes, I knew her well, I loved her. But...

"No." He shook his head. "I've never seen her before." It felt like a lie but it was the truth. Wasn't it?

Columbo nodded. "You just stumbled across her then?"

"That's right. I was coming home from Buena Vista Park. I heard a scream. And..."

"Did you see anything? Did you see it happen?"

He shook his head again. "No, I just heard a scream. By the time I got here, she was lying there...like that." He looked around at the crowd of onlookers. "Didn't anyone else see anything?"

"Officers are canvassing the area, asking." Columbo scrutinized him. "I'm more interested right now in what you know, what you saw." He paused. "What were you doing in the park this time of night?"

He shrugged. "Taking a walk. Enjoying the night air."

"What do you do for a living, Mr. Kole?"

"I'm a theoretical physicist. I teach at UC in Berkeley." He studied the detective. "Does it really matter?"

Columbo shrugged. "Are you sure you didn't see anything?"

He thought for a moment. Maybe he did forget something; he was so taken aback by the dead girl's familiarity and his own inexplicable feelings for her.

"Well?"

"I think I remember seeing someone running away." He ran a hand through his hair.

"You think you remember, Professor? Like a…*theory?*"

Now he really scrutinized the detective. What kind of crack was that? "No, not a theory. I remember...I saw someone running away, toward the Lower Haight and Fillmore."

"What did he look like?"

He shrugged. "I couldn't even say it was a *him*. It was just a dark figure."

Columbo sighed. "Tall or short? Fat or thin?"

"Not fat but too far away and too dark to tell whether tall or short." He shrugged again. "Just a shadow, really."

Columbo nodded. "Anything else?"

He shook his head.

The detective handed him a business card. "Call me if you remember anything...anything at all."

He took it, looked at it. It didn't say Columbo but instead McGrath. He stuffed the card in the pocket of his jeans and stared down at the love of his life lying in a pool of her own blood at his feet.

"You can go, now, Professor Kole."

He nodded but didn't move. He was afraid to leave, afraid to look away. He would never see the dead girl again, and he wasn't sure he could live with that horrible fact. How could he go on without her now that he knew she had existed?

"Professor?"

"Huh? What?" He looked up.

"Are you sure you don't know her?"

He stared down at the girl. "I'm sure."

The cop had a strange look on his face. "You can go."

Reluctantly, he turned away. As he walked up Haight toward Stanyan Street and home, he couldn't help feeling that his life would never be the same. He would never be able to get this girl out of his head, out of his heart. With her dead, he now knew he would be forever alone.

Lost in grief, he walked with his head down until another strange feeling came over him; he felt as if he were being watched. Glancing up, he caught a glimpse of a familiar face standing in the crowd, on the other side of the yellow tape. He stopped cold, but in an instant, the face was gone, ducking back and disappearing into the surrounding onlookers. He blinked and searched the crowd but to no avail. He hadn't even gotten a good look at the face, couldn't even be sure if it was a man or a woman, so how could the face seem so familiar? And why would he think this person was watching him?

Gooseflesh crept along his extremities, across his scalp. He shivered and walked on, unable to shake the weird feeling of being watched. And not only watched but in danger from whomever was doing the watching. By the time he reached his home, he had worked himself up into full-fledged paranoia, looking over his shoulder, seeing peril behind every tree and hidden in every shadow. He climbed the wooden steps to the front door of his duplex that he rented in the old Victorian. He took out his key. His hand trembled slightly, hindering his ability to unlock the door and get inside. A cold wind stirred around him like invisible phantoms coming to visit. The phantoms planted cold kisses on his neck and playfully ruffled his hair. Before they could get too intimate, he managed to open the door and get inside. He slammed the door, shutting out the unwanted advances.

Inside, he still felt watched, not safe. He couldn't explain it. But, then, there was so much he couldn't explain.

With growing unease, he went to the kitchen, retrieved a beer from the refrigerator, and drank it as he readied himself for bed. He plopped himself into bed after brushing his teeth, pulling the covers to his chin. How was he going to sleep? He couldn't get the girl out of his head. He couldn't shake the odd and inexplicable feeling of being watched in his own home. Maybe the beer would help. Maybe he should have another one. Maybe…

He rolled over onto his side.

Gemma spooned him. She nuzzled his neck and whispered, "Are you up?" Her hand slipped down his stomach and into his pajamas.

He moaned. "I am now."

"I'll say you are." She gently caressed and stroked him.

He moved to the rhythm of her strokes. "You're bad."

"Mmm, you like me that way."

He smiled. He did. He had to admit it.

"Should I stop?"

"No, definitely not." Her hand felt so soft, so warm, he could hardly contain himself. "Never stop."

"Never's a long time." She stroked a little harder, a little faster.

He groaned as he quickened his rhythm in time with her hand. "Not long enough."

She kissed his cheek, ear, and neck as she continued her hand job. "Never long enough." But she abruptly stopped.

He rolled onto his back. "You said you would never stop."

She smiled. "Not stopping. Just pausing. I think to make sure you never get away, I should take you as my prisoner." She climbed on top of him, straddling his midsection. Producing leather straps seemingly out of nowhere, she proceeded to tie his hands and feet to each bedpost.

He now was splayed out on the bed like a cadaver ready for an autopsy. He didn't resist. He could never resist her. "Do with me what you will."

She giggled. Straddling him, she reached behind her and again took him in hand and began to stroke. "I plan to."

He groaned, squirming with delight underneath his love. "Forever?"

She leaned over, her lips lightly touching his, and whispered, "Time is then, forever now."

As he came, she disappeared as if she were nothing more than an apparition.

He woke with the girl's name on his lips. "Gemma…"

His hands and feet were bound to the bedposts, just as in the dream. He struggled to get free.

"Gemma?"

Darkness surrounded him, but soon his eyes adjusted. He was in his own bed, at home. But she was nowhere in sight. Of course not, she wasn't real. She was the spitting image of the dead girl, but really was nothing more than a figment of his imagination, his dream. Her name probably wasn't even Gemma. How could it be? Still, into the darkness, he whispered, "Gemma…"

"She's dead. Three times dead now."

The voice came from somewhere out of the dark shadows.

"What?" He practically choked on the word. He swallowed hard. "Who the fuck?" He struggled against his restraints. "Who's there?"

A malicious laugh answered. A figure stepped out of the shadows, towards the bed. The table light switched on, revealing the intruder.

He couldn't believe his eyes. He couldn't speak, couldn't even breathe, as he stared into a face that was a mirror image of his own.

"Surprise," his doppelgänger said. A sneer spread across his face.

"Who the fuck *are* you?" he choked out, voice sounding like rusted hinges.

The mirror image cocked his head. "I'm you." The sneer widened even more. "Well, I'm you from a world that exists side-by-side with yours."

"A duplicate? You're fucking crazy."

"That's interesting. If I'm a duplicate and I'm fucking crazy, then it stands to reason that you're fucking crazy too, doesn't it?"

He struggled. The leather straps cut into his wrists and ankles. He struggled harder but couldn't free himself. Maybe this duplicate was right. Maybe he was crazy. His entire world was spinning out of control.

"And who's to say that you're not the duplicate." Wyatt II laughed, a malicious and mocking cackle. "But if it makes you feel better, I'll play the part of duplicate to your original. Doesn't matter to me. You're me and I'm you, just in different spacetime."

"What?"

"Come on, Wyatt, don't play stupid. We're both physicists. We know the theories concerning the existence of parallel universes. We've read papers written by Hugh Everett. No self-respecting physicist hasn't. He first conceived the idea way back in 1957."

"Sure, I've read Everett," he conceded. "And Fred Alan Wolf too. And others. But if you're me from a parallel universe, how did you get here? And how in the hell did you get me tied up and why?"

Wyatt II laughed again. "You were strangely cooperative in letting me tie you up.

It was no problem. Only your boner got in the way."

He would've felt embarrassed, but he had bigger problems than having a hard-on, like being tied up and at this guy's mercy.

"Were you dreaming of Gemma?" Wyatt II asked.

Gemma? Hell yes, he had been dreaming of her. She had tied him up in the dream. No wonder he cooperated. In his sleep, he wanted to be tied up.

"She's a bitch, you know."

The surprises kept coming. How did this doppelgänger know the dead girl? Even more surprising, was her name really Gemma, like in his dream? And if so, how would either of them know that?

Then something else dawned on him, hitting him like a speeding freight train. "It was you. *You* killed her, didn't you?"

Wyatt II nodded. "Three times now. The first time in my universe." He took a deep breath. "It was deliciously satisfying. At first, anyway. Then I felt the need, the urge, to kill her again. But how do you kill someone twice?" He looked off, as if gazing into nothingness. "I found a way." He focused again. "You were destined to meet her tonight, you know. That's how I knew where she'd be." He laughed. "Having *you* find her corpse made the kill even more delicious."

"Why? Why would you want to kill her? She was perfection."

Wyatt II nodded. "She was, and I loved her madly. That's why I killed her and will continue to kill her as many times as I can." He paused. "I saved you a lot of heartache in the end. She really was a bitch."

He couldn't believe his ears. This mirror-image madman had stolen Gemma away before he could even meet her. And knowing they were destined to meet, knowing that they had met many times in many realities, made it even worse. That's why she seemed so familiar to him. It's why he instantly fell in love with her, even as she lay dead. Somehow, one reality bled into another.

"If everything you've told me is true, then you know there are infinite possibilities, just as there are infinite universes. That means just because Gemma hurt you in some way doesn't mean she'd hurt me. In my universe we could've been happy…happy forever."

"True," Wyatt II agreed. He shrugged. "But why take the chance."

He again struggled with his restraints. He wanted to kill this asshole who looked like him. Obviously, their physical resemblance and their similar occupations were all they had in common. He would never harm Gemma, not for anything, whether she hurt him or not.

Wyatt II laughed. "Better to kill all the Gemmas, in all the worlds, rather than take that chance."

Tired, his wrists and ankles bleeding from struggling with the straps, and not wanting to hear anymore insanity on the subject of murder, he steered the conversation toward science. "How in the hell did you pull this off? Traveling to parallel universes, which also would involve time travel, isn't possible, at least not yet, not in my universe anyway."

Wyatt II laughed again, a mad cackle. "The future communicates with the present and the present communicates with the past. Time is not fixed, my friend. We're not stuck in it like flies in honey. You of all people should know that, if you're half the physicist I am."

His eyes grew big, like a kid's at Christmas. "You discovered a way to create an artificial spacetime warp?"

"Bingo." Wyatt II sneered. "When a guy's motivated by hatred, he can move mountains, time, and dimensions."

"But I thought you said you loved her madly."

Wyatt II shrugged. "Love…hate…same thing…different sides of the same coin." He shrugged again. "I'd love to talk to you more about it, explain the science, but it's really time for you to die."

At that, he pulled frantically on his restraints. His breath and heart began a foot race. Perspiration plastered hair to his head and glistened across his torso. But fighting the straps was to no avail, and soon he tired again. Breathless, he asked, "Why kill me?"

"I'm going to take your place for a while," Wyatt II confessed, "at least until I can move on to the next universe. I need time and resources to open up another portal. You can give me both. It's the perfect murder because for all intents and purposes you won't be dead. No one will even be looking for you or your body." He shrugged. "I'll literally be you." He laughed. "And I'll have all the resources that the lab at Cal Berkeley can offer to open that new portal. Then it's off to kill me another Gemma."

"How can you be me?" He wondered aloud. "How can I be you? How can *we* be so crazy?"

Wyatt II spread his hands out as if to say, *who knows*.

That's when he noticed the hypodermic needle in the duplicate's hand.

"What is that?"

Wyatt II wrapped a latex band around Wyatt's arm.

"This is a cocktail of my own making," Wyatt II answered.

He was injected with the poison.

"It will be relatively painless. I'd much rather have the pleasure of caving your skull in, but I can't afford all that blood. I need to be able to clean up and dispose of your body with relative ease if I'm to successfully take your place."

He immediately felt the concoction course through his veins, setting his blood on fire. His abdomen cramped. His throat gurgled with bile.

Wyatt II leaned forward. "Your time is up."

He glared at his doppelgänger and grinned. "Time is then…" he croaked "…forever now."

Isn't that what Gemma told him in the dream?

Wyatt II scoffed. "You're a fool."

He closed his eyes and gave in to the inevitable.

It was Gemma's face he saw in his last moments and not the mad doppelgänger's that loomed over him. His final thoughts were of following her into whatever dimension of time and space in which she now existed and reuniting with her in infinite possibilities.

He slipped into death, her name on his lips. "Gemma…"

"Wyatt…" she answered.

Fred Wiehe

The End

The end is near
It stalks me
I fear
Following closely behind
Hiding in shadows and
Lurking nearby
It will never give up
It will always abide
Yes, the end is near
I need to consent
I need to concede
I need to swallow my fear
For the end is here

A̲b̲o̲u̲t̲ ̲t̲h̲e̲ ̲A̲u̲t̲h̲o̲r̲

Fred Wiehe teaches Creative Writing to children of all ages and adults. He is also a professional, bestselling writer and a member of the Horror Writers Association. However, his novels, books, short stories, and screenplays crossover genres into urban fantasy, science fiction, supernatural thrillers, paranormal suspense, and more. He writes for both adults and young adults. *Strange Days*—a supernatural crime thriller—was called "a creepy, hair-raising, chill bumping read" and "a winner in its genre" by Midwest Book Review. His other books include the science fiction novel *Starkville*, the horror/suspense novel *Night Songs*, and the dark fantasy novel *The Burning*. His short story *Trick or*

Treat; It's the Puppet People was published in the 2007 Halloween edition of *Sinister Tales Magazine*, and his short story Trick or Troll was published in the 2008 Halloween edition of *ShadeWorks*. Both stories are included in the anthology *Holiday Madness* published by Black Bed Sheet Books. Recently his novel *Fright House*, about an insane asylum turned Halloween attraction, gained enormous critical acclaim. "Creepy and highly entertaining," says Jonathan Maberry, New York Times bestselling author of THE NIGHTSIDERS and ROT & RUIN. Another recent novel of critical acclaim, *Aleric: Monster Hunter*, is a must-read for Wiehe fans. He and his family reside in California's Bay Area as he continues to release new and amazing works, and watch for more to come!

Website: **http://www.fredwiehe.com**

Look for us wherever books are sold.

If you thought *this book* was cool, check out these other titles from the #1 source for the best in independent horror fiction,

BLACK BED SHEET

www.blackbedsheetbooks.com

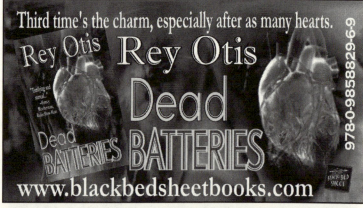

www.blackbedsheetbooks.com

Made in the USA
Middletown, DE
07 July 2024